Lucky Beach

JOANN BASSETT

Lucky Beach
Copyright © 2016 JoAnn Bassett
All rights reserved.
Printed in the United States of America

Published by Lokelani Publishing
Green Valley, AZ 85614
www.joannbassett.com
***
This book is a work of fiction. Places, events, and situations in
this book are purely fictional and any resemblance to actual
persons, living or dead, is coincidental.
***
Also by JoAnn Bassett:

"THE ISLANDS OF ALOHA MYSTERY SERIES"
Maui Widow Waltz
Livin' Lahaina Loca
Lana'i of the Tiger
Kaua'i Me a River
O'ahu Lonesome Tonight?
I'm Kona Love You Forever
Moloka'i Lullaby
Hilo, Goodbye

"THE ESCAPE TO MAUI SERIES"
Mai Tai Butterfly

Discover the latest titles by JoAnn Bassett at
http://www.joannbassett.com

ISBN-13: 978-1530270736
ISBN-10: 1530270731

For Koma, always.

CHAPTER 1

Everybody loves a winner.

Anyway, that's what I'd always heard. But like a lot of things I used to believe, it turns out it's not true. In fact, it's flat-out bogus. People *pretend* to love a winner. They smile in your face and tell you how happy they are for you. They congratulate you on your good fortune and wish you well. But don't believe it. When your back is turned they give you the finger. They call you a selfish bitch. Soon, a bone-deep resentment snuffs out any good feelings they ever had for you. Believe me, I know.

For the past year I've been rich. I'm talking seriously well-to-do. Before that I was poor. Not snotty-nose kid poor, but poor enough that when I'd see a guy scavenging pop cans along the side of the road I'd wonder how much he'd get for them. Before I got rich I had friends, lots of friends. I had old high school friends, and work friends, and girls'-night-out friends. People in my neighborhood would invite me over to watch the Super Bowl or to grab a beer after work. But now that I have a ton of money, the friends are gone. Every single one.

"The movers called, Miss Gomez," said my assistant, Chloe. "They're running a little late, but they'll be here by noon."

I'd asked Chloe at least a dozen times to call me "Monica" but it never stuck. She'd do it a time or two and then she'd go back to "Miss Gomez." I figured it had to do with her upbringing. I know when I was little, my *abuela*—my grandmother—would scold me if I called an authority figure by their first name. So, even though I was twenty-nine and Chloe was just six years younger, she didn't feel right calling me by my first name. I wasn't her friend, I was her boss.

"Thanks, Chloe. Do you know where I put my keys?"

Chloe pointed to the end of the kitchen countertop where I usually dropped them.

It was a Tuesday, the third of March. I remember the date because it was the day I moved three thousand miles from home. I wasn't taking the move lightly. It'd weighed on my mind for some time that I was leaving everything I'd ever known and moving to a place I'd never been before. But I didn't know what else to do, or where else to go.

"Oh, and your lawyer called again. He said he needs to talk to you before you go."

I had no intention of calling him back. The last year had been nonstop aggravation. My life had been sucked dry with trips to the attorney's office, the courthouse, and an unmarked back door to a bank in Tucson. I was done with all that.

The flight to Maui took a little over five hours. It would normally take longer but I wasn't flying a commercial airline. Instead, I'd chartered a small jet. In the cabin it was just me, Chloe, and my miniature Schnauzer named Pima. An old-school flight attendant who actually wore a navy-blue suit with a skirt instead of pants fussed over us as if we were British royalty.

There were two guys in the cockpit: a fiftyish pilot with thinning brown hair that looked like it'd been touched up with "Just for Men," and a co-pilot who appeared to be only a few years older than me. The co-pilot had dark curly hair, icy blue eyes and yummy broad shoulders. He also sported a three-day scruff that got my juices flowing. I swear the guy could've modeled CK underwear in his off hours.

When we shook hands, I considered asking him if he'd like to join me in the tiny lavatory to see if we could make the smoke detector go off. In the past year I'd become shameless about checking out guys. Not that I hadn't done it before, but lately it'd become something of an obsession. I could tell you, to the exact hour, the last time a man touched me. Since I won the money, the only physical contact I've had with men is shaking hands with old guys like my lawyer, my accountant and my banker. One time a cute salesman gave me a hug after he'd sold me a ridiculously expensive watch, but that doesn't count.

My cell phone rang as we touched down at the Kahului airport on Maui.

"Aren't you supposed to have that thing turned off?" Chloe's face looked like we were about to cart-wheel down the runway in a ball of flame.

"That's a myth," I said. "The airlines tell you it messes with the navigation system to keep people in coach from strangling each other over 'yakking while flying.'"

Still, I turned off the phone after checking the caller ID. My lawyer. Again.

The tires bounced once and the thrusters roared as we skidded to a quick stop.

"I can't believe we're really here. Thank you again for bringing me, Miss Gomez. I've always wanted to go to Hawaii."

I'd always wanted to go to Hawaii, too. But in my imaginary trip to paradise I'd clutched my new husband's beefy bicep as I watched ocean, palm trees, and sugar cane fields slide by the window as we arrived for our one-week honeymoon. We'd kiss each other—one more time—and squeeze our entwined hands in anticipation of blissful days of beach, beverages, and bed. Not necessarily in that order.

But here I was, sneaking into Hawaii like a woman on the run. Probably because that's exactly what I was.

⊖ ⊖ ⊖

The day I won the money is clearly etched in my memory. It was a clear April morning, a Saturday. I'd gotten up to make coffee when I heard someone pounding on my front door. I figured it was a neighbor wanting to borrow something or to ask me to watch their kid for a half-hour while they ran to the market.

But it wasn't.

The guy standing on my doorstep was way more colorful than most of the people you see on the streets of Rio Blanco, Arizona. He had a cheddar-cheese fake tan, a haystack of copper-colored hair (bad hair plugs or a bad piece, I couldn't tell) and a wide veneered smile that looked like the entrance to a carnival ride.

"You're our grand prize winner! You're our grand prize winner!" He didn't look at me as he screeched. Instead, he beamed into the silvery lens of an ominous-looking black video camera. The camera was balanced on the shoulder of a guy silently gliding toward me. The video guy reminded me of that TV show, "Shark Week," where the sharks stealthily approach their prey and gobble them down in one or two well-placed bites.

"So, whaddaya say?" Haystack Hair yelled. "You're our grand prize winner in the Mega-Magazine Multi-Millions Jackpot!" He handed me a huge balloon bouquet but as I reached out to grab it, the strings slipped through my fingers. A dozen shiny Mylar balloons drifted up and away so fast it was as if they'd never existed.

I stood there shifting my eyes from person to person. I'd seen these things on TV and the winners always screamed and tore their hair. Sometimes they cried or fainted. I was too confused to do any of that. I was sure the guy had made a mistake. The last thing I needed was a YouTube video going viral that showed me freaking out while the fake-tan guy checked his prize-winner information and realized he'd come to the wrong house.

"Who are you looking for?" I said.

"We're on a mission to locate a Miss Monica Gomez of 335 East Coyote Wash Drive in beautiful Rio Blanco, Arizona!" He shouted it really loud, like a street corner preacher trying to draw a crowd. He could've saved his vocal cords. My neighbors from three blocks around were already in the street, staring at my house as if a big drug bust was going down.

"That's me," I said.

"Well then," he lowered his voice then built to a big crescendo. "I'm David Michael Corcoran, and I'm here with the Multi-Millions Prize Posse to announce that you're our newest Mega-Magazine Multi-Millions Jackpot *winner*!"

The guy talked so fast, it was like he'd gone to auctioneer school or something. I was impressed by his ability to keep all the M-words straight.

"Wow," I said. I felt kind of bad I couldn't bring myself to jump up and down and act all pee-my-pants crazy, but I still had visions of that guy from *Punk'd* bounding out of the Prize Posse van.

"Would you like to say a few words to the folks out there?" David Michael Corcoran pushed the mic in my face.

I cleared my throat. "Thanks. If this is really true, it's great."

"Well, I must say, you're about the coolest customer we've ever had. Are you by chance *already* a multi-millionaire, Ms. Gomez?"

"No."

"Well, you are *now*!"

A bleach-blond guy standing by the Prize Posse van began waving his arms and yelling to the crowd to get them to cheer and applaud. My neighbors clapped half-heartedly. From the looks of things, they were also wary someone from *Punk'd* might be lurking around.

Arturo, a single dad from across the street, came over to the cheerleader guy. After a short exchange Arturo turned and glared at me as if he'd just been told I'd been caught trafficking in child pornography.

That was the day that changed my life. That was the day I learned that in real life, *nobody* loves a winner.

CHAPTER 2

The little charter jet had come to a stop, but we had to wait while the flight attendant unlocked the door hatch and lowered the steps. Chloe scooped up Pima and clipped a leash onto her collar before handing her over to me.

"You're a Hawaiian dog now, Pima," she said. "You're going to have to learn to do the doggie hula."

Pima whined as we made our way down the outside stairway. I carried her, since going down steps always freaked her out. She sniffed the unfamiliar air with the ferocity of an overprotective mother checking whether the milk had gone sour. I petted her to calm her down, but it probably wasn't much help. My hands shook as the full impact of what I'd done began to sink in.

Nothing was familiar. The air was fresh and fragrant, but the change in humidity from the desert southwest was palpable. My waist-length hair was probably already well on its way to frizzing into something resembling the black veil on the Bride of Frankenstein. But what did I care? I didn't know anyone here but Chloe, and she'd tell me I looked great even if I had a wad of spinach stuck in my front teeth. One of the upsides of having "help" is they boost your self-confidence. The downside is you can never believe them.

The flight attendant stayed aboard while the pilots walked us over to the private terminal. I dropped back a few steps to get a good look at the co-pilot's buns. Whew. Good thing the guy was scheduled for a quick turn-around or I'd probably be saying something inappropriate. I certainly was thinking it.

Chloe interrupted my reverie. "So, do we have a car or something? I mean, how're we supposed to get to the hotel?"

For an assistant, she sure left a lot up to me. But it was okay. I'm a control freak (or so I've been told) and I like to be in charge. Even when I was still working, my favorite part of the job was handling details and solving problems. I liked it when my boss would call me into his office all flustered and fuming. He'd rant about how we were *ruined* and the company would be *taking a huge hit*. I'd make some calls, hire some temp workers, or buy something we needed, and poof! twenty minutes later, problem solved.

Steven Harrow had been my boss. I hadn't worked for the guy for almost a year, but he was still in my life every single day. He was the reason I'd packed up and vamoosed without leaving a forwarding address. He was the source of ninety-five percent of my stress. He was the guy who'd cost me my friends, my reputation, my self-esteem—and now my home.

ᕲ ᕲ ᕲ

I told Chloe I'd ordered a town car and it should arrive shortly. We entered the small terminal and a smiling young woman in a tight pink tank top and a really short Hawaiian-print skirt handed me a *mai tai* in a plastic cup as she welcomed me to Maui. I lifted my hair off my neck as she placed a fragrant *lei* of white flowers over my head. I asked her if she'd please get Chloe a *lei* and a drink as well.

She bobbed her head and said, "No worries." Then she trotted over to a little rattan bar in the corner of the room to get them.

The *lei* felt cool against the back of my neck. When the hostess returned with Chloe's *lei* and *mai tai*, I asked the pilot and co-pilot if they'd like anything. They both ordered Pepsis.

"Isn't this great?" Chloe said. "I always thought Hawaii would be nice. I'm glad I was right."

I wanted to tell her it was doubtful that people arriving at the main airport would get free *mai tais*. And they'd probably only get a *lei* if they paid for one in advance. I was pretty sure people who flew into the regular Maui airport probably spent their first hour of vacation waiting for their luggage to come down the carousel and then standing in line at the car rental place. But I kept all that to myself. Because even though Chloe and I were close in age, she was miles behind me in street smarts. I loved her sunny naiveté and didn't want to wreck it by pointing out the distressing parts of life she'd managed to artfully dodge for the past twenty-three years.

While the pilot was in the men's room, the co-pilot asked if I'd enjoyed the flight. I told him it was fine. He said he was new with the jet service and his company would probably be sending me an email survey to fill out. I was tempted to tell him I would've given him higher marks if he'd offered to induct me into the "Mile High Club," but he looked like the kind of guy who'd take me seriously, and I didn't need the grief.

He said, "Well then, Miss Gomez—"

"Please, call me Monica."

"Uh, okay then. Uh, Monica, if you're happy with our service we'll be heading out to catch a few winks before our turnaround flight. Thanks again for flying with us today. We at Desert High Jet Service appreciate your business."

He reached over to shake my hand and I grasped it a bit longer than necessary. Then I caught his eye and gave him a wink. He gave me back nothing. No smile, no "backatcha sweetie," nothing but a blank stare.

"I think I see our town car out front," said Chloe.

Good old Chloe, always stepping in to save me from myself.

We emerged from the terminal building into brilliant sunshine, and I was struck by the never-ending vista of green. Even at this general aviation area with its beige modular buildings and long stretches of gray tarmac there were shoulder-high flowering bushes and palm trees everywhere. The palms sported thick green crowns. In Arizona we had palm trees, but they always looked as if they were pleading for more water. Here, the palms appeared unaware that water could ever be scarce.

"Oh, and don't forget to turn your phone back on," said Chloe, as we tumbled into the back seat of the town car.

"I'd rather leave it off," I said.

"Yeah, but...well, you know," she said. She pinched her mouth into a tight circle. "Do you think it's really over?"

"I don't know what to think," I said. "But it's over for me. I'll go along with whatever the lawyers hammer out. I'm done bickering."

"But hey! We're in Maui," Chloe's voice rose to a triumphant crow. "And that's not too shabby."

Pima let out a doggy sigh and wriggled deeper into my lap.

The last year had been a disaster, but I'd persevered and left it all behind me. I'd made it to Maui. And from here on out, there'd be no looking back.

CHAPTER 3

The Monday after the Prize Posse showed up, I quit my job. In my resignation letter I gave two weeks' notice, but my boss shook his head and said, "Like I'm going to pay you to sit around here and gloat?"

I packed up my stuff and left.

The local media had a field day with my winning. I was interviewed by all the major TV channels. Even the *Arizona Republic*, the big Phoenix newspaper, came down to talk to me. When I saw myself on TV I thought I looked like a hiker who'd been found in the desert after going missing for a couple of days. Shocked, happy, but utterly clueless.

The reporters all pretty much asked the same dumb questions, *What's it like to suddenly become a multi-millionaire? Did you ever think this would happen to you? How are you going to spend your fortune?*

One reporter, a guy from the Tucson paper, the *Arizona Daily Star*, asked me to walk him through the whole thing—from when I first entered the contest to the day I learned I'd won. I couldn't imagine why anyone would be interested in the details, but he seemed to think that readers, especially superstitious readers, would love to know if there were any secrets to winning forty-five million bucks.

I told him I'd been the office manager at Az/Mex Produce, one of the many produce distribution centers in Nogales, Arizona. More than twenty billion dollars' worth of fresh produce comes into the United States through Arizona every year, and Az/Mex is one of the major players in the industry. Among my many duties as office manager was sorting the incoming mail and tossing out anything not relevant to the business.

One day, a big yellow envelope from the Mega-Magazines contest came in the mail. I put it in the toss pile. But later, while eating lunch at my desk, I opened it and filled out the entry. I guess I must've been bored. That afternoon I put it in the outgoing mail and forgot about it.

Almost four months later the Prize Posse showed up at my house. To say I was surprised would be an understatement. I'd completely forgotten I'd even sent in the entry.

"So, your secret is you entered the contest while you were at work?" he said.

"I guess so."

Looking back, I should've kept my big mouth shut.

ฦ ฦ ฦ

The town car pulled up at The Ali'i Royale in Wailea. We got out and the hotel staff didn't look any too pleased to see me carrying Pima through the open-air lobby. The guy at the front desk made it clear pets must be kenneled at all times, even in the room.

"How are you going to enforce that?" I wasn't trying to be pissy, I really wondered how they could tell if a dog was in or out of the kennel once the guest closed the door.

"If we see your pet through the window or if a member of our housekeeping or room service staff reports it, I'm afraid we'll need to request your immediate departure."

Okay. Chloe had clued me in this wasn't a pet-friendly place when she'd gotten the reservation, but I thought since I'd booked their biggest suite they'd cut me some slack. Apparently not.

Pima's forced incarceration pushed looking for a permanent residence to the top of my to-do list. I'd hoped to kick back and enjoy the spa, room service, and several on-site restaurants for a couple of weeks while I looked at houses, but Pima didn't take well to kennel-dwelling. It would be only a matter of time—and no doubt a pretty short time—before we got turned in and turned out.

It was too bad we'd be leaving soon because the suite was magnificent. It had four main rooms: two spacious bedrooms, a well-appointed living room and a full kitchen. It also included two of the biggest bathrooms I'd ever seen. Even Chloe's slightly smaller bedroom suite was nearly the size of my *abuela's* entire house back in Rio Blanco.

Whenever I got to thinking about my *abuela*, it knocked me down a few notches. I'd missed her so much in the past year. She was a no-nonsense, practical woman who would've been a huge help in dealing with the stuff that happened after the Prize Posse showed up.

My dad had been killed doing his job. He was a Border Patrol agent until he got gunned down by a couple of drug runners packing marijuana from Mexico into Southern Arizona. I was twelve when he died. It was the worst thing that could happen to an only child. Especially to a daughter who worshipped her father and was pretty much ignored by her mother. My best guess is my mom resented having to compete with me for my dad's attention so she chose to pretend I wasn't there.

My mom didn't cope well with my dad's death. That's putting it mildly. She became the town drunk and a few other choice things. One night after closing down her favorite watering hole, she plowed her car into a light pole and went to join my father.

After she died, I moved three blocks away to live with my *abuela*, my father's mother. I'd pretty much been living at her place since my dad died anyway, so it wasn't that big a deal to move the rest of my things over there. The woman was a saint. I know everybody says that about their grandmother, but in my case it's one-hundred-percent true. She endured the cold stares and gossip-mongering about my mother but she never rose to the bait. My *abuela* died ten years ago, when I was nineteen. For the entire time I lived with her she never uttered one bad word about my mother. I appreciated that, a lot.

The funny thing is, since I'd spent my middle school years feeling mortified by my mother's behavior, when the crap hit the fan after I won the Mega-Millions money it wasn't as upsetting as it might have been. I'd been toughened up. I was already used to being the brunt of gossip. Of course when I was a kid, the talk had been about my mom. Now the talk was about me. But still, it helped that I'd already grown a thick skin.

Chloe unpacked our suitcases while I walked Pima. I asked at the front desk if there was a dog *exercise area*—a nice way to say a *poop yard*—and they said there was one a couple of blocks away. I tucked a plastic bag in my pocket and we started out.

The walkway along Wailea Boulevard was cool and leafy, the trees covered in flowers. I'd never seen anything like it. Although for nearly a year I'd had enough money to go anywhere I wanted, I rarely left my house except for the occasional blow-out shopping trip. I had a full schedule with attorneys and court dates and depositions, not to mention financial planners. If I'd taken off, even to simply spend a week at a place like the Miraval Spa Resort up in Tucson, who knows what would've happened?

I turned into the dog park and Pima started seriously checking the local pee-mail. It was always a long process whenever I took Pima to a new place. So many doggy smells, so little time. She sniffed and squatted and finally came up with the thing we'd come for. I put it in the bag and deposited it in a trash barrel. Pima wanted to hang out and sniff around some more, but I wanted to go to the beach. I hadn't stood at the ocean's edge since before my dad died.

We were on the sidewalk trotting back to the hotel when I saw a *For Sale* sign on a fantastic house up on the sloping hill above Wailea Drive. It had wrap-around windows facing what must've been a one-hundred- and-eighty degree ocean view. I hurried Pima along. I had barely an hour to spend on the beach before dinnertime. Tomorrow wouldn't be a beach day. I had to find a real estate agent and seriously start looking for a place to live.

🐢 🐢 🐢

"That guy from the *US Star Weekly* called again," Chloe said as I came into the suite. "He was kind of a butt when I told him you were out. I don't think he believed me."

"Did he leave a number?" I usually didn't talk to reporters, especially ones who were trying to dig up dirt.

"Yeah. I told him you probably wouldn't call him back, but he made me take his number anyway. Are you gonna call him?"

"I am. I think I might be able to make his snooping work for me."

I punched in the number on my cell phone.

"This is Sam Sullivan, so this better be good," he said when he picked up.

If that was how the guy answered his phone, he obviously hadn't been raised by my *abuela*.

"Hello, Mr. Sullivan. This is Monica Gomez, the Mega-Magazine prizewinner from Arizona. I'm returning your call."

"Whoa, you actually called me back? Give me a second here. I need to grab a de-fib machine. My heart's gonna need a jolt."

I thought, *Nobody likes a smart ass, Mr. Sullivan.* But I didn't say anything. Instead, I waited for him to put on his big-boy pants and start acting like a professional.

"Heh, heh," he chuckled as if he'd cracked me up with his antics. But only one of us was laughing. "So, Ms. Gomez, are you willing to talk on the record about winning the big jackpot?"

"I don't know. You didn't leave a very detailed message with my assistant so I'm not sure what you're looking for."

"Yeah, well here's the gist. Everyone wants to know how ordinary people cope with coming into a zillion bucks out of the blue. And from what I understand you've been involved in some prolonged litigation over the Mega-Magazine prize money. Is that correct?"

"There were a few initial concerns, but they've been cleared up. Next question?"

"When did they get cleared up? I'm looking at a court document that shows—"

I didn't want to pick at old scabs with a guy who could splash my picture on the front page of a sleazy tabloid that would grace every grocery check-out line in the country. Been there, done that.

I interrupted him. "As I said, Mr. Sullivan, there were some preliminary misunderstandings, but they've been ironed out. I'm sure a story about people quietly settling their differences won't sell many gossip magazines. Sorry, but as you said earlier, I'm afraid this is a waste of your valuable time."

"Then I guess you haven't heard." The annoying chuckle was back in his voice.

"Haven't heard what?"

"Your former employer, Steven Harrow, filed a new lawsuit against you today. This time he's asking for fifty million dollars."

"What? Fifty million? But after taxes I only got about thirty million."

"Is that your statement, Ms. Gomez? Can I quote you on that?" The guy sounded positively giddy.

"No you may *not* quote me. I said the matter has been resolved. Your source is obviously misinformed. *That's* my statement." I hung up.

What was that weasel Harrow up to now? Maybe I should've taken my lawyer's calls after all.

CHAPTER 4

The next morning I got up and took Pima out for a quick trot before calling the real estate agent whose name was on the For Sale sign in Wailea. I wasn't sure I wanted to live in that part of the island, but I figured if she was the listing agent for that gorgeous place she'd probably know about other houses I'd like.

"This is Bev Strong."

"Hello Ms. Strong. My name is Monica Gomez and I'm interested in the house on the hill above Wailea Drive."

"You mean 1616 Honopua? The asking price on that one's pretty steep."

I was used to remarks like that. My young-sounding voice and Hispanic name probably conjured up visions of a hotel maid or maybe a community-college student, not a woman with a multi-million dollar balance sheet.

"I'm sure it's quite expensive, but it appears to be a very nice house. Is there a time this morning when you could show it to me?" Now was the moment of truth. If Bev blew me off a second time, I'd hang up and move on to someone else.

"Sure. The property's vacant. I have a sales meeting until about nine-thirty but we could run by there around ten. Do you want to meet me at the property or should I pick you up?"

"I'm staying at The Ali'i Royale in Wailea, Suite 1140. Would you mind giving me a call when you're on your way?" I said. "I can either meet you in the lobby or you can come up to the suite."

"Why don't I come to the suite? I'd like to show you the brochure I've had printed up for 1616. And it would give me a chance to answer any questions you might have before we tour the property."

In other words, she wanted to size me up before taking me through a house that was probably priced well above seven figures. I didn't take offense. If I were in her shoes I'd have done the same thing.

ɕ ɕ ɕ

Bev Strong arrived right on time. She was your stereo-typical high-market real estate agent: expertly-cropped blond hair, skinny build, and a bird-like face with eyes that seemed to take in everything in about six seconds. She wore a pale yellow linen pants suit with creases across the front of the pants. That's why I avoid linen, you can never keep it from wrinkling.

When she arrived, I went to the door myself rather than send Chloe. Bev shook my hand on her way in.

"These suites are nice, don't you think?" she said. "You've got it all—plenty of room, a full-on oceanfront view and, best of all, they replace these lovely custom furnishings every six months whether they need it or not."

I nodded. I wasn't buying the suite so why was she trying to sell it to me? Oh well. Maybe she was just warming up her sales pipes.

"Ah," she chirped as if I'd reached out and goosed her. "I see you have a dog. Does the front desk know about this little cutie-pie?"

Pima had come over to check out Bev. When Bev didn't reach down to pet her, I assumed she held the same jaundiced view of dogs as the folks who manage The Ali'i Royale.

"Yeah, they know," I said. "And they've made it crystal clear they're not running a dog kennel. That's one of the reasons I need to find a house right away. If anyone who works here sees Pima out of her kennel they've threatened to toss us out."

Bev eyed me as if trying to fit the puzzle pieces together. I loved that part of the meet and greets I'd had since winning the money. People usually tried to figure out my story before they had to ask. I'm sure a few had me pegged as a Mexican soap opera star or maybe even the daughter of a key player in a drug cartel, and I got a kick out of seeing how long I could keep them guessing. But I was desperate to find new digs, so I didn't allow Bev's confusion to simmer too long.

"I know I'm probably younger than most of your clients," I said. "But I assure you, the house on the hill isn't out of my price range. I've recently come into a large sum of money, and I intend to pay cash for whatever property I buy. I'm new to the island and hope to make Maui my permanent home."

"Uh-huh. Well, let me go over this brochure with you." Bev dug out a folded flyer from a tasteful Vera Bradley-print bag on her shoulder. "I'm pretty proud of how this turned out. It gives you a glimpse of the fantastic architecture. And check out that view!"

At this point, Chloe came ambling in from the kitchen. "Can I bring anyone coffee?"

Once again, Bev looked confused. Who was this person who resembled me enough to be my little sister? And how did she fit into the equation?

"Chloe, this is Bev Strong, my new realtor." Bev perked up at my use of the phrase, *my new realtor.* "She's going to be showing me some properties this morning. Do you want to come along?"

"I guess so. If you want me to."

"I'd appreciate it if you would," I said. I turned to Bev. "Chloe is my assistant. She helps me keep track of my day-to-day affairs." The way it came out it sounded like Chloe was my pimp. If only.

"Excellent," said Bev. "The more eyes the better. I'm sure Monica will appreciate having another woman's opinion."

"Yes, I'm sure *Miss Gomez* would," said Chloe, emphasizing her more formal approach to my name. "That's what I'm here for."

I kenneled Pima and she began howling. I was pretty sure she wouldn't let up until we got back. Maybe the racket would convince the pet-a-phobes at the front desk they should let the owner decide where their dog should hang out.

"Should we take my car?" said Bev.

"I 'spose so, since Miss Gomez doesn't even have a car," said Chloe. I shot her a *let me handle things* look and she gave me her *sorry* face in return.

"My car's being freighted over from the mainland," I said. "They told me it's going to take a couple of weeks to get here."

"Of course. It's best that I drive anyway since I know my way around. You've probably noticed that all our streets have Hawaiian names. And with only twelve letters in the Hawaiian alphabet it can get a bit perplexing. For example, we have an island right off the southwest coast of Maui called, "Lana'i." It's spelled L-A-N-A-apostrophe-I. But here in the islands we also call a balcony a "lanai." It's spelled the same way but without the capital letter and the apostrophe. You say the words slightly differently because of the apostrophe, but when you look at the written words they look pretty much the same."

"Are we going to have to speak Hawaiian if we live here?" asked Chloe.

"No, in fact native Hawaiians are kind of fussy about their language. It's okay for a *malihini*—that's a newcomer like you—to use basic words like *mahalo* for 'thank you' and *aloha* to say 'hello' and 'good-bye,' but other than that, it's usually best to stick with English."

"They use the same word for 'hello' and 'good-bye'?" said Chloe. "So, how do you know which one they're saying?"

I smiled at Bev and she smiled back. I loved having Chloe around. Besides her many other wonderful qualities she always made me feel like I could qualify for the Mensa Society.

Bev showed us through the four-thousand square foot house on Honopua. It was more house than I needed, but Bev explained that most ocean-view homes were that big or even bigger. She said it didn't make sense to put a small house on a million-dollar lot.

That morning we looked at homes in Wailea, Lahaina, and Ka'anapali. I told Bev I liked the ambiance of the west side of the island a bit more than the south side.

"Yes, the Lahaina side's nice, but you know Oprah Winfrey has two homes here on Maui. One is on the flanks of Mount Haleakala, above Wailea, and the other is way out in Hana."

"You mean we could be neighbors with Oprah?" said Chloe.

"Not really," said Bev. "She has estates, with acres of land surrounding her homes. I don't think you could ever find a house close enough to go borrow a cup of sugar. But we love the idea that Lady O chose our island. I mean, she has homes all over the world, but she spends a lot of her time right here."

After touring five more houses—all with spectacular views—I was convinced I could pretty much live any place on Maui and be happy.

"I don't know," I said. "They're all great. What do you think, Chloe?"

"I liked the one where the second bedroom had that awesome deck."

"It's called a *lanai*," said Bev. She shot Chloe a patronizing smile.

"I thought you said we didn't have to speak Hawaiian," said Chloe.

Score one for Chloe.

"Before you decide," Bev said. "I have one more house to show you. I like to leave the best for last. This home just oozes the 'wow factor.'"

We drove up a smooth multi-lane road which Bev said was called the Honoapi'ilani Highway. "This is a very important road to remember. It connects West Maui to the rest of the island."

"Well, maybe it's important, but it's going to take me a month to learn how to say it," I said.

"Honoapi'ilani? It's not that hard. In Hawaiian you just take each syllable one at a time. So it's Ho-no-a-pi-i-la-ni. Just like that. It looks more difficult than it is. It's like the Hawaiian State fish—*humuhumunukunukuapua'a*. When you see it written out, it's ridiculous. I mean, it's twenty-one letters long, for heaven's sake. But when you break it into syllables it's not that hard to say."

"Sounds hard to me," muttered Chloe from the back seat.

The house was in Kapalua, on the northwest side of the island. It sat up high on a wide expanse of lawn. As we drove down the private drive, Bev said the architecture was called "pavilion style" which meant it had a main living area surrounded by a number of free-standing "pavilions" housing different bedroom suites. Bev explained that each of the suites had its own roof and was connected to the main house by an open-air walkway. There was also a pavilion with an immense *lanai*, or flagstone patio, along with a saltwater swimming pool.

"Wow," said Chloe. "This house sounds great."

"Well, I know we haven't had a chance to chat much about price," said Bev. "But if you can swing it, this is hands down the best deal on the island. The owners moved to Bali, if you can imagine that. Anyway, they're selling it completely turn-key. Furniture, linens, artwork, kitchenware—it comes with everything but a toothbrush."

"Oh, you don't have to worry about price with Miss Gomez," said Chloe, as if I wasn't sitting two feet away. "She's loaded."

I turned around and shot Chloe a dirty look.

She shrugged. "Well, it's true."

"That's great to hear," said Bev. "Because at four and a half, this home is probably your best bang for the buck on the market today."

"Four and a half *million dollars*?" Chloe's voice came out as a high-pitched squeak.

"Yes, and it's worth that and then some," said Bev. "The home is surrounded by nearly two acres of oceanview property. And wait 'til you see what's inside. The Roman-themed marble bath in the master is to die for."

We got out and Bev fumbled through a tangle of keys in her bag and then she unlocked the front door. As we went from room to room, Chloe's jaw gaped so wide you could practically count her molars.

"Miss Gomez, you should get this one," she said when we'd finished looking around. "After everything you've had to put up with, you deserve this—big time."

It was a spectacular house and the owners had done it up in grand style with teak floors, quality tropical-themed furniture and artwork that rivaled pieces you'd find in a museum. The kitchen had not one, but two, free-standing islands. Bev said one was for food prep and the other for informal counter-style dining. The counter-tops were the most beautiful granite I'd ever seen.

"This looks like a mural," I said.

"You have a good eye, Monica," said Bev. "This granite is called 'Pittoresco.' It's from a small quarry in the Umbria region of Italy. The swirls and colors are reminiscent of a Renaissance painting. "

Bev had obviously boned up on the details of the house.

"You sure know a lot about this house," said Chloe, as if reading my mind.

"Well, actually this house is another listing of mine. I probably should have mentioned that earlier."

"But there's no sign out front," I said.

Bev raised an eyebrow. "You'll never see a For Sale sign on a house of this caliber in this type of neighborhood. It would be considered quite tacky."

"Would *I* also be considered tacky?" I said. I was pretty sure I wouldn't have to explain what I meant to Bev.

"Oh, not at all," she said. "We have quite a diverse group of residents up here in Paradise Ridge. People from the software industry, a couple of sports figures, and of course, everyday people like you and me. You would probably be one of the younger homeowners, but to be frank, there are also a few so-called 'trophy wives' up here who're probably younger than you are."

"Do you live up here, Bev?" I said.

"Actually, I do. And it's fabulous. We have two championship golf courses, three wonderful restaurants and a great group of folks in the homeowners' association. Look, Monica, I'm sure you'd enjoy living in any of the homes we toured today. But I can assure you, I wouldn't have brought you to Paradise Ridge if I didn't think you'd love living here as much as I do."

How much was it worth to me to know that at least one of my neighbors would be happy to see me move in? Apparently, four point five million dollars.

CHAPTER 5

Chloe, Pima, and I moved into the Paradise Ridge house eight days later, on a Friday the thirteenth. True to her surname, Bev Strong had badgered the sellers into allowing me to move in before the final closing documents were signed. I'd put down a hefty earnest money deposit and Bev had assured them there was no way I'd back out. At the hotel, sweet little Pima had been spotted outside her cage at least twice, and after the second infraction the front desk advised me I was one Milk Bone away from living on the street.

Moving day was a non-event. Since the house already had furniture and pretty much everything else, the only things Chloe and I brought with us were a few suitcases along with Pima's things. For such a well-heeled woman, my closet was pretty empty. When I first won the money I'd gone on a handful of shopping sprees but it hadn't been much fun. Where's the fun in going shopping by yourself and having suck-up clerks in fancy stores take sneaky iPhone shots of you to sell to the tabloids? It wasn't like I was one of the Kardashians, but the very public battle over the money I'd won had made me somewhat famous. Actually, "infamous" is probably a more accurate description.

So, I'd switched to buying stuff online. I had about five dozen pairs of shoes from Zappos.com and a mountain of things from online versions of stores you'd see in the mall like Anthropologie or BCBG, but it was hard to buy stuff without trying it on. I never sent anything back. If something turned out to be ugly or didn't fit, I just crammed it in the back of my closet and forgot about it. When the movers came to pack our stuff for Maui, Chloe helped me sort through everything and pick out the few things I loved. In the end the "leave it" pile was ten times higher than the "take it" pile. Goodwill made out like a bandit.

By that weekend, we were completely moved in to Paradise Ridge. By Sunday night, I'd looked through every nook and cranny and determined that even at four and a half million dollars I'd definitely gotten a deal.

🐾 🐾 🐾

"Are you happy here?" Chloe said on Monday. We were finishing our lunch at the kitchen island. The beautiful granite countertop was only marginally less dramatic than the eye-popping ocean view.

I started to reply before realizing she was talking to Pima, who was sitting at her feet. The dog wagged her stub of a tail as if answering for both of us.

Chloe looked over at me. "So, what do we do now? I mean, it's nice here and all. But what're we going to *do* all day besides look at the pretty view?"

Once again, she'd read my mind. Although most people probably thought Chloe had a dream job, they had no idea what her life was really like. She worked for a woman who'd been called a cheat and a liar in both the local and national news. I'd even been accused of grand theft. Chloe had no doubt lost friends over it, just as I had. And she never complained. I paid her well, but probably not well enough to make up for leaving her entire life behind.

My love life had certainly suffered from the bad press, but from all appearances hers was no great shakes either. I think she'd had a boyfriend for a month or so during the past year, but one day when I'd asked about him she'd shrugged and said they'd broken up. She said he'd grilled her constantly about what was going on with me: the money, the lawsuits, the whole more-money-than-she-could-ever-spend fantasy. She said she decided he was a jerk. I hadn't heard a peep about any other guy in her life after that.

"I think I might take up golf," I said. "Do you want to join me?"

"Golf? Isn't that like an old man's game? I mean, golf courses are pretty and all, but I don't know if I want to spend my whole day trying to make a little ball go in a hole. It looks totally boring."

I knew something about golf because I'd worked in the Rio Blanco Golf Course pro shop for a couple of years before I went to work at the produce warehouse. In fact, after I won the money, I'd gotten a call from an old boyfriend who'd been the assistant pro at the course. He offered to take me out for coffee to catch up and reminisce about old times.

When I got to the coffee shop he blind-sided me by hauling out a thick file folder and starting in about a "fantastic investment opportunity." He knew a guy who had an idea for a whole new type of golf course that could be played rain or shine, in cold or in heat. I thought it sounded like indoor miniature golf, but when I said that, he seemed to take offense and told me I was underestimating the concept. They needed some serious cash to get it going, but in return he'd give me a ten-percent stake in the business. I politely declined. That was the first, but certainly not the last, time I was called a *bitch* to my face. It stung for a moment, but then I recalled I'd heard the b-word countless times before. Seems dear ol' mom and I ended up with the same nickname.

"Lots of young women play golf," I said to Chloe. "You ever hear of Michelle Wie? Wie's a professional golfer who qualified for the pro tour when she was only fifteen. So you see, she isn't old and she's not a man and she plays golf."

"It still doesn't sound very fun. You go ahead, though. You want me to call and get you a reservation?"

"It's called a tee-time. And first I want to take a few lessons. Come on, at least take a lesson with me."

Another great thing about Chloe is she doesn't make me issue orders. She knows when I say, *come on*, it carries the same weight as an order.

I drove the rental car to the Paradise Ridge pro shop the next morning. Chloe wasn't exactly pouting, but she wasn't her usual sunny-side-up either.

"We don't have any golf clubs," she said as we watched a foursome of two gray-haired men and their chirpy pastel-clad wives unload their clubs at the bag drop area.

"Don't worry. They'll be happy to loan us clubs. It comes with the lesson."

The golf pro who'd be conducting our lesson was a woman my *abuela* would've called a "lady in comfortable shoes." I was never sure in my later years if that was her way of referring to a lesbian or a woman who didn't give a rip about vanity, but whatever it was, it applied to the female golf pro signaling for us to follow her out to the range.

"Why didn't we get *that* guy?" Chloe said under her breath.

She nodded toward a young male pro giving a private lesson to a woman who probably fit Bev Strong's definition of a "trophy wife." The guy was handsome in a Bradley Cooper sort of way. He had thick dark hair and a sinewy build with well-muscled arms that looked like he could crush the ball three hundred yards. He had his arm around the woman's waist and he was showing her how to twist her body when making a tee shot.

"Ah," I said. "He's helping her with her swing."

"I'd like to show *him* a thing or two about swinging," Chloe muttered.

Our instructor had speed-walked to two empty spots on the practice tees. With both hands planted on her ample hips, she turned and scowled at us to catch up.

The lesson went well, especially for Chloe. It seemed she was a natural. Her swing was powerful and fluid. After only a few attempts, her drives were consistently flying nearly two hundred yards straight down the middle. Her putting was measured and accurate.

"Hey, that was pretty fun after all," she said when we'd finished. "I like bashing that little ball. And it's exciting when it finally goes into the hole."

Our instructor tapped Chloe on the forearm. "Do you want to go out on the course? Your friend here needs a bit more practice, but I think you're probably ready to try a short round."

"Uh, I, well," Chloe stammered. This is how it was with us. She needed my permission to do anything. After all, everything she did from eight in the morning until six at night was on my time and my dime.

"I think that sounds great," I said. "Do you have the time to take her out? I'll stay and hit another bucket of balls."

"I can't," said the pro. "I've got another lesson scheduled right away. But I'm pretty sure Jason could take her. He's free until five."

She nodded toward the Bradley Cooper guy. I prayed Chloe would be able to refrain from peeing her pants.

"Can I?" said Chloe in a voice way too pleading to sound anything but desperate.

"Of course," I said. "Let's see if Jason's available."

Turned out, Jason was available in more ways than one.

"When do I need to be back?" Chloe asked. Her eyes made Pima's pleading puppy-dog face look like a rank amateur.

"Take the rest of the day off," I said. "Not much going on anyway. But try to be back before dinner."

She shot me a look of gratitude that was worth much more than an afternoon of her companionship. But as she and Jason pulled away in the golf cart, I figured the odds of Chloe getting back before dark were probably way south of fifty-fifty.

CHAPTER 6

The next morning, Chloe would barely make eye contact with me at breakfast.

"Are you okay?" I said. "You're acting weird."

"I'm, uh, fine." She hunched up her shoulders and peered out from behind her long bangs. "I guess I'm just feeling a little bad about something."

"Oh, what's that?"

"Well, Jason and me really hit it off, you know? I mean, he's so...so..."

"Gorgeous? Hunky? Sexy?" I said.

"Yeah, but he's way more than that. He's like the perfect guy for me. I can't get over meeting him so soon after we got here. And I feel bad because you're the one who wanted to play golf, and you paid for it and everything..."

"Hey, I'm happy for you, Chloe. But I still need you to be my assistant. No talking on the cell and texting all day. No coming in so tired after a night with Jason that you can't do your work, okay?"

It was a ridiculous thing to say. After all, what *was* Chloe's work? Essentially, it was keeping me company. She'd helped out a lot when I'd had a tight schedule of lawyers and financial planners, but now her job was pretty much reduced to walking the dog, going to the grocery store once or twice a week, and keeping an eye on the cleaning ladies and other workers who showed up at the house.

"Oh, believe me, Miss Gomez, I'm clear about that. When it's work time, I work. When I'm off, I can do my personal stuff. Besides, Jason's at the golf course from ten until six, even on weekends. But since we live close by, I could walk up there and see him when he gets off work, right?"

"It's about a mile and a half, uphill, to the pro shop, Chloe. But if we're going to be golfers, I think I should buy a golf cart."

"Yay! Would you let me drive it?"

"Sure. We'll use it to play golf, and you can use it to get around the neighborhood until my car gets here. I'll be glad to get rid of this rental car so you can drive."

The car rental people had made it clear Chloe was too young to be allowed to drive their precious Nissan Altima. So, for the past couple of weeks I'd done all the driving.

"Oh, by the way," I went on, "I'm thinking of going down to that big grocery store down on the highway. You know, the one on the way to Ka'anapali," I said. "Do you want to come?"

"No thanks. I'm going to walk Pima and then I'm going to take an inventory of the kitchen stuff. I think this place has everything you want, but I like to be sure."

Chloe was about the most organized person I'd ever met. I loved her little checklists and inventories. She'd kept me sane in Arizona when an avalanche of legal documents had threatened to bury me in paper, and she was correct in assuming I'd want to know whether we had the right type of corkscrew, and whether we had a manual can opener as well as an electric one.

"Okay then. Do you have a grocery list for me?" I said.

"Right here." She handed me a list of six items written in precise block letters.

"I'll be back in an hour or so. Do you know where I left my keys?"

She pointed to the end of the kitchen counter. We'd kept the running gag about the keys going across three thousand miles of ocean.

About twenty minutes later, I pulled into the Times Market just off the Honoapi'ilani Highway. The store was unremarkable, but adequate. Bev had mentioned there was a farmer's market just up the road in Honokowai, but it was only open three days a week and I'd forgotten which three days they were.

I picked up the items on Chloe's list and then cruised the aisles trying to acquaint myself with the store. There had all the usual things we had in Rio Blanco: Rice-a-Roni, Special K, and Grey Poupon. There were also some new things. In the fish case there were trays of chopped red fish with stringy green stuff mixed in called *ahi poke*. And in the canned foods aisle, I came upon an entire section of Spam—at least a half dozen different flavors including hot and spicy Spam, honey Spam, and something called "wasabi" Spam.

In the produce section there were more fruits I couldn't recognize than ones I could. One of the mystery fruits was a fist-sized oval green fruit labeled *lilikoi*. I picked up a *lilikoi* and sniffed it.

"I see you're into passion fruit," said a man's voice behind me. The voice was smooth and low, as if he was kidding around with someone he knew.

I turned. His eyes slid down my body. I felt like he was undressing me right there in the produce section of the Times Market. I glanced down to make sure I hadn't missed a button on my blouse.

"Passion fruit?" I said. "The sign says *lilikoi*."

"Yeah, that's 'cause *lilikoi* is the Hawaiian word for passion fruit." He smiled. His teeth were white and straight, his lips more luscious than any of the fruit on display. I shifted my gaze and took in the rest of him. If Chloe's Jason was Bradley Cooper, this guy was Dwayne Johnson, aka The Rock. He was about six-foot-five of solid muscle, with thick black hair and piercing dark eyes. He shot me an *Aren't I somethin'?* grin that he'd probably been perfecting in the mirror since he was twelve years old.

"Huh, that's interesting," I managed to say.

"You eat it by cutting it in half and sucking out the seeds. A lot of people squeeze it for the juice. It's real *ono*—good."

"I'm sure it is." I'd heard about getting picked up at the grocery store, but maybe he was a chef or something and was simply bragging up the local bounty. I smiled and pushed my cart to the next bin where pineapples were neatly stacked in a tall pyramid. I poked through the pineapples, but didn't pull one out for fear of bringing the whole thing crashing down.

He followed me. "You a visitor?"

He seemed to be getting quite a kick out of watching me stutter-step through the display of foreign fruit. No doubt he was well aware of his intimidating physique and he enjoyed the effect he had on women.

I flashed back on what a former friend in Rio Blanco had told me about how her life had dramatically changed when she'd gone from a B cup to a D cup via an expensive boob job. She said she relished nothing more than walking into a room wearing a down-to-there V-neck blouse and watching the guys scramble to pick their tongues up off the floor. Seems Mr. Lilikoi got the same kick running his pickup lines on female tourists.

"Actually, I just moved here," I said. "For good. I bought a house up in Kapalua."

"Ah, so you're a *malihini*."

I remembered Bev mentioning that word. "A newcomer. Yes, that would be me."

"*Ho'okipa* to our island. I hope you'll like it here." He extended his hand. "I'm Keokoa Kekane. Keo for short."

Was the guy a real Hawaiian? Bev had also told me that only about ten percent of Hawaii's population was ethnically Hawaiian, but maybe Keo Kekane was his womanizer name. Maybe the name on his birth certificate was more along the lines of Steve Jones or Bob Smith.

We shook hands. His grip felt warm and strong. "I'm Monica. Monica Gomez, from Arizona."

"Ah. Well, Monica Gomez from Arizona, I'm glad to meet you."

We stood there for a couple of beats. I didn't know what else to say, and apparently he didn't either. The silence started sliding into awkward territory.

"I'm happy to meet you because I actually came in here today on business," he said. He pulled out a plain white business card and handed it to me. "I manage the local food bank. I spend a lot of time prowling the stores trying to get them to toss a few things our way. It's a non-stop job trying to round up more food and cash donations. We've got twice as many people asking for help as we did just a few years ago. And with the downturn in the economy, we've got half as much food on our shelves."

I stepped back. Who was this guy? How had he picked me out of all the people in the entire store to hit up? Did I have a sign on my back that said, *I won millions*? I felt stalked. I'd been on Maui only a few weeks and already a complete stranger had sidled up to me and stuck his hand out for a donation.

"Uh, I'm sure the food bank's a great charity. But I've got to run. Nice meeting you, Keo."

I left my full shopping cart in the produce section and race-walked to the door. I didn't take a full breath until I drove through the guard gate at Paradise Ridge. How far would I have to go before people would stop hounding me?

CHAPTER 7

A few days after my humiliating exit from the grocery store, I spent the morning puttering around the house, tidying drawers and straightening the pictures on the walls. At lunch, Chloe asked me once again when my car was due in from the mainland.

"Why do you keep asking? Do you want to use the car to go visit your new boyfriend? Take the golf cart. Or, better yet, maybe he should act like a gentleman and come down here and see you," I snapped.

"His brother's in the hospital and he loaned his car to his sister-in-law since they don't have one," she said. "But I wasn't asking about the car for me. I've just noticed you've been acting kind of antsy. I thought maybe you'd feel better if you had some familiar things around."

"Oh. Well, the car's due in sometime next week. I'm sorry if I seem cranky. I'm just starting to wonder if moving here was such a good idea after all."

"Why would you say that?" she said. "Back home, you constantly got calls from crazy people claiming to be your relatives. Or guys who wanted you to invest in some stupid invention or help them out with questionable medical situations. And, don't forget all the times you had to meet with your lawyer. Your name was always in the news, and not in a good way. Over here, there's none of that. It's calm and quiet. Look around, Miss Gomez, this really *is* paradise."

She was right, of course. At night we didn't even bother closing the sliding glass panels to the lanai. I'd sit at the dinner table and gawk at the ocean view until it got dark and then I'd slip off to bed. The temperature varied only slightly from day to night, and the ever-vigilant security guards at the gate house kept out intruders and looky-loos. But something was nagging at me. As much as I tried to push it out of my mind, after meeting Keo I realized Maui probably didn't feel like paradise to the people waiting in line at the food bank. Not only did they not have an ocean view, they didn't even have enough to eat.

"I met a guy at the store on Tuesday," I said.

"I thought you'd blown off going to the store. You didn't bring home any of the stuff on my list."

"I know. I went to the store, but I left before I could buy anything because I met a guy in the produce section and I got flustered."

"He must've been pretty hot to make you forget you're out of wine." Chloe fanned her face with her hand.

"No, it wasn't like that. He's the guy who runs the local food bank. He said he was at the store looking for donations."

"Oh no, here we go again," she said.

"Yeah. But you know, I've been thinking. Maybe I need to be more generous. I mean, even after paying cash for this house, I've still got tons of money. Probably more than I'll ever need. I should *do* something with it, don't you think?"

"Depends. How cute was this guy?"

I must've blushed because she gathered steam.

"Did you find out if he's married? Because before you go writing a check, you should probably find out if he's available, don't you think?"

"That's not the point, Chloe. I should help him out because there are people on this island who go to bed hungry every night. And because I remember what it feels like to eat nothing but pinto beans for dinner."

"Then go to the food bank and give him some money. Do you want me to go with you?"

"No, that's okay. I looked it up on the Internet. It's in Wailuku, all the way on the other side of the island. I'll drive the Altima over this morning and give the food bank some money. Then I'll check at the harbor and see when my car's coming in."

"Well, if you're cool going there by yourself, would you mind dropping me off at the driving range on your way?"

I rolled my eyes.

"It's not what you think, Miss Gomez. I'm not going up there to see Jason. I just want to hit some balls while you're gone. I want to practice so you and me can play golf together."

I couldn't really argue since taking up golf had been my idea in the first place.

After I dropped off Chloe, I tapped the address on Keo's business card into the GPS. The directions said Wailuku was thirty-three miles away. They also said it would take almost an hour to get there.

I hesitated. An hour to go a little over thirty miles? Why would it take so long? In Southern Arizona, you can go thirty miles in about twenty minutes. But for more reasons than I cared to think about, I wasn't in Arizona anymore.

I turned onto the Honoapi'ilani Highway and headed out.

Ꮬ Ꮬ Ꮬ

The highway that goes from one side of the island to the other was clearly marked and well-maintained, but there were a lot of twists and turns through hills separating West Maui from the rest of the island. And, once I'd made it to the other side, I ran into a string of traffic lights that all seemed to prefer the color red. I relied on the GPS to tell me where to turn because, as Bev Strong had pointed out, it was impossible for me to decipher the road signs. Every street name was a word with mostly vowels. It was hard to decipher between all the o's, a's and e's on the little street markers .

The GPS lady told me to turn at Ho'okahi Street and then to turn again on Kolu. I found myself in an industrial area of windowless one-level warehouses. I should have just mailed Keo a check. There was no way I'd find the number on the business card among the labyrinth of identical gray and beige metal buildings. The GPS kept chirping, *You have arrived at your destination*, so I knew it was around there somewhere, but I saw no signs or addresses on the buildings. Which one was it?

I wanted to ask someone if they knew where the food bank was, but the entire place appeared deserted. When I was about to give up and just go out to the harbor to check on the car, I turned a corner and saw a large panel truck with the Maui Community Food Bank logo painted on the side. It was parked at an open loading dock. I parked on the street and got out. As I approached the loading dock, a young woman with braids pinned across the top of her head rushed out of a nearby door and ran toward me.

"I'm glad you made it. No worries, we're just getting started." She handed me a white cotton apron with the food bank logo on it and a plastic shower cap. "The others are already inside. *Mahalo* for coming in on such short notice."

I wondered if Chloe had called and told them I was coming. But that didn't make sense. I'd left Chloe at the driving range, and besides, she wasn't inclined to take matters into her own hands when it came to meddling in my personal life.

I'd planned to write a check to the food bank, go down to the harbor and ask about my car, and then drive right back home. But back home to what? I didn't have anything waiting for me there but Pima, and she slept all afternoon anyway.

I slipped the apron over my head and tied it in back. When I donned the shower cap I had to twist my long hair into a sloppy bun to fit it inside the cap. Having my neck exposed felt weird.

"I'm Leilani, Lani for short," said the woman who'd given me the apron. She held the warehouse door open for me. "You'll be sorting today. We got some good produce from Foodland this morning so it should go pretty fast. No rotten stuff. All pretty nice."

As the door closed behind me I felt a chill. They must've had the A/C going full blast. Lani gestured toward a box of disposable rubber gloves. "You need to put those on. They make your hands kind of sweaty, but they keep the food clean. Besides, some of this stuff has bugs."

I put on the rubber gloves and walked behind her as she ushered me to a spot on what looked like an assembly line but was actually just a series of folding tables shoved together.

"You'll be working with Max today," Lani said. "He'll show you what to do."

Max turned out to be a tall guy about sixty to seventy years old. He had a pleasant face and he wore his shower cap about halfway back on his head since he appeared to be completely bald. He looked more like the old guys I'd seen teeing off at the Paradise Ridge Golf Course than someone I imagined working at a food bank.

"Is there someplace I can lock up my purse?" I said.

"Stick it under here," Max said, pointing to a spot under the table. "Nobody'd dare take it."

A few seconds later two fork lifts began bringing in stacks of sagging cardboard boxes. They stacked three boxes by each of the tables and then beep-beep-beeped back out to retrieve more. Max instructed me to just observe for a while.

"It's not brain surgery," he said. "But there's a rhythm to working side-by-side like this."

I stepped back and watched as Max quickly unpacked a box of iceberg lettuce and inspected each head. Most of the lettuce he replaced in the box, but occasionally he'd make a face and throw a head into a big trash can alongside the table.

"See? It's not hard. Look for bad spots or rot. If it's a little damaged, that's okay. Just pick off the worst of it. But if it looks totally rotten, throw it out. This lettuce looks pretty good, although it's not very nutritious. But I guess when you're hungry, anything's better'n nothin'."

I stepped up to the table and began grabbing heads of lettuce as fast as I could. Every now and then Max would signal to the fork lift operator to pick up our finished boxes and bring us more. After a while the lettuce stopped coming and bananas took over. Many of the bananas had started to freckle and I was throwing out more than I was boxing up.

"Whoa," said Max pulling a big bunch of bananas out of the trash can. "These aren't so bad. This one here's kinda funky, but the rest are okay. If you find a bad one, just rip it off and box the others up. We never get enough fruit so we can't afford to waste it."

At two o'clock an air-horn sounded and everyone started ripping off shower caps and snapping off gloves. Max went down the line of tables and picked up the last of the bananas and put them in a box. The rest of the workers cleared out so fast you would've thought someone had sounded a fire alarm.

"Where'd everybody go?" I said.

"Quittin' time around here's called '*pau hana*.' When they're done, they're done," he said. "So, can I buy you a cup of coffee?"

The guy was old enough to be my grandfather, but he seemed nice enough. I followed him to a back part of the warehouse. There was an area in the corner that had been walled off with sheets of unpainted plywood. Through the open door I saw it was a make-shift break room consisting of three rectangular folding tables and a garage-sale assortment of chairs.

I followed Max into the room where nine or ten other people were already seated. Everyone had a mug of coffee in front of them and more than a few of them had the fidgety look of someone who normally enjoys a cigarette with their coffee. The walls were littered with *No Smoking* and *Clean Up This Area* signs, making the room look more like the cafeteria back at my high school than a place to reward weary volunteers.

"What're you here for?" said a nearly toothless guy of about fifty with a deep scar running from the edge of his mouth to his right eye.

"Excuse me?" I said.

"I said, what're you here for?" The guy said it slower and louder, as if he figured I had a hearing problem.

Max spoke up. "That's off-limits and you know it, Del. The lady's here for her own reasons. It's none of your business and you could get written up for asking."

I was about to ask Max if we could step outside so I could ask what the heck was going on when I heard a familiar voice behind me. Oh great. I looked like something that should've been tossed the in the trash can, and now he decides to shows up.

I put on my game face and turned around.

CHAPTER 8

Was it even possible that Keo could look even sexier than he had at the grocery store? I guess the answer was *yes*, because he did.

I tore off my shower cap and shook my hair out, hoping it didn't look as sweaty and tangled as it felt.

"Monica, right?" Keo said.

He came over and rested a hand on my shoulder. I was stunned he remembered my name. Max came back from getting us coffee and he set a chipped mug of thick black coffee down in front of me. I looked around for cream and sugar but didn't see any.

Before he sat down, Max asked Keo if he'd like a cup. Keo thanked him but said he could only stay a few minutes.

Keo pulled a folding chair up next to me. "I gotta say, Monica, I'm surprised to see you here."

Oh damn. He must think I'm pathetic, hunting him down at work. Especially after my less-than-appropriate departure from the grocery store. He probably figured me for some kind of lunatic. Why hadn't I just dropped off the donation check like I'd planned?

"Yeah, well, you know…" I couldn't for the life of me think of how to finish. Should I tell him I simply came to drop off a check but got conscripted out in the parking lot? Maybe I should ask if we could go somewhere private to talk. No, that really sounded like something a lunatic stalker would say.

"Did you work here today?" Keo asked.

I nodded.

Max butted in. "She sure did. A full four-hour shift. Didn't even take a break."

"Working here's a real a win-win, don't you think?" said Keo. "I'm glad you decided to check us out."

I wanted to say, I came to check *you* out, not the rotting produce and this motley crew of twitchy food sorters.

Keo went on. "So, was it what you expected?"

"Well, I'm not used to standing so long," I said. "But the time went by pretty fast."

"Not fast enough for me, sister," said a woman at the next table. She looked ancient, with rheumy eyes and gnarled hands curled around her cup. "I gotta put in five more hours in this joint and then I'm done."

I leaned forward. "What's going on?" I kept my voice low so only Keo and Max could hear me. "What does she mean she's got five more hours?"

Keo gave me a wink and touched my shoulder again as he got up.

"Gotta do the rounds," he said.

After Keo was out of earshot, Max said, "Most everyone here is working off court-ordered community service time. Not everyone, of course. Some people, like me, are volunteers. I figure it's the least I can do, being's how I'm a *haole* living in another man's country."

I must've looked confused because he went on.

"You know, the United States stole Hawaii from the Hawaiian people. Just up and took it a hundred and fifty years ago. So I do what I can to make amends. I work here and I also tutor kids up at the high school in math and science. I enjoy it and it makes me feel better knowing I'm giving back a little. But there's really no way to undo what was done, is there?"

A big dark-skinned guy with a shaved head came over and clapped Max on the back. "Hey man, you know they don't allow no politics in here, eh *brah*? But jus' let me say as far as I'm concerned you're good people. *Haole* or no."

Max grinned. "*Mahalo*, Timo. Sorry for talking outta turn. But this little gal needs to be brought up to speed. Most mainlanders don't have a clue about the sovereignty issue."

Keo was in the back corner saying his farewells to what looked like a group of girl gang-bangers. He came back by our table on his way toward the door. "I've gotta run, but it was good to see you again, Monica. Be sure and check with our volunteer coordinator before you leave. She'll sign your timesheet."

I'd scooted my chair back and was about to follow Keo outside so I could clear up the misunderstanding when the break-room door flew open. A young woman in black leggings with a skimpy black tank top burst into the room. As if the Mortitia Addams look wasn't already well-established with her outfit, she had scary-looking skull tattoos trailing from shoulder to wrist on both arms. Her stringy long hair had been dyed a dull blue-black.

She spotted Keo and ran over to him, flinging her arms around his neck. "*Ku'u ipo!*" she cried. "I haven't seen you for a whole two days. I was getting worried."

"I'm sorry. I've been working 'til late. C'mon, walk with me." He expertly disentangled himself from her embrace. He grasped one of her hands in both of his and his face softened. He held her gaze until she dropped her eyes.

"Why didn't you come over last night?" she murmured in a pouty voice. "I waited for you. I even got us pizza and everything."

He whispered something in her ear and the two of them left together.

"Who was that?" I said.

"Her?" Max shook his head. "She's Keo's girl, or so she claims. But who knows? He's way too wily to own up to what's going on with the two of them."

I didn't let on I was shocked. Instead, I changed the subject. "So what's that word mean? You know, *haole*?"

"It's kind of a bad word," Max said. "It means a foreigner."

"But I thought a foreigner was a *malihini*. My neighbor Bev told me I'm a *malihini* because I just moved here from Arizona."

"No, *malihini* is a friendly word. It means a newcomer. *Haole* is a more derogatory term, a racial thing. It means a Caucasian, or someone of a race other than Hawaiian or Polynesian."

"So, if someone calls me a *haole*—"

Max interrupted. "It's *definitely* not a compliment."

I thanked Max for showing me the ropes and then I got up and rinsed my coffee cup in the sink. I was halfway across the parking lot when Keo caught up with me.

"Hey, Monica. I wanted to give my *mahalo* again for coming," he said. "You know, I've got good instincts about people. I had a feeling when I met you at the store the other day I might be seeing you again."

I wanted to ask him if he'd pegged me for a common criminal, but instead I flashed him my fake *no problem* smile. Fifteen years of playing the "Little Orphan Annie" card in Rio Blanco had made me pretty good at camouflaging my emotions, and a year of being called a cheat and a thief had made me even better.

"Yeah. Well, meeting you made me curious. I wanted to see how things worked here at the food bank," I said.

"What do you think?" he said. "Were you able to make some new friends?"

Oh, yeah, Keo. Like I'm real eager to get up close and personal with folks working off their DUI time or their plea bargain for peddling drugs to school kids.

"It was an interesting experience. Very informative. Nice to see you again, Keo." I reached to grab the door handle on the Altima, but Keo got to it first. He held the door open for me. I glanced over his shoulder to see if Tattoo Girl was lurking around. I could just imagine her watching Keo playing Sir Lancelot and then tailgating me all the way back to Kapalua so she could beat me up.

I considered telling Keo the truth about why I'd come out there, but I didn't want to embarrass us both. Instead, I climbed in the car and drove off.

I looked at the clock on the dash. It was almost three o'clock. I had plenty of time to go to the harbor and check on the ship bringing my car over, but I wasn't in the mood. It would get there when it got there. For the past year I'd been obsessed with managing everything. Managing my money, managing my reputation, managing my mouth. I'd moved to Hawaii to get away from all that.

I pulled onto Waiehu Beach road and drove back to Paradise Ridge following the GPS lady's instructions as if she were talking me down off a ledge. The garage door was sliding up when it dawned on me I'd forgotten to pick up Chloe on my way back. It'd been more than six hours since I'd left her at the driving range.

I pulled out my cell and called her. She answered on the second ring.

"I'm sorry it took so long," I said. "Are you still at the range?"

"No, I'm here in the house. I just saw you pull in. Are you okay? You sound funny."

"I'm fine. Just kind of tired."

"Jason's here," she said. "I hope that's okay. After you didn't come get me he brought me home in his golf cart." She giggled and I flashed on an image of them in a compromising position.

"No problem," I said. "I'll be in soon. I need to grab a few things out of the trunk."

I sat in the car listening to the car engine tick as it cooled. I could just imagine Chloe and Jason scrambling to get halfway decent before the "boss lady" showed up. It made my clumsy attempt at going to the food bank to connect with Keo just that much more humiliating.

CHAPTER 9

To say the weekend was unremarkable would be an understatement. I played computer games and tried to finish reading a book I'd started weeks ago, but my mind kept wandering back to the food bank. Maybe it hadn't been so bad working there. At least while I was there time had passed quickly and I felt needed.

On Monday morning I was on the lanai when Chloe placed a cup of steaming Kona coffee in front of me. The aroma was so wonderful it felt like a waste to drink it.

"Do you have any plans for the day?" she said. Maybe I was imagining it, but I detected a slight chiding for my slothful behavior over the weekend.

"I'm going to the other side of the island to do a little shopping," I said. "The cleaning ladies will be here this morning. Would you make sure they vacuum inside my closet? I don't think they got in there last time."

"Sure, Miss Gomez. Anything else?" Chloe was eyeing me like she had when the first nasty article about me had come out in a notorious gossip rag. The look wasn't as much pity as concern.

"Uh, let's see. I also need you to call around and find someone to power wash the driveway. I think it looks stained."

"Didn't Ms. Strong tell us they did all that before they put the house on the market?"

"They said they did. But I still think it looks stained. See if you can find someone who can clean it up, okay?"

"No problem. Mind if I go hit some balls over my lunch hour? Jason said he'd pick me up. He promised to have me back here within an hour."

"Fine. But if the cleaning people are still here, I'd like you to wait until after they're finished so you can lock up."

"Of course, Miss Gomez."

I chewed on half a coconut bagel while I planned my day. I'd decided I'd run by the food bank and drop off the check I'd neglected to give them on Friday. If Max was around I'd see if he could join me for a cup of coffee, but I wasn't going to hang around hoping to see Keo. I was only going over there because I'd made a commitment to myself to finish what I'd started—nothing more.

After that, I'd stop at the big mall in Kahului and try on some new shorts and maybe look at sandals. Before coming back, I'd find the harbormaster's office and see if they could give me an idea of when my car would arrive. When I'd shipped it they said it would take ten to fourteen days, and it was already going on three weeks.

I got to the food bank at ten. This time no one came out to intercept me. In fact, the parking lot was empty. I tried the door by the loading dock and found it unlocked. The place was dark and deserted. There was a crack of light coming from under the break room door so I figured everyone must be in there. I hustled past the empty sorting tables and took a deep breath before opening the door.

Tattoo Girl was the only one in there. She had her head down and was picking at her ghoulishly-patterned arm as if trying to dislodge a tick. Her head shot up when the door slammed behind me.

"I remember you," she said. She'd attempted a smoky-eye look with gobs of eye shadow and liner, but instead of looking hot she looked more like she'd come out on the short end of a street brawl. "You worked here last week."

"Yeah, I came in on Friday. Why isn't anyone working today? Is it a holiday or something?"

"Duh. The sorting line's only open on Tuesdays and Fridays." She went back to picking at her arm.

"Do you know if Keo Kekane is here?"

She looked up and narrowed her eyes to mere slits. "What do you want with him?"

"I'd like to sign up as a volunteer."

"You don't bother Keo with stuff like that. I'm in charge of volunteers."

"Okay, but I'd like to talk to him about when it would be best for me to come in. You see, I live on the other side of the island and it's a long drive over here. I want to check and make sure I only come in on the days when the volunteers are here."

"*I* can give you the volunteer schedule," she said. "I'm here every day. On Mondays we do deliveries, on Tuesdays and Fridays we sort fresh stuff, on Wednesdays we box up the canned food, and on Thursdays we go to the pantries and sign up new people and do emergency deliveries."

"Oh. So, every day is different," I said.

She rolled her eyes. "Don't you hear good? I just told you we sort fresh food on Tuesdays *and* Fridays. Those days are the same."

Her sneer made me want to punch her in the face. I'd probably get away with it since her eyes already looked like she'd been smacked around a little. I hadn't been in a cat fight in more than a dozen years so it was debatable how well I'd fare. Although she was scrawny, she looked tough. She might have the upper hand when it came to hurling jabs and ducking blows.

"Is Keo out making deliveries?" I said.

"How should I know? When he's working I don't bug him. When it's our private time, then he's all mine."

Thankfully, the door opened and a stocky woman in a faded blue *mu'u mu'u* entered the break room. She had smooth brown skin and she'd wound her shiny black hair into a little round ball at the crown of her head.

"*Aloha*! My name's Makaila. How you doin'?"

"*Aloha*. I'm Monica."

She came over and put out her hand. I stepped forward to shake hands but instead she grasped both my hands in hers. "Nice to meet you, Monica. You need a little *kokua* today?"

"Food? No, I'm doing okay for food."

"*Kokua* don't mean food, dummy," said Tattoo Girl. "It means 'help'. She asked if you need help."

Her snarly voice and the "dummy" thing just added to my bewilderment of why Keo was involved with her, but then I reconsidered. Men love to lament, *what do women want?* but one of the few upsides of being female is we know exactly what men want. Although it was hard for me to picture the two of them sharing the same sheets, maybe she had secret talents that only a pierced tongue could maneuver.

I turned to Makaila. "No, thanks. I came in to work, but I see nobody's here today."

"You jammed up with the court?" Makaila said. "Maybe I can find somethin' for you in the office. Get you filing or some such. I could prob'ly get you at least a couple hours."

"Oh, thanks, but I'm not here for community service hours. I just had a little time on my hands today and thought I'd come volunteer."

Tattoo Girl broke in. "She's really here lookin' for Keo."

Makaila laughed. "Oh, honey. Every red-blooded *wahine* on this island be lookin' for a man like Keo."

Tattoo Girl snuffed loudly and swiped the back of her hand under her nose. Then she held up a fist. "Don' you go talkin' about my man like that. You hear?"

"Sure, Starshine. No beef. Jus' kiddin' around." Makaila turned to me and nodded toward the door. "C'mon, I'll walk you out."

As Makaila and I went back through the dim warehouse, a shiver snaked down my spine. When I'd left on Friday the place had been ablaze with light and buzzing with activity. Now, as I trailed after Makaila through the gloomy high-ceilinged space I could hear the trade winds whistling through the cracks in the corrugated metal walls.

"Kind of spooky in here," I said.

"Not nowhere near as spooky as that little girl back there," she said in a low voice. "Keo's the only one who can handle her. What he sees in her, I'll never know. But do yourself a favor and steer clear. She's got a real short fuse."

When we got outside, I dug around in my purse and came up with the check I'd written to the food bank. "Would you do me a favor and give this to Keo when you see him?"

She took the check. When she read the amount her jaw dropped. "You sure? This here's a lotta money."

"Keo said it's been a tough year," I said.

"It has been. And a lotta people's situation don't look like it's gonna get better any time soon." She held out her arms, then gripped me in a pillowy hug. It felt so much like hugging my *abuela* I had to shake off the urge to hang on.

"*Mahalo nui* for this," she said flapping the check back and forth as she stepped back. "You have no idea how much this is gonna help."

"It's my pleasure," I said.

🐢 🐢 🐢

I pulled into the Queen Ka'ahumanu Center Mall but then left before parking the car. I wasn't in a shopping mood. When I'd first gotten the money I'd spent entire days prowling the upscale shopping malls around Tucson and Phoenix. La Encantada, Scottsdale Fashion Square, Biltmore Fashion Park. I'd hauled more merchandise out of those places than UPS.

In fact, the same day I was told to leave my job, I drove up to La Encantada Mall in Tucson and plunked down twenty-eight hundred bucks for an orange Louis Vuitton handbag. I'd actually pronounced the brand name, "Lo-is Vitten," but the sales clerk didn't correct me. I handed over my credit card like I regularly bought designer stuff and this was no big deal, but my heart was pounding. I hadn't actually received the prize money yet. What if the bill came before the money hit my bank account? Or worse, what if Haystack-Haired David Michael Corcoran was a fraud and the Prize Posse was really a bunch of unemployed actors with too much time on their hands? I'd have to hawk my car to pay for the bag.

I pulled out onto Ka'ahumanu Avenue and turned left at Wharf Street. Then the GPS lady told me to make a quick right onto Ala Luina. I wasn't exactly sure where I was going, but this was the definitely the harbor area and hopefully the harbormaster would have some information about my car.

I stopped at the gatehouse guarding the pier. Beyond the gate I saw a couple of fire trucks parked on the dock and about a dozen guys in firefighter gear milling around.

"Can I help you?" said the guard.

"I've come to find out when my car's supposed to arrive."

The guy twisted his mouth to one side as if I'd told him I'd like him to let me in so I could set fire to the pier.

"You know you can look it up online," he said.

"I have been looking it up. All it says is it's 'in transit.' That's not much help. I was told it'd take ten days to two weeks and it's been way longer than that."

"How much longer?"

"It's nearly three weeks now."

The guy turned to watch the activity on the dock. Then he looked back at me and gave me a *shaka*—that ubiquitous thumb and pinkie-finger wave I'd learned could stand for *hi*, *how's it going?*, *take it easy*, and probably a dozen other things I hadn't figured out yet.

He smiled. "Look, over here we run on 'island time.' You'll get your car when your car shows up. No way to hurry the ocean."

"Look, it's not floating in on the tide. It's on a ship or a barge or at least something with an engine. Can't you look it up and see where the ship is?"

"Might could. But we're kinda busy right now. And besides, all the manifest will tell me is when it left LA. All heavy freight goes to Honolulu first. They wait until they get a full barge before they bring it over here. What I'm tellin' you is—your guess is as good as mine."

"What's with the fire trucks?" I said, nodding toward the activity on the dock.

"We had a couple dock workers go in."

"You mean, in the *water*? A couple of guys fell off the dock? How'd they manage that?" I tried to stifle the smirk in my voice but I must've not been very successful because he shot me what Bev refers to as "stink eye."

"It's serious," he said. "They could've drowned."

I murmured I hoped they'd be okay. Then I threw the rental car in reverse and did a three-point turn to get out of there. I headed back to the West Side. It'd been a totally wasted morning, but at least I'd managed to burn up a few hours.

When I got home Chloe handed me a telephone message. The message was from a Stan Phizer calling from Kahului Harbor. "He said it's about your car."

Great. After getting the "island time" excuse from the guy at the guard gate, it looked as if my car had been there all along. Oh well, it wasn't as if I didn't have time to drive back over. But ever since I'd won the money I'd become used to people catering to me. How hard would it have been for the guard guy to check and see if my car was there? Okay, so it was a little hectic with the fire trucks and all. But does that mean everything just shuts down while they pluck a couple of hung-over dock workers out of the water?

It seemed to me that "island time" was just the local way of saying "not my job."

CHAPTER 10

I called the number on Chloe's note and it rang about six times before somebody picked up.

"Harbor Master's office, Phizer speaking." The voice was gruff, as if I'd interrupted something terribly important like a video game or a nap.

"I'm returning your call," I said.

There was no ready acknowledgment, so I went on. "This is Monica Gomez. I believe you called me a little while ago about my car?"

Silence.

I must've been right about the nap and the guy wasn't awake yet. "I shipped it over here from the mainland. It was supposed to arrive more than a week ago. I was told it would be coming in on a barge from Honolulu, and today I got a call about it."

Still, nothing. Geez, did I have to draw the guy a picture?

Finally, he said. "What kind of car? Color, make, model?"

"Don't you keep records on these things?" I said. "It's a Lexus LS 450. White. I have the shipping documents. I'll bring them with me when I come. If it's okay, I'll come tomorrow. I live over on the West Side and I already went to Kahului once today."

He snorted. "Save yourself the trip. 'Fraid the only one who'll want to see those shipping docs now will be your insurance agent."

"What?"

"Lost a few things this morning, your car being one of them."

"Lost?"

"Yeah. Never seen anything like it. The barge came in, and we were starting to unload it when a rogue wave slammed us. Big sucker. Nothin' we could do. Your car and a cargo container went right over, along with a couple of my guys. One helluva mess, let me tell you."

"I was out there. I saw the fire trucks. What happened to my car?"

"My guys are both going to be fine, thanks for asking."

I wanted to tell him I already knew that, but then realized I didn't. "Well, that's good to hear. So, about my car?"

He chuckled. "Well, like they say, you're gonna always know where it is, 'cuz it's not goin' anywhere. It's gonna make a nice home for the fishies."

"That car was nearly new. It cost seventy-five thousand dollars."

"Oh, well then it's gonna be a *real nice* home for the fishies. Come over when you get a chance and we'll get you the 'lost in transit' paperwork. You'll need it for your insurance claim."

I didn't say anything. It stung that my one small touchstone from home—my car—had been swallowed up by the vast ocean that separated me from everything I'd ever known and loved.

When he spoke again, he sounded more sincere. "Sorry, but these things happen. Just a bit of bad luck, I'd say."

🐢 🐢 🐢

The rest of the week slipped by in a flurry of faxes, early morning phone calls, and filling out forms. My Tucson-based insurance agent seemed to have a hard time picturing "went to Davy Jones' locker" as a possible covered loss for someone who'd bought her car at Desert Sun Lexus.

"Bob, I don't live in Arizona anymore."

"As of when?"

"As of early March this year."

"You should've notified our office of your address change. Your coverage in Arizona may or may not include flood-related loss."

"It didn't flood, Bob. It slipped off a barge and went into the ocean."

"Yeah? Well, that still makes it a water-related loss. I don't know if we'll be able to cover that."

🐢 🐢 🐢

By the time Friday rolled around I was thrilled to see Bev Strong's name on my caller ID. After nonstop calls from my lawyer, my insurance agent, and a local used-car jockey who offered to "hook me up with a sweet ride" after being tipped off by his longshoreman neighbor about my car going in the drink, it was great to get a personal call.

"Bev, good to hear from you," I said.

"Monica, I'm feeling real uncomfortable about something and I had to call and confess."

"What's up?"

"I've been meaning to host a little 'meet and greet' for you here in the neighborhood and it's just been one thing after another. I know it's *très très* last minute, but is there any way you could fit it in your schedule to come over for a little get-together tomorrow evening? Nothing fancy. Just a few of the more social neighbors. I'm embarrassed to throw this at you last-minute, but my calendar has been brutal. I'm sure yours is just as full."

Did I dare confess my calendar looked like the proverbial white cat in a Rocky Mountain blizzard? Probably not such a great idea to a woman who was putting in twelve-hour days writing up listings and hosting open houses.

"It's kind of you to think of me, Bev. Let me check my schedule." I held the phone away from my ear for about five seconds before saying, "Looks good. What can I bring?"

"Absolutely nothing but yourself, dear. I'm having Kitty, from Kapalua Katering, bring over some snacks for us to munch on. She makes the best coconut calamari. To die for. Plan to get here around, say, seven? And, as for dress, let's keep it casual. Don't you even *think* about going shopping for a new frock."

I was about to ask if I could bring Chloe when Bev signed off with a cheery "See you tomorrow" and hung up. I considered calling her back, but realized Chloe would probably consider it work. No doubt she'd rather spend the time with Jason anyway.

෯ ෯ ෯

I got to Bev's at ten after seven. There were only three cars in the driveway. Maybe the other neighbors had walked over. A well-scrubbed young man in a freshly pressed aloha shirt and white pants answered the door and handed me a drink festooned with a tiny pink paper umbrella, pineapple spear, cherries on a plastic toothpick and so on. I took a sip to steady my nerves as I stepped from Bev's gleaming white marble foyer toward the great room with its fifteen-foot ceiling and full-on ocean view. The drink tasted like it was about ninety-percent dark rum, for which I was thankful.

"Ah, darling. You're here," Bev swooped over wearing an outrageous silky thing that looked like she'd repurposed a brightly-colored parachute from one of the local parasail operators.

"Wow, that's amazing," I said, eying her get-up.

"Oh, this old thing?" she said. "It's been in my closet for years." She leaned in to whisper. "It's kind of a bitch to get everything back in place when I have to pee, but it's so comfy I couldn't resist."

I looked down at my lackluster attempt at Hawaiian casual: aquamarine palm-patterned sleeveless top and white cropped pants. I'd taken my sandals off at the door like everyone did in Hawaii, but they were nothing spectacular—simple white flip-flops I'd paid way too much for at J Crew. At least when I'd gone for a pedicure I'd opted for little palm tree decals on my toenails. On my wrist I wore a southwest-style turquoise and silver bracelet that my *abuela* had given me when I graduated from high school. I was sure the stones were fake, but I'd always worn it when I faced something daunting, like my first day at work or my driver's test.

"I love, love, love your chic little Navajo statement piece," Bev said, tapping a carmine-red nail on the largest chunk of turquoise plastic in my bracelet. Could she tell? If so, she kept it to herself.

"We're a few people short of a full house," she went on. "But that's fine. Because there's someone here I'm dying to introduce you to. And it will be *so* much easier for you two to get to know each other with fewer people around."

I looked around the spacious great room and into the open kitchen. There were about ten people, total. I caught Bev's eye and it dawned on me. This was a fix-up. A blind date. A gotcha. In the past year I couldn't recall the number of times I'd been shanghaied into meeting the favorite nephew, younger brother, or "newest member of our firm" in a bald attempt to find me a gigolo who'd act as a snitch-baby if I even dreamed of taking my business elsewhere. The professionals in charge of managing my winnings weren't about to take "your services will no longer be necessary" lying down.

I did my best to flash Bev a smile, but it must've fallen short.

"Oh, don't look like you're about to be shot at dawn," she said. "You'll love Derek. And don't worry, he's not after your money. He's got more than plenty of his own."

She touched my elbow and guided me outside to the pool area where three men were sharing a hearty laugh. As soon as we got within earshot, they froze. They each wore the expression you'd expect from a group of fourth grade boys when Sister Mary Catherine shows up at the paper drive and catches them enjoying their first glimpse of a Playboy magazine centerfold.

"Bev, great party," said fourth-grader number one. He was a guy of about sixty, with a self-assured shock of startling white hair and mischievous navy-blue eyes.

"Yeah, we were all just remarking how fantastic your view is," said the second guy. "Best in the neighborhood." Number two was about twenty years younger, with a shaved head and about forty extra pounds around his midsection.

The third guy looked more my age. And whether he had money or not I was still interested. He had piercing green eyes, with thick dark lashes and eyebrows—sort of like Ben Affleck. His hair was blond, though. It kind of clashed, the blond hair with the dark eyebrows, but it was sexy as hell. He was only three or four inches taller than me, but height had never been a deal-killer as far as I was concerned.

He held out his hand to shake mine and the other guys watched like zookeepers watching a couple of pandas who'd been brought together to mate. Would we hit it off? Would the male lumber away disinterested? There was no way the female would be pulling the snub. I was practically panting.

"Monica, I'd like to introduce you to Derek Chambers." Bev's voice was a low purr. "I thought you two might have a lot in common."

"If we don't now, I'm sure we will soon," said Derek. Oh goody, he was glib as well as gorgeous.

"Nice to meet you," I said. Okay, so when I'm in lust I don't do glib very well. Derek didn't seem to mind.

"Bev's told me a lot about you. I hear you're something of a tabloid celebrity back on the mainland. Just think, our own Kate, Duchess of Cambridge, right here in Paradise Ridge."

"Unfortunately, I'm afraid I'm more like the Octomom or Casey Anthony than Kate Middleton. Notorious rather than glamorous."

"You look pretty glamorous to me," he said.

Bev sidled between the other two guys and grabbed their arms to steer them back inside. They seemed disappointed to miss out on the mating ritual but the steel in Bev's grip no doubt let them know she wasn't about to let their rubbernecking foul up her world class matchmaking.

I leaned in to Derek. "So, you say Bev's told you about me, but I'm afraid she hasn't told me anything about you."

"Oh?" A crease wrinkled his impeccably-tanned forehead.

"Probably she wanted to allow me the pleasure of finding out for myself," I said. "Like a wonderful present I get to unwrap."

Whoo-hoo. I gave myself like a hundred glib points for that one.

We found a cozy loveseat by the gas fire pit and Derek told me his story.

"I've been very fortunate," he said. "I got into the oil and gas game when things were still controlled by a few key players. I worked hard, made some risky moves. One winter in Denver I actually lived in an RV. I had to move from campground to campground every time I got busted for overstaying my welcome. Shale oil was about to make a comeback, but nobody was looking. And natural gas? I've got a one-word answer for stopping terrorism by Islamic extremists."

I gave him my best, *Oh, do go on,* look.

"It's 'fracking.' Simple as that. We're sitting on so much natural gas in the Midwest it's ridiculous. Us buying oil from the towel-heads is like Eskimos buying Frigidaires. Doesn't make sense."

"But isn't fracking where they pump arsenic and a bunch of other weird chemicals into the earth and contaminate the ground water? Isn't it bad for the environment?" I said.

"I'll tell you what's bad for the environment. Crashing planes into skyscrapers in New York City and ISIS blowing up our embassies. If we'd just suck it up and let the oil and gas industry take over a few hundred square miles of godforsaken prairie land, we could be energy self-sufficient in less than ten years."

"But what about the people who live there?"

"What about 'em? You see the people of North Dakota whining about getting truckloads of cash for drilling on their farmland? They never made cash like that fretting over the price of winter wheat."

After a couple of Bev's high-caliber cocktails, I wasn't that concerned about fracking, winter wheat, or ground water in the Midwest. I was focused on trying to remember whether I'd put on my good Victoria's Secret lace panties or if I'd opted for my ugly, but more comfy, Hanes cotton ones.

My underwear hadn't mattered for more than a year. Now, thanks to Bev, it looked like it could matter a lot.

CHAPTER 11

My *abuela* was hard-nosed about what she called "giving *leche* for free," which was her short-hand way of reminding me that men have no reason to buy a cow if they can get the milk for free. Sleeping with a guy on the first date (or, heaven forbid, after meeting on a blind date) was so frowned on in her household that I'd gotten something of a reputation in high school as a prude and a tease.

So, when Derek nuzzled my neck and asked me if I wanted to come over to his place to "see his etchings"—okay, his offer wasn't that lame, but just about—I demurred.

"I really need to be getting home," I said. The dark rum was whispering, *"Your* abuela *will never know,"* but old habits die hard.

"Do you want me to come down to your place and tuck you in?" he said.

I said, "No thanks," but caught myself nodding, *yes.*

My rum-soaked brain was yelling at me that I was a consenting adult and it was time to stop acting like a coy teenager. But try as I might, I just couldn't get myself to agree to something that would require a walk of shame in the morning.

Finally, Derek backed off. "Look, I get it. But we both know it's just a matter of time. And, lucky for you, I've got lots of time."

He walked me out to my car. I dug around in my tiny Tiffany clutch and couldn't find my keys. Here's a tip for avoiding DUI: if your keys hide from you it means they don't think you're fit to drive.

I could see lights on in my house only a few hundred yards below.

"I think I'll walk," I said. "I've had a bit to drink and I wouldn't want to mow down an unsuspecting neighbor."

"I'm completely sober," Derek said. "I'm happy to drop you off."

Since my *abuela* also had a thing about girls not walking alone at night, I took him up on his offer.

When we pulled up at my driveway, Derek had to get out and push the iron gate open. I'd disabled the locking mechanism because it seemed silly to live in a gated community behind another locked gate. But I always closed it when I left, just to give the illusion of additional security.

We got to the front entryway and Chloe came to the door and poked her head out.

I rolled down the passenger window. "It's just me, Chloe."

"Miss Gomez? Are you okay?"

"I'll be in shortly. I'm fine."

Derek had a hand on my thigh and he gave it a little squeeze. "You certainly are," he said in a husky whisper.

For some unfathomable reason, that made me laugh and I giggled as I fumbled for the button to get the car window to close.

Derek wasn't laughing. In fact, his expression looked stern as he leaned over and placed his lips on mine. The feel of his warm, soft lips sent my spasms of laughter scurrying somewhere deep in my belly. I put a hand around the back of his neck and pulled myself closer. His tongue found mine and together we slid down a slippery slope of desire.

I wasn't sure how long we'd been at it when all the exterior lights on the house snapped on. A few seconds later I saw Chloe's face glaring from the sidelight window next to the front door. I flashed back to sixth grade when José Moreno had walked me home from a middle school football game and we'd begun making out on my front porch when my dad ripped the door open and ordered me inside.

Remembering how my father had looked at me sobered me up in a hurry. "I'm sorry," I said to Derek. "I need to go in."

"You got something to tell me?" Derek said.

"What?"

"You got a boyfriend? Maybe a girlfriend?"

"Uh, no. You mean the person who turned on the light?" He nodded.

"That's my assistant, Chloe. She's kind of protective of me."

"You want protection, you should get yourself a dog."

"I've got a dog. I've also got a very sweet, very loyal assistant."

We locked eyes. "I really need to go in."

"See you tomorrow?" he said.

"I guess," I said. "Call me."

"No, you call me. Here's my number." He popped open the center console and handed me a business card printed on heavy card stock. I rubbed my thumb along the raised embossed lettering.

I sat still for a few beats to see if he'd leap out and get my door for me but when he didn't, I groped for the door handle. The cold metal required a pretty good tug to release the door latch.

"So, are you gonna call?" he said.

I leaned back inside. "Sure."

"Just so you know," he said. "I take commitments, even half-hearted ones, seriously."

"So do I."

As I got out, I took a good look at the car. It looked like a Mercedes Benz, but it didn't have the three-point star emblem on it anywhere. It had four doors, but was low and sleek. Even in the meager glow of the porch lights I could see it was two-tone, gold or light brown on the bottom and a darker color on top. The wheels were black spoke-type, not the flashy chrome I'd expected.

Before I closed the passenger door, I leaned back in. After all, I was in the market for a new car, and this one was sleek and beautiful.

"What kind of car is this?"

"It's a Lorinser, made by Mercedes Benz," he said. He shot me a cocky smile.

"How much does a car like this cost?"

"Wrong question," he said.

"Okay."

"What you meant to ask was how fast can this sucker go?"

"Okay. How fast?"

"Over two hundred miles an hour, no sweat. Zero to sixty in less than four seconds."

I shrugged. We lived on an island with no freeways and only a precious few stretches of straight road with more than one lane on each side. Why would it matter how many seconds it took to reach sixty miles an hour?

My face must've signaled my indifference.

"Okay, since you asked," he said. "This baby cost eight-hundred grand, plus freight and taxes. Talk to you tomorrow."

I'd barely gotten the door closed when he threw the car into reverse and shot back toward the gate, tires squealing.

ဆ ဆ ဆ

Chloe was waiting on the other side of the door when I got inside.

"Whew, who was that?" she said.

"That was Derek Chambers. Bev fixed us up at her party."

"Some fix-up. Is he as gorgeous as the car?"

"More."

"Seriously?" she said.

"He's handsome, rich, and a really good kisser."

"Makes you wonder why he's still available," said Chloe. She seemed to think better of it and then said, "Uh, I didn't mean it that way. What I meant was, how lucky for you he's a friend of Bev's."

"Don't apologize for questioning what's the deal with him," I said. "Believe me, I've been thinking the same thing."

We went to our respective bedrooms and I got into bed. I hadn't been that drunk for more than a year, and I hadn't been kissed like that for even longer. As I lay there, my brain was making so much racket it was impossible to get to sleep. I kept coming back to the same thing: who pays more than three-quarters of a million dollars for a car? Even if I could afford it, and I certainly could, I'd never waste money like that. What if it had been Derek's precious Lorinser that had gone in the drink at Kahului Harbor instead of my Lexus? Aren't some things just a silly extravagance, regardless of how much money you have?

The next morning I noticed I'd gotten a text message on my cell phone. It was from Keo and it'd come in last night. How'd he get my number? Then I remembered filling out the volunteer form at the food bank. I read the text: *Hrd u came by fd bnk Mondy. Sry I missed u. R U cmg in Tuesday?*

What was that about? Maybe he'd taken the time to Google my name and he'd ramped up into full-blown fund-raiser mode. Or maybe he and Starshine had had a tiff and he was lining up possible replacements. Whatever the reason, I wasn't going to respond. I'd moved on.

I called Derek at eleven.

"Sleep late?" he said.

"No, but I didn't want to call too early and wake you."

"Sweetheart, there's no way you could call too early. I work on Greenwich Mean Time, which means I'm up way before the sun."

"But today's Sunday."

He laughed. "No rest for the wicked. I work every day. The energy business runs twenty-four seven, three hun-dred-sixty-five. Say, you up for a sail this afternoon?"

"Sounds great. Although Bev may have told you I come from the Arizona. I can't remember the last time I was on a boat."

"Look, Monica, I'm not recruiting deck hands," he said. "You're only job will be to look gorgeous and enjoy your-self."

"What should I wear?"

"Something skimpy."

"No, seriously," I said. "What should I wear for a boat ride?"

"I'm equally serious. Wear as little as possible. We might want to take a dip. I've got towels and plenty of sun-block, so come as naked as you dare. I'll pick you up in an hour."

☟ ☟ ☟

Derek showed up exactly an hour later and Chloe an-swered the door. I'd thrown clothes all over my room trying to figure out what to wear. White cropped pants? No, I'd worn a pair last night. I didn't want it to look like I'd slept in them. How about my navy pin-dot sundress? No, that retro look made me look like a housewife from a 1960's sitcom.

I settled on a black and white one-piece bathing suit I'd bought a few years ago for a girls-only trip to Puerto Peñasco, Mexico. We hadn't realized it was Spring Break for the University of Arizona and the place was packed with rowdy college kids, but that made it all the more fun.

I slipped a white mesh topper over my arm and sauntered out to the great room. Chloe, in good old Chloe fashion, let out a low whistle. "You look great, Miss Gomez. Like a swimsuit model or something."

Derek's eyes stayed fixed on my legs. "Yeah. But why not a bikini? Over here no woman under forty swims in full-body armor like that."

I looked down. "This is the only swimsuit I have."

Did I dare let him know I had no intention of getting wet? I didn't know how to swim. My idea of going to the beach was a three-hour drive to the Sea of Cortez to sit poolside and sip two-dollar happy hour margaritas so strong they'd dissolve the paint off a barn.

"Looks like you girls need to go shopping," he said. He winked at Chloe, but she didn't smile back.

"I think Miss Gomez looks fabulous just the way she is," she said. She turned to me, "But if you'd like me to find you some new swimsuits I will."

"We'll talk about it when I get back."

Derek followed me outside. There was a shiny red Corvette convertible parked in the driveway. The top was down.

"Yours?" I said.

"Yeah. I don't like to take the Lorinser out in traffic. And today being Sunday there's going to be a lot of locals hanging around town and tourists parked at the harbor."

"How many cars do you own?"

He laughed. "More than I should, I suppose. But don't hold it against me. I swear it's my only vice."

CHAPTER 12

We drove to Lahaina Harbor going the "long way" as Derek put it. We turned off the Honoapi'ilani Highway at Front Street and took the smaller road through neighborhoods and past the neon *Jesus Coming Soon* sign that looked like it'd been there for at least fifty years. I guess *soon* is a relative word in Biblical terms.

When we got to Papalaua Street with the Hard Rock Café on one side and Longhi's Restaurant on the other, the traffic slowed. The four-block crawl down the main tourist drag of Front Street from Papalaua to Dickerson took almost as long as it'd taken us to drive in from Kapalua. We turned into the harbor area and I started looking for a parking place.

"Whew. It's crowded today," I said. "Looks like we may have to go around the block a few times before something opens up."

Derek smiled. "No problem. I don't sweat stuff like that."

He pulled in front of the Pioneer Inn and an earnest-faced bellman raced out to the car. "Will you be staying with us, sir?"

"Sure am. Just checking in. You know someplace safe where I can park?"

"Don't worry, sir. I'll park it for you." He scribbled something on a ticket and ripped off the lower half. "Here you are, sir. Just ring the bell station when you want your car brought around."

"Thanks. Will do," Derek said.

He pulled out his wallet and handed the valet a folded bill. From where I was sitting I couldn't determine the denomination, but when the bellman glanced down at it his eyes widened.

"Sir, this is very generous. Usually guests tip when we bring their car back around."

"Well, that's to make sure you *do* bring it back around. And in perfect shape." Derek said. "If there's so much as a thumbprint on it I'll alert your supervisor."

"No worries, sir. It will be totally safe with me."

We got out and the valet slid into the driver's seat. He pulled away at a snail's pace. I'm sure he would've loved to leave a little scratch on the pavement, but he puttered along as if he was parking his grandma's Buick Roadster.

"You're not staying here, are you?"

"No, why would I?" It took Derek a couple of beats to figure out why I was asking, and then he said, "Oh, that line about 'am I checking in'? Yeah, I learned that a couple years back. It's a little game I play every time I come down to use the boat. That guy's gotta have figured it out by now that I'm handing him a line but trust me, he doesn't care."

Derek's "boat" turned out to be what I would've called a "yacht." I hadn't grown up around water and, until I'd gone to Puerto Peñasco, I hadn't been in any type of watercraft other than the two-man rowboat my dad used for fishing at Patagonia Lake. Still, I figured something longer than an eighteen-wheeler would definitely be called a "yacht."

"Wow, it's beautiful," I said.

It was. The sleek hull gleamed a brilliant white in the noon-day sun, and the windows sparkled like highly-polished sapphires. There were at least three levels—a smaller upper deck, topped by a bunch of antennas and a large round ball I assumed had something to do with navigation radar, a middle deck that took up most of the length with a small open area in the back and a chrome railing that went all the way around to the front of the boat, and then a lower deck that skimmed along the waterline with several oval-shaped portholes.

"This is a yacht, right?" I said.

"I s'pose, since the salesman kept calling it that. I'd hoped for something bigger, but they have size restrictions in this harbor. If I was in Honolulu, I'd have more to choose from. But who wants to live in a freakin' city, right?"

We boarded the yacht. I don't know what I expected, but I hadn't expected to see pristine ivory carpet and miles of built-in white leather couches. The cabinets and wood furniture were so shiny they looked like plastic. And the kitchen—Derek called it a "galley"—was outfitted in stainless steel everything, including a half-size SubZero refrigerator.

"You could live here," I said.

"Yeah, I guess a person could. I'm too much of a landlubber to ever consider it, but the salesman said the original owner used to sail it back and forth to Seattle. So, it's definitely a seagoing vessel."

"Is there a bedroom? Or do these couches make up into a bed?"

Derek laughed. "Oh, sweetie. There's no couch surfing required. This thing's got four bedrooms and four heads."

"Four bedrooms? My *house* has four bedrooms. And what's a 'head'?

"A 'head' is the nautical term for a toilet or a bathroom. In this case, the master 'head' has a Japanese soaking tub, a rain shower, and marble countertops."

"Wow. I'm happy just looking around. We don't have to even leave the harbor."

"No, we're going out. In fact, I need to check and see if Larry's warmed up the engines. I haven't been aboard for a few weeks."

He left to go deal with getting the boat underway and I went down a tiny stairwell to peek into the bedrooms. There were two main bedrooms equipped with queen-sized beds and large marble-tiled "heads." The two smaller sleeping rooms had twin bunk beds and more modest toilet accommodations.

I climbed the steps to the third deck where Derek was sitting in the captain's chair. Next to him was a scruffy-looking guy in jeans and a t-shirt. He stood when I entered and stuck out his hand.

Derek said, "This is my friend, Monica."

"I'm Larry," he said as we shook hands. "I take care of Mr. Chamber's fleet."

Fleet? Derek had a fleet? What kind of guy has a *fleet* of anything?

"Larry takes care of my vehicles," Derek said, clearing up the mystery. "My cars, this boat, the motorcycles..."

"Don't forget your airplane," said Larry. He beamed as if Derek's abundance of motor-driven conspicuous consumption somehow reflected well on him.

"Larry's a first-class mechanic. Hard to come by in these parts." He clapped Larry on the shoulder. "So, whaddaya say about me taking this baby out this afternoon?"

For a split second I thought he was talking about me. Like he was asking Larry to weigh in on my date-worthiness.

"You want me to pilot it out of the harbor?" said Larry.

"Nah, I can handle it."

"You sure? It's been a while, sir."

Derek shot Larry a look that could freeze tequila. "I said I've got it, Larry. But before you leave, why don't you take a few minutes to scrub out the head in the master suite? Last time I looked I thought it could use a good cleaning. And don't forget to put out a new toilet paper roll."

Larry hung his head and mumbled, "Nice to meet you, Monica," before slinking out to go downstairs.

🐢 🐢 🐢

About fifteen minutes later, Larry waved from the dock to let us know he'd disembarked.

"So, can you really drive this thing all by yourself?" I didn't mean to sound skeptical; it just seemed it might be a tight squeeze to get a boat of that size in and out of the crowded harbor.

"Of course. I'm going to ask you to mind the stern, but this thing practically maneuvers itself."

"Stern?"

"Yeah. That's the back of the boat. Make sure we don't get too close to anything as we're pulling out."

"What should I do if we come too close?"

He slowly spun around in his captain's chair to face me. "Yell 'Stop.' I'll have the intercom on. Think you can handle that?"

I guess I'd asked for that one.

We pulled out into open water and the sky seemed as vast and blue as the ocean below. I remained on the second deck until we'd cleared the harbor. Then I went upstairs to be with Derek. I marveled at how close the neighbor islands appeared and asked him to point out which islands were which.

He nodded his head slightly to the left. "Over there is the island of Lana'i. And the one to our right is Moloka'i."

I could clearly see the clefts and ridges of Lana'i, but no buildings or harbors. In fact, there seemed to be no sign of civilization at all.

"Have you ever been over there?" I said.

"To Lana'i? Of course. In fact, I own property there. In my opinion, the best golfing in the islands is on Lana'i."

"I've recently taken up golf," I said.

"Really? That's great. I'll take you to Lana'i sometime. It's got two amazing courses."

We chugged along for ten more minutes and then Derek cut the engines to a mere rumble. "You want to take a swim?" he said. "I've got a hydraulic swim platform off the stern."

I glanced nervously toward the back of the boat.

"You worried about sharks? Well, don't be. They don't hassle people in deep water like this. And besides, they don't like the engine noise. Keeps 'em away."

Sharks were the least of my worries.

"I've got to tell you something," I said.

He laughed. "What? You got hydrophobia or something? I don't see you foaming at the mouth."

"Hydro-what?"

"Hydrophobia. It's Latin. It means 'fear of water.' It's one of the key symptoms of rabies."

"Are you saying if I don't want to get in the water I have rabies?"

"No. Forget it. It was a joke."

"I've never liked water," I said. "Don't get me wrong. I think water's okay to drink. And I like Jacuzzi bathtubs and taking a shower every morning, but jumping into a lake or swimming in the ocean isn't for me. I hope you're not disappointed."

He held out his arms. "Come here. Staying dry is fine with me."

I snuggled into his embrace. We hugged for a while and then he slipped a hand under my swimsuit and started working his way around to my breasts. It felt good to be touched. I reached back and started to undo the strap at my neck. I hadn't gotten the hook out of the loop when Derek grasped the sides of my suit and attempted to pull it off me. The force of his pulling must've bent the hook because the straps gave way with a snap.

"Whoa, cowboy," I said. "What's the rush?"

"Hey, I said we don't need to swim," he said. "So, how else will we get our exercise?"

He tipped my head up with a thumb under my chin and leaned in as if to kiss me. But instead of a kiss, he locked a forefinger across my upper lip and held my jaw tightly closed between his thumb and finger. I felt a flush of panic as I tried to remove his hand and found I couldn't.

"Mmmh," I said, pulling back.

He dropped his hand.

"You're right," he said. "This isn't the best place for this. C'mon."

He grabbed my upper arm and pulled me downstairs to the sumptuous master sleeping cabin. I gasped as he slid his gym-strong arms under me and lifted me up onto the bed.

"I don't know—"

"Shh," he said. "Let's not kid ourselves. We both know what we want."

He was right, of course. But somehow this didn't feel right.

"We need to get you out of that thing," he said. He yanked at my bathing suit and my breasts popped free like twin clown heads popping out of a jack-in-the-box. I couldn't hold back a nervous giggle.

"What's so funny?" he said. His face was blank; his eyes like hard green stones as he gaped at my naked breasts.

"Nothing. I just thought my boobs kind of looked like—"

"Your boobs look great. And, now I'll show you something equally great."

He slipped off his swim shorts and, *whoa*. It'd been a long time since I'd glimpsed anything quite like that, but it wasn't just absence that made my heart grow fonder. His "manly parts" were quite impressive.

I tried to take it slow, but failed.

"You're quite the little eager beaver," said Derek. "I like that in a woman. But now let's do it again and go through all the gears this time."

Over the course of the afternoon we made love three times. By number three, my breathing was getting ragged. As I lay there panting my way back to something approximating a normal heart rate, I had the same comedown feeling I'd experienced after winning the money.

Before I was rich I thought if I could ever get to a point when I didn't have to worry about money, my life would be perfect. Since childhood I'd enjoyed excellent health, decent looks, and a pretty good head on my shoulders. But once I started working, I spent more and more time fretting over how to pay my bills. After winning the sweepstakes that burden was lifted. All that stood between me and my imagined "perfect life" was finding a sweet, handsome, loving guy who was interested in me and not just my money.

Derek was a sweet guy. He was affectionate and fun in bed. And, from the looks of things, he had plenty of money and wasn't afraid to spend it. We motored back to Lahaina Harbor a few hours after sunset. I stood beside Derek as he skillfully maneuvered the boat back into the slip, but I couldn't shake the sense that something wasn't right.

It was the same hollow feeling I'd had after the prize posse had driven away and the enormity of winning was beginning to take hold. I felt jumpy and insecure. As if the only way forward was through uncharted territory with no way back.

What was wrong with me? Why is it every time I get what I want it makes me uneasy?

CHAPTER 13

W hen Chloe came into the kitchen Monday morning I was flipping through the *Maui News* on my iPad. I heard her but didn't look up. She poured herself a cup of coffee and then came over and stood at my elbow. I tried to ignore her but she was so close I could smell the coconut conditioner in her hair. Pima was whining and doing her *feed me* dance at Chloe's feet.

"What is it?" I said, still not looking up from my iPad.

"Guess who's flying here to Maui this afternoon?"

"Santa Claus?" I said.

"You don't pay me enough to laugh at lame jokes, Miss Gomez. I'm serious. You need to hear this."

I put the iPad down. "Okay, shoot."

"Your attorney, Mr. Dease. He's arriving at 2:45 at the little airport."

John Dease III, Esquire, was my favorite attorney in my legion of lawyers. He'd held my hand from the very beginning and always said the right things at the right time. I'd watched him change his strategy from pit bull to Scooby Doo to lap dog as the situation warranted, and I trusted him implicitly.

"Why's he coming over?"

"He said you've been putting him off for weeks and it can't wait."

"He's landing at Kapalua?" I said. "He's gonna love that."

Kapalua Airport, or the West Maui Airport as it's sometimes called, is only a short drive from my house. It's on a bluff in the middle of what used to be pineapple fields. The community of Kapalua's claim to fame, aside from world-class golf courses and wealthy residents, is it is always windy. The runway at West Maui Airport is extremely short so only small prop planes can land there. Bev Strong had warned me that passengers sometimes scream like teenagers on a roller coaster as the planes make quick lifts and dives on take-offs and landings.

John Dease hated to fly. In fact, when I'd had court hearings at the Arizona state capital he'd always opt to drive the two hours from his office in Tucson to Phoenix rather than fly, even though by plane it only took half-an-hour.

"So, how did your date with Derek go yesterday?" Chloe said, changing the subject. Lucky for me she was digging in the pantry for Pima's kibble or she'd have no doubt seen the hot flush that scorched my cheeks.

"It was fine," I said. "Great, actually."

She popped her head out. "Great? Like in, 'hot' great? Or great, like in 'nice guy, but no cigar'?"

"Oh, there was definitely a cigar." As soon as I said it, I felt my blush deepen.

"Oh, yeah? Details?"

"Look, before John gets here, I've got to get some things done. And aren't the window washers coming today?"

Chloe nodded.

"Then we'd better get going. I still haven't showered yet."

🌺 🌺 🌺

Derek called while I was toweling off. "Hey, love," he said. "How're you faring this morning?" For some reason, he'd affected a slight British accent.

"Wonderful," I said. "How about you?"

"Couldn't be better." A beat of silence went by while I wondered if he'd just called to check on my health. Then he went on, "I was hoping to come down to see you. I got an urgent call from a business associate in the Middle East and I need to pop over there for a few days. But before I go, I wanted to say good-bye."

"Come anytime."

He laughed. "Now that's what I like my girls to say. I'll be there in, oh, ten minutes or so?"

He showed up in the Corvette.

I ushered him into the foyer. "You're taking your 'Vette to the airport?"

He was wearing a crisp white dress shirt, tan slacks and a soft brown suede bomber jacket. Way too much clothing for a leisurely day on Maui, but probably completely appropriate for a thirty-hour flight to the Middle East.

"No way," he said. "My company's sending a limo. I parked at the airport one time and learned my lesson. You'd be surprised at the number of bozos who steal cars here. It's an island, for God's sake. It's not like they're gonna get away with it for long, but they can sure do a lot of damage trying."

I offered him something to drink, but he declined. "I just wanted to see you again. You're so gorgeous. I woke up this morning and had to pinch myself. How's it possible that my dear neighbor lady, who's been trying to fix me up for the better part of a year, could've finally come up with someone so perfect?"

He draped his arms around my shoulders and pulled me close. I smelled his spicy scent—aftershave, leather and pine-scented soap. I nuzzled into his chest. Derek seemed the perfect match for me, too.

"Well, I gotta go," he said. "I'm catching Qantas to Sydney and then it's Air Emirates nonstop to Dubai. I should be back within a week, maybe sooner."

"Wow, Dubai. Sounds exotic."

"It's not. It's nothing more than Las Vegas on steroids. Fancy hotels, fake everything, and people with more money than God."

"Why would God need money?"

"See, that's what I like about you. You're funny. Besides being the sexiest woman on this rock." He bent in and kissed me, hard. I pulled back and touched a finger to my lip to make sure it wasn't bleeding.

"My bad," he said. "I just want to make sure you don't forget me while I'm gone."

"A split lip isn't a great souvenir."

"You're right," he said. "Kiss me. I'll be gentle this time."

We kissed slow and deep. My awareness collapsed into a deep well of pleasure and longing. Even though I was still a bit sore from our love-making on the boat, I felt myself gearing up for more. I could feel Derek rising to the occasion, as well.

"I really hate to say it, but I've got to go," he said. He pulled back and held me at arm's length. "I'll be back as soon as I can. Where I'm headed, the women wear black tents from head to foot, so no fair checking out the nearly naked guys on Ka'anapali Beach, okay?"

"Don't worry. I'll be right here when you get back."

"I'll call when I get to Dubai," he said.

He hopped in his car and left. I stared at the empty driveway feeling alone and adrift. I still had a nagging feeling that something was off, but I chalked it up to a year of paranoia. I willed myself to relax and enjoy the moment. I reminded myself there's nothing more fun than the first blush of desire. When you can't get enough of each other and every kiss, every caress and every moment of passion is white-hot. I smiled as I made my way back to the house. Derek had just left but I already missed him.

Thankfully, getting ready for my attorney's arrival that afternoon didn't leave me time to mope. I decided to dress up a bit to mark the occasion of my first mainland visitor. I put on long white pants, a royal blue silk blouse and a thick gold necklace I'd bought during one of my early shopping binges. John Dease was at least twenty years older than me, probably around my dad's age if he'd lived, but he treated me like an equal. He always made me feel as if my questions were brilliant and my decisions admirable.

I felt a bit guilty for not calling him before I left Arizona. He'd left messages nearly every day for the past three weeks. I'd more or less forced him to take the six hour flight to meet me face-to-face and I knew how much he hated flying. Then I chuckled to myself. Knowing John, he'd bill me for every minute and throw on a bit more for aggravation, so I really didn't need to feel *that* bad.

I fired up my computer and opened my email. I had two-hundred-eighty-two unread messages. I looked at the dates and realized I hadn't sat down at the computer for nearly a week. I searched for John's name and came up with thirty-six unopened e-mails.

It wasn't as if I didn't know what he was going to tell me. That wise-ass *US Star Weekly* reporter who'd called the day I'd arrived in Maui had tipped me off. My former boss and year-long nemesis, Steve Harrow, had apparently upped the ante. And, as much as I wanted to ignore him like a kid hiding under the covers to keep the bogeyman at bay, it wasn't working. Seems the bogeyman was pinching my toe and wasn't about to stop until I gave him his due.

ↄ ↄ ↄ

When I picked John up at the airport, his plaster-white face and damp handshake discouraged me from asking if he'd had a good flight. Instead, I gave him a quick hug and hustled him out to my car. We made small talk as I drove up to the house. I asked how mutual acquaintances were doing, and he asked how I was enjoying life in Hawaii.

When I pulled through the gate John let out a soft whistle. "Whew. Looks like I win the bet," he said. He pulled out his phone and took a picture of my house.

"The bet?"

"Yeah, I made a bet with my new secretary that your place wouldn't be on the beach. She was sure it would."

"The beaches on this side of the island are mostly over-built," I said. "Lots of condos, and lots of big hotels. I love it up here on the bluff. But it's windy most of the time."

"Tell me about it," he said. "When that pilot nose-dived onto that little runway I was waiting for him to yell 'Allahu Akbar' and plow right into the hill. Worst plane ride ever."

"We'll rebook your flight home. If I drive you over to the big airport at Kahului you can fly in a nice wide-body jet all the way back to Phoenix. No problem."

"Speaking of problems," he said. "We've got some."

While Chloe made John coffee—I'd never seen John when he wasn't clutching a coffee cup, day or night—he told me about Steve Harrow's latest scheme. He reiterated what I'd already heard from the reporter. My former boss had filed a suit against me for fifty million dollars. He'd also requested to be reimbursed for all his attorney's fees and court costs to date.

"The man's insane," I said. "He's the one who initiated all the lawsuits, racking up tens of thousands in legal fees. And besides, I've already won this case once. Isn't this double jeopardy? What happened to the settlement we agreed on before I left Arizona?"

"That agreement stands. But a few days before you moved over here, Mr. Harrow got some bad news."

"What? He get hit with a paternity suit? Or has his bookie threatened to bust a kneecap for unpaid debts? Whatever it is, I'm sure it's not my problem."

"I'm afraid it may be. Seems while you were running his front office you failed to adequately vet some of the workers. Immigration agents raided Az/Mex a month ago and found thirteen illegal workers with falsified documents. Every one of them had been signed off by you."

"What? That's impossible. I used the E-Verify system the feds put together. How could so many illegals slip through?"

"That's what Mr. Harrow wants to know. He's facing stiff fines and may possibly lose his business license."

"But fifty million bucks?"

"That's what he claims the business is worth."

I put my head in my hands. "This is a set-up. But what can I do? If those people gave me false documents that were good enough to fool the system, how could I have known? And I swear, I didn't know."

"I came over to hear your explanation and that's good enough for me," John said. "I've been digging into this, hoping to find a precedent. But so far, no luck. This may turn out to be a test case. Makes sense, you've got deep pockets and the feds love to make headlines by getting tough on immigration. But it's not all gloom and doom. I still haven't gotten to the bottom of it yet."

"Isn't Harrow at least partly responsible? I mean, they were his workers. He was their boss after I left. If he had any doubts he should've looked into it."

"I agree. And that's my going-in position. But I want you to know what we're up against. The court of public opinion isn't behind you on this, Monica. There are a lot of folks who believe you weren't entitled to keep the contest money and this will just galvanize their position."

"But I won that case. The jury agreed I'd sent in the entry on my own time since it was my lunch hour. And Harrow was unable to prove I'd used the company postage meter to mail it. Besides, that has nothing to do with this. They're two different things."

"I agree. But the problem is we'll be hard-pressed to come up with a second jury who'll not be influenced by what happened in the first case. You know how it is."

He looked out at the spectacular view of sunshine flashing like diamonds on the peaks of the ocean waves. "I'll do everything possible to protect what you've got here, Monica, but you need to be prepared to fight."

I groaned. That was the last thing I wanted to hear. I'd moved three thousand miles away, but the tentacles of greed and envy still had me firmly in their grasp.

CHAPTER 14

John stayed until Tuesday. That afternoon I drove him to the airport in Kahului to catch a nonstop flight home. I pulled up to the white zone out front.

"You're sure I'm on a big plane this time?" he said.

"Yep, I checked. You're on a Boeing 767. It's non-stop and I promise this flight will be much smoother than the one you had coming over. I also confirmed you're in first class."

"Good. I'm gonna start drinking as soon as I buckle up."

"Take it easy. You know you'll still need to drive a hundred miles to Tucson after you land in Phoenix."

"I get in at midnight. I'll stay at a hotel tonight and drive home tomorrow. There's no law against driving with a blinding hangover."

"Whatever works," I said.

We both got out, much to the consternation of the chubby guy wearing the neon orange security vest at the far end of the loading zone. He started hustling toward us, pointing to his watch to signal my time was limited.

John got his small carry-on out of the trunk and I gave him a quick hug. "I'm sorry you had to come all this way. I'll keep my phone on from now on, and I promise to answer your calls and emails within a day."

He shot me an annoyed look. It wasn't classic laid-back John, but I attributed his crankiness to his dread of spending the next six hours in the air.

"You do that," he said. "If I have to fly over here again, I swear I'll hand your case over to Patterson."

Jeb Patterson was the managing partner in John's firm. I'm pretty sure the guy had won the Bar Association's "Curmudgeon of the Year" award for the past twenty years, and had probably been nominated for lifetime achievement in that category. He was ancient, mean, and had a deep-rooted case of halitosis. He also won ninety-five percent of his cases.

"I'll be good," I said. "Cross my heart."

John disappeared into the shady recesses of the open-air ticket lobby and I roared away as Mr. Security began a stereo recitation of the litany playing over the loudspeaker: *The white zone is for loading and unloading of passengers only. No parking!*"

I took the Altima to the car rental place and told them my personal car had been lost while being shipped over. I said I'd need to keep the car for another few weeks.

"We can't allow you to have this car for more than twenty-eight days," the agent said.

"Why?"

"Because we're not licensed to do leasing."

"I don't want to lease the car. I just want to rent it for a little longer."

"Yeah, but if we rent you a car for more than a month it becomes a lease."

"What?"

"Yeah, that's the law."

"I've never heard of that," I said.

"And you can't lease a car here unless you're a resident."

"But I *am* a resident."

The clerk peered at my driver's license. "This is an Arizona license."

"I know. I haven't had time to change it. But I moved here almost a month ago."

"If you need to lease a car, you'll need to qualify for a valid Hawaii license. In any case, I can't renew your rental. This car's already reserved for next week."

"I'll take a different car."

"We're totally booked. Spring break, you know."

"Maybe I'll try another car rental company."

"Good luck with that. Every year it's the same thing. During Spring Break nobody's got cars."

I still had nearly a week to go on my rental, so I drove back to West Maui. I'd have to buy a new car soon, but I didn't want to deal with it right away. I'd gotten used to driving the Altima. Maybe I'd lease one for a while. Derek's ridiculous eight-hundred-thousand-dollar car was beautiful, but after a year of *money's no object* I'd grown tired of buying expensive stuff just because I could. And besides, I was trying to blend in. It's hard to blend in when your car cost more than most people's houses.

I punched in the address of the Department of Motor Vehicles office in Lahaina. It turned out it was in a shopping mall across the highway from the Long's Drug Store. When I turned into the parking lot, the GPS kept saying, "*You have arrived at your destination*," but I couldn't find it. Had they moved?

I parked and walked the length of the strip mall. Much of it was empty. The vacant buildings looked no more than five years old. Probably a vestige of the real estate crash a few years ago. I was about to give up and head back to my car when I passed an unmarked beige storefront with a white poster in the window. It said, "Document Guide for

Driver's License, Permit, and State ID Card." The list showed twenty or more documents that could be used as proof of identity for a Hawaii Driver's License. I already had a driver's license. I figured I'd just trade the Arizona one for the Hawaii one. Slam dunk.

I went in and took a number. When a breathy disembodied female voice called my number and urged me to go to the assigned window, I pulled out my Arizona license.

"I'm here to swap my Arizona driver's license for a Hawaii license," I said. "I moved here a few weeks ago."

The woman behind the counter looked at me as if she recognized me from a wanted poster at the post office. "I'll need to see some ID," she said.

I slid my license across the counter so she could read it. "Here. It's my Arizona license. I just want to trade it for a Hawaii one."

"We can use this as *one* of the forms of ID we require," she said. "But I'll also need proof of legal presence and your social security number. Here are the documents we'll accept." She handed me a sheet with the same list of documents as the poster in the window. "Any of these will do, but people usually bring in their passport or birth certificate for legal presence and their Social Security card to validate their social security number. It has to be the original; no copies. And, I'll need to see proof of Hawaii residence."

"But I had to show my birth certificate and a bunch of other stuff to get this Arizona license," I said. "You can't get a driver's license in Arizona if you're not a U.S. citizen. They're kinda touchy about that."

"Good. Then it shouldn't be a problem for you to provide it again this time."

"But if I have a valid Arizona license, it means I've already shown proof of citizenship. Don't you see?"

She slid the Arizona license back to me. "Come back when you have the required documents," she said. "Oh, and *aloha*. Welcome to Hawaii."

I picked up the list but didn't look at it until I got back outside. My passport was in the wall safe at my house but I wasn't sure if my original Social Security Card was in there too. I hadn't needed it since I'd stopped working. The other two documents they'd accept were both work-related: a recent paystub or a W-9 wage statement from my employer. Too bad I didn't have a job. They'd also take a Medicare card or a Social Security Benefit Statement but I had more than a few decades to go before I got my hands on either of those.

So there it was. If I couldn't find my Social Security Card I couldn't apply for a Hawaii driver's license. I could get a replacement card, but who knew how long that might take? Without a Hawaii license I couldn't lease a car. It looked like my only option was to buy a new car before I had to turn in the rental.

I drove to Kapalua pondering whether to get a boring car that blended in or go for something flashy like Derek's Corvette. I had a four-car garage so I could have both if I wanted. No need to buy them both at once. Maybe I should buy the practical car first and then...

My musing was cut short when I rounded the turn leading to my gated driveway. The gate was standing open. Two huge yellow Maui Fire Department fire engines blocked the driveway, lights flashing and engines rumbling.

CHAPTER 15

I hopped out and sprinted the length of the driveway. Two official-looking guys wearing heavy firefighter coats and white helmets stood at the back of one of the fire trucks. I sniffed the air but didn't smell smoke—a good sign.

"Hi," I said. "I'm Monica Gomez, and this is my house."

The first guy extended his hand. "Deputy Chief Cicero. I'm IC here." I must've looked confused because he went on, "I'm the Incident Commander."

The second guy also introduced himself but I didn't catch his name.

"What's going on? Is my house on fire?"

"No, I'm afraid it's sort of the opposite," Cicero said.

Again, his communication skills fell a tad short.

"You've got a major water leak which has created a sinkhole situation. Come see."

I followed him around the side of the house and, *whoa*, my saltwater swimming pool was no more. In its place was a gaping hole. I should say a *deep*, gaping hole. Large chunks of tile and pieces of concrete were scattered along the bottom of the pit.

"What happened?" I said.

"We're still trying to sort it out. We're speculating you must've had a slow leak in the pool and it finally gave way. The soil up here on these bluffs is pretty unstable. When they built these homes they probably didn't tamp it down properly. They're supposed to let the ground settle after they excavate, but most times builders are in such a hurry to make a buck they just go ahead and build."

"But why did it swallow everything up like that?"

"When you were a little girl did you make mud pies?"

"Not really. I grew up in the desert. Arizona, actually."

"Well, here we've got porous volcanic soil with lots of voids, like bubbles or spaces in the earth. You add water and you create a potential for sinkholes. It doesn't happen often, but when it does, it's a nasty mess."

"Is my house safe?"

"That's why we're here. We're monitoring the situation. So far, we haven't seen further expansion of the breach, but you're gonna have to bring in a geologist and an engineer to evaluate the ongoing risk. Until then, I'm afraid you and your family can't stay here."

"Where will I go?"

He smiled. "One thing we got here in West Maui is lots of hotels. I suggest you get on the horn and find one. We got Spring Break comin' up so it may take a while, but from the looks of things you can afford a high-end place. Those don't tend to get booked up with the college crowd."

"Can I go inside?"

"Yeah. We'll stick around another few minutes while you gather your things. You got other family members living here? No one came to the door when we knocked."

Chloe couldn't be at the store since I had the car. And she'd taken Pima on her walk earlier that morning. Where was she?

༖ ༖ ༖

I ran through the main part of the house calling Chloe's name. She didn't answer, but Pima came slinking out from behind the sofa looking like she'd done something back there she'd rather I didn't notice.

I scooped her up. She was shaking so hard it was like holding a furry twelve-pound vibrator.

"It's okay, you're okay," I said. I stroked her bony little head and her shaking went from "high" to "medium" but she still wouldn't make eye contact.

"Don't worry about it," I said, glancing at the sofa. "I'm sure your pile is nowhere close to the big pile of crap that used to be my swimming pool." Why is it we think dogs can understand us? Maybe it's because as soon as I said it she settled down and licked my hand.

I ran into Chloe's room but there was no sign of her. Had she fled after calling 9-1-1? It didn't seem like something she'd do. From the very beginning Chloe had been more stalwart than me in facing tough times head-on.

Back in Arizona a photographer had camped out on my street for two days. He was probably hoping I'd come out so he could snap a photo of me looking like the greedy thief Steve Harrow had made me out to be in the media. When we ran out of dog food, Chloe had had enough. She snatched a corn broom from the hall closet and went outside and whacked the guy over the head with it. When he complained to the police, she told the cops she'd gone outside to sweep the sidewalk and the photographer had startled her. She alleged it was strictly self-defense.

I went into my room and packed an overnight bag with a change of clothes and some basic toiletries. I picked up Pima's doggie bed, scooped some kibble into a plastic bag, and snapped on her leash. I opened the front door and Pima's ears went up. The sound of throbbing diesel engines and the sight of a half dozen firefighters in turnout gear must've been too much for her. She dashed through my legs trying to get back inside. I jerked her leash, feeling bad about nearly strangling her, but we had to get out of there. It turned out to be tough duty to drag a twelve-pound dog down a fifty-yard driveway while wheeling an overnight bag and clutching a bulky fleece dog bed.

Three media vans blocked my way to my car. As I pondered how I'd get past them, a solemn-faced young woman dressed in a soft-blue *aloha* print shirt and white slacks climbed out of one of the vans and came toward me. She was followed by an equally earnest-looking guy lugging a video camera. It seemed news of my yawning sinkhole had been picked up from emergency scanners.

Deputy Chief Cicero popped up out of nowhere.

"You ready to leave?" he said.

"It looks like I won't be able to get out."

"No worries," he said. "Cops got guns, but we got a bigger ride."

He signaled to the driver of one of the fire engines to move out. The driver gunned the engine and threw it in reverse. An earsplitting *'beep-beep-beep'* sent the reporter and cameraman scurrying.

"People have a right to know," the reporter huffed, now in full retreat.

"Yeah, and people have property rights, too," Cicero said. "Next time, park on a public street."

"Isn't this a public street?" she said over her shoulder.

I could barely hear her over the continuing shriek of the reversing fire truck.

Cicero yelled, "This street, hell, this entire neighborhood, is as private as it gets, sister."

She got in the van and slammed the door.

I turned to the deputy chief. "How'd those media vans get past the guard at the gate?"

He rubbed his thumb and fingers together. "Guards make minimum wage, you know. Doesn't take much."

I thanked him for his help and then flashed back on the army of media vans that had descended on my home when I won the sweepstakes. After my boss filed his lawsuit I'd had to move from my modest bungalow in Rio Blanco to a sprawling *ranchette* outside of town. Reporters and photographers blocked my street and harassed my neighbors for weeks on end. If the Rio Blanco Fire Department had cleared the street like the Maui FD had just done, I'd have sent free pizza to the fire house for the rest of the year.

🐟 🐟 🐟

I drove up to Bev's house but she wasn't there. As much as she loved selling houses, she loved neighborhood gossip even more. She'd be royally ticked she'd missed getting a first-hand glimpse of the sinkhole before it made the TV news.

I left a message on her cell and drove down to Ka'anapali Beach. There were dozens of wonderful hotels along the beach walk. Surely at least one of them would have a vacancy. Pima presented a bit of a problem since people rarely bring their pets on vacation to Hawaii, but I'd decided that, if need be, I'd sneak her in. After all, we'd only be there a few days.

I booked a two-bedroom suite at The Jolly Harpooner, a pricey high-rise with a somewhat repugnant name. The guy at the front desk asked if I was joking when I inquired about their pet policy, so I mumbled something about being allergic to cats and left it at that.

My suite was on the seventh floor. I hid Pima in a large duffle bag for the trip through the lobby and explained to her that she'd have to keep the noise down while we rode in the elevator. Once again, I was amazed by her ability to rise to the occasion and act as if she'd understood me.

I called Chloe's cell phone every ten minutes for the next two hours, and left at least six messages. By four-thirty, I still hadn't heard from her so I stopped calling.

At six-fifteen my cell phone chimed and I snatched it up. "Chloe? Where have you been?"

No answer. I looked at the phone to see if the call had been dropped, but the seconds were still ticking by on the screen. I noticed the incoming call wasn't from the Arizona 520 area code on Chloe's phone, it was a local call, 808.

"Hello?" I said.

"*Aloha*, Monica?" It was a man's voice. "Are you okay? I saw the news."

"Who is this?"

"It's Keo Kekane. I heard your name on the news and when I saw the video I couldn't believe it. How're you doing?"

I choked on my answer. "I'm...uh, I mean..."

What was it about this guy that brought out the schoolgirl in me? I shocked myself by starting to cry. "I'm sorry. It's just that my friend Chloe's missing, and I'm worried she might've been swallowed up in the hole. I don't know what to—"

"Are you home?" he said.

"No, I can't stay there. I'm at Ka'anapali Beach, at The Jolly Harpooner. Room Seven-Fourteen." By now I was boo-hooing so hard everything was coming out choked and garbled.

"Got it. Jolly Harpooner, seven-fourteen. I'm coming over," he said. "I'll be there in half-an-hour."

ᕦ ᕦ ᕦ

Twenty minutes later my cell phone rang again. I looked at the caller ID. Once again it was an 808 number.

Maybe it was Keo calling back to say he couldn't make it after all. Starshine must've put her toe-ringed foot down.

"Hello," I said.

"Hello? Miss Gomez?" It was Chloe.

"Chloe, where are you? I've been worried sick."

"I'm sorry, Miss Gomez. I shouldn't have left without calling you, but I was so upset I forgot."

"Where are you? And why aren't you calling from your own phone?"

"I'm calling from Jason's cell. My phone died."

"Are you okay? Were you scared when the firemen showed up?"

"Firemen? What firemen? Is your house on fire?"

I told her about the sinkhole.

"OMG, this is like the worst day *ever*."

"What's going on?"

She sniffled. "Jason's leaving. He has to go back to California."

"Where are you?"

"At Jason's. He's only here for a few more days. Can I take a couple of vacation days? I want to spend as much time with him as I can before he has to leave."

"Sure. But won't you need some clean clothes? I can come get you and we can go over to the house tomorrow. I think they'll let us in so we can pack."

"I'm good. I probably won't be wearing much in the next few days." She giggled.

Good ol' Chloe, the queen of TMI—too much information. Too bad she didn't give me the information I really wanted, like why was Jason being sent back to the mainland. Was he a convicted felon who'd failed to check in with his parole officer? Or maybe an AWOL soldier who'd finally been flushed out by the Marines?

There was a knock at the suite door. "Chloe, someone's at the door. I've got Pima and we're staying at The Jolly Harpooner on Ka'anapali Beach. Call me later, okay?"

"I will. And thanks, Monica. I really appreciate it."

I smiled. Chloe calling me by my first name was all the thanks I needed.

I hung up and answered the door. There stood Keo with a big bundle of tropical flowers wrapped in a cone of lavender-colored paper.

"Thought you might need a little cheering up," he said. His eyes squinted in concern, but his smile gave him away.

"Go ahead, say what's on your mind," I said.

"I've been trying to come up with a clever line all the way over here," he said. "Best I could do was, 'Classiest homeless shelter I've visited all week'."

"Yeah, well, thanks for the flowers. They're beautiful. What are these spiky ones called?"

"Those are protea. They grow in upcountry Maui." He bent down to give Pima a quick scratch behind the ears. When he stopped, she jumped up, whining for more.

"She's insatiable when it comes to attention," I said.

"I've heard dogs take after their owners. You think it's true?"

I chose to not respond to his snide inference, but instead said, "Where's Starshine tonight?"

"She's at a meeting. I need to pick her up in an hour."

"You're sneaking out?"

He shot me a puzzled look. "It's cool."

We both allowed a beat of silence to pass and he went on, "So, tell me what happened. On TV, your place looked like a scene out of a horror flick."

"That's pretty much it. The fire chief told me there must've been a leak in the swimming pool. The salt water must've undermined the unstable ground and created the sinkhole. I've never seen anything like it."

"Me neither. You know, that bluff up there was one of the last tracks of land to get built on in West Maui."

"I can see why," I said. "The slope is pretty steep."

"That, and few other things," he said.

"Can I get you something to drink? Water, pop, maybe something stronger out of the mini-bar?"

"*Mahalo*, but I'm good with water."

I got us each a glass of ice water and we went out to the lanai. The lanai was huge, running the full length of the ocean view suite and wrapping around the corner. From there it was possible to see it all: views of Lana'i and Moloka'i to the front, and the green peaks of the West Maui Mountains behind.

"I like it down here by the water," I said. "The sound of the waves is peaceful. And it's fun to people-watch everyone coming and going along the beach."

We looked down seven floors to the Ka'anapali Beach walkway below us. The walkway was lit with flaming tiki torches, illuminating a lively beach bar scene along with a few ocean-side restaurants. A lone singer with a guitar was performing at an open-air bar right below the hotel.

"If you like people so much, why do you spend all your time alone?" Keo said.

"What do you mean? I don't spend *all* my time alone. I have friends."

"Yeah? I was hoping to see you back at the food bank, but it's been more than a week now."

"Just because I don't spend every waking hour volunteering for the less fortunate doesn't make me a hermit," I said. "Or a Scrooge."

"Who said anything about you being a Scrooge? I thought since you were new to the island you'd volunteered at the food bank to make friends. But you only came in once."

"It's a long drive, Keo. And besides, I've been making friends on this side of the island. You might know one of them—Derek Chambers. He told me he sponsors a bunch of charities here on Maui."

Keo smiled, and then shook his head. "Ah yes, Mr. Chambers. A real prince of a man. Do you know what he does for a living?"

"He's in the energy business."

"That's what he told you? '*The energy business*'?"

"Yeah. Oil and gas exploration and distribution. He says this country is sitting on enough oil and natural gas to be a hundred percent energy independent, but we refuse to allow the energy companies to tap the resources we have."

"That's not why we aren't energy independent. We're stuck buying oil and gas from hostile countries because of guys like your buddy, Derek Chambers."

"What?"

"He's a speculator, Monica. A bottom-feeder. He makes millions gouging people, especially poor people. Have you noticed what a gallon of gas costs over here? And it'd be even higher if the state of Hawaii hadn't stepped in and capped the price. People like Derek Chambers manipulate the price of oil by playing footsie with shady characters from OPEC and oil billionaires here at home. He doesn't want this country to be energy independent any more than I want Maui kids to go to bed hungry."

A warm gust of wind swirled around us as if the Almighty was adding His two cents. The sky along the horizon was turning navy blue, and a sallow moon had peeked above the top of the green hills to the east.

I got up. "Thanks for stopping by, Keo," I said. "And thanks for the flowers. It was thoughtful of you."

Keo followed my lead and stood. "Yeah, I should be going. And, again, *mahalo nui loa* for your generous donation to the food bank. But do yourself a favor, okay? Check into Derek Chambers. I don't know you very well, but I have a hard time imagining you hanging out with a scum sucker like that."

I walked him to the door. It felt odd not to give him a hug or even offer a handshake, but all I wanted was to get him out of there. I'd endured a year of rants by jealous people bent on destroying my reputation, so I wasn't about to listen to more of it directed at a friend of mine. In the past twelve months I'd developed a keen nose and I could smell sour grapes a mile away.

Keo may think feeding the masses with his non-stop begging and his felony-fueled workforce is noble but it's not. It's puny and pathetic. The way to truly make a difference is to enlist people with money, like Derek and me, to fund his cause. Bad-mouthing the one-percenters may be popular with the do-gooders and tree-huggers, but it's counter-productive.

As I closed the door it occurred to me that maybe snarky Keo Kekane and his jealous, tattooed girlfriend might actually be a pretty good match after all.

CHAPTER 16

April Fool's Day fell on a Wednesday. Since I'd given Chloe the next few days off, I was alone with Pima in our fancy digs at The Jolly Harpooner. The direct oceanfront view got me thinking. Maybe I should fix the sinkhole at my house in Paradise Ridge and then sell the house and move to the beach.

Life was short, and I had no reason not to be enjoying it, especially since money was no object. Bev Strong might try to dissuade me—no wait, she'd be thrilled. The real estate commissions she'd earn on the sale of the Paradise Ridge house and then my purchase of a new beach house would probably prompt her to get a tattoo with my name in it.

And speaking of tattooed women, how disappointing had it been to hear Keo admit to squiring Starshine to and from her so-called "meeting," and hear his jealous socialist rant about Derek's job? I could hardly wait for Derek to come home so I could tell him what Keo said. It seemed I missed my new beau more than I cared to admit.

I smuggled Pima through the lobby to go outside for a walk and when we got back upstairs I got right to work. Now, not only was I going to have to deal with the insurance company about the loss of my car, but I was also going to have to put in a claim for the sinkhole mess. The fire department guy had told me to contact a geologist and an engineer. Probably best to start there.

"Island Geo. This is Marv," said the guy who answered the phone.

"Hello Marv, I'm looking for someone to come to my home to give me an estimate for repairs."

There was a pause and the guy said, "We're engineering geologists. We don't do home repairs."

"I'm sorry, I should've been more specific. I need my yard repaired, not my home."

"Well," the guy dragged out the word, as if he were thinking of how to explain something simple to a dull-witted person. "Then I suggest you call a landscape service. They're the ones who fix yard problems."

"Did you watch the news last night?"

"Yeah."

"Did you see the big ol' sinkhole that opened up in Kapalua?"

"Wow, are you serious? That's *your* place?" He went from patronizing to positively giddy in record time.

"Yeah, that's me. And the incident commander from the fire department said I needed to get a geologist and an engineer to evaluate the situation and recommend repairs."

"As I said, we're engineering geologists. We can do it all. We'll assess the situation and we can recommend contractors who'll be able to mitigate whatever damage we find."

There was a muffled sound on the line. A second later, I heard a whoop of joy in the background.

"Excuse me?" I said. "What's going on in your office?"

"Oh, sorry," he said. "I just told my colleague you're calling about the sinkhole. We rarely get to work on something this big."

"How soon can you come out?" I said.

"We're pretty busy with a hotel project in Wailea, but let me look at our schedule and I'll give you a call back. What's your number?"

I gave him my cell number.

"Marv, this is urgent. I'm staying in a hotel until I can move back home. I'm on the seventh floor and I've got my dog with me. Dogs aren't allowed here, so ... you get the drift. The fire department won't let me return until I get your blessing."

"I understand."

"Oh, and Marv, let me add that money isn't an issue. I want this fixed, and I want it fixed fast. Whatever it takes."

"Are you counting on insurance to cover this? If so, you better talk with your claims adjuster. They might consider this an 'act of God.' Acts of God usually aren't covered."

"I'm pretty sure God had nothing to do with this. From all appearances, it was caused by a leaking swimming pool. But rest assured, regardless of what the insurance company says, I will pay cash for whatever it takes to get this handled ASAP. You hear what I'm saying, Marv?"

"Yep, got it. I'll check the schedule and be back to you within the hour."

ᗧ ᗧ ᗧ

Now that I'd got things moving on the sinkhole, I turned to my car. I'd be able to keep the rental car for only four more days. Since I was no longer at home where at least I could ask Bev to help me out, it felt even more necessary to find reliable transportation. I drove across the island to the Lexus dealer in Kahului. I wasn't sure what model I wanted, but I'd loved my recently drowned Lexus so I'd decided to stick with the brand.

I parked and had no more than stepped onto the dealer lot when a smiley young woman about five feet tall race-walked over to me.

"*Aloha*, and welcome to Lightner Lexus. My name is Ana Pueo. And you are?"

"I'm a woman who needs to buy a car."

She chuckled. In the past year I'd learned that high-end sales people are usually astute enough to laugh at rich people's attempts at humor. No matter how pathetic or biting.

Her eager smile shamed me into not making her ask again. "My name is Monica."

She reached out to shake hands. "Monica, nice to meet you. Well, again, welcome to Lightner Lexus. We're the largest Lexus dealership in the islands."

"Really? No offense, but this doesn't look like a very big dealership."

The place took up less than half a block. Back in Tucson, there were mega-car dealers with sales lots covering acres of ground. This place looked more like the mom-and-pop used car lot we had in Rio Blanco.

She narrowed her eyes and crossed her tanned, toned arms. "We are absolutely the largest Lexus dealership in Hawaii. Our flagship showroom is in Honolulu, and we have satellite locations on each of three neighbor islands— Maui, Kaua'i, and the Big Island of Hawai'i."

Her defensive little spiel sounded rehearsed. I had a hunch she was bucking for manager, or at least salesperson-of-the-month.

"Well, good to hear," I said. "I'd like to buy a car, today. I used to drive a Lexus LS and I loved it, but I'm thinking I may want something a little sportier. Maybe an IS convertible."

A flicker of uncertainty interrupted her gaze. "You want a new car right away? How about your LS? Will you be trading it in?"

"I'd love to trade it in, but I doubt you'd give me much for it." I was messing with her again, but hey, I'd had a rough couple of days.

"I can promise top dollar."

"Sight unseen?" Now I was *really* messing with her.

"Yes, as long as you have the title. Just give me the VIN number and I can look it up and give you a firm quote. You can even use the trade-in for your down payment."

I backed off. "Thanks, but that won't work. You see, my car isn't here."

"Is it back on the mainland? We have partner relationships with most of the major Lexus dealers along the West Coast."

It was beginning to get embarrassing. "Look, let's forget about the trade-in. I just want to test drive a new IS convertible. If I like the car and I like the color, I'll buy it."

She looked around the lot as if searching for something she'd misplaced. "I'm afraid I don't have a convertible here at the moment. We have one or two at our Honolulu location, and I believe they may still have one over on the Big Island, but here on Maui we usually sell our allotment of convertibles as soon as they come in."

"So, where do we go from here?" I said.

"I'd be happy to look up the details on the IS convertibles in Honolulu. Then, you could test drive the IS sedan we have here. If you love it—and I'm sure you will—we can negotiate a deal on the convertible model. We'll order one sent over. We'll even pick up the tab on the freight charges. Easy-peasy." She grinned as if she'd puzzled out the final question on *Who Wants to be a Millionaire*?

When I didn't say anything, she went on.

"Really, it's no big deal. We do it all the time. I can have your car here by the end of the week. We'll get it detailed and ready for delivery by Saturday, Sunday at the very latest. It won't be a problem."

I laughed.

"Monica?" she said. "I see you're laughing. I know it sounds kind of complicated, but it's not."

"I'm not laughing because it's complicated," I said. "I'm laughing because the last time I had a car freighted over here it ended up at the bottom of Kahului Harbor."

"Oh, my goodness. That was *you*? I heard about that. That's the first time anything like that has happened since I've lived here." She reached over and touched my arm as if offering heartfelt condolences. "And I've been on Maui almost eight years now."

"Yeah, so you can understand why I'm a little gun-shy about putting my new car on a barge. I've been driving a rental for almost a month."

Ana dropped her eyes and leaned in to whisper. "I didn't want to say anything earlier because, well, you mentioned you wanted to try the IS," she said. "But if you've previously owned the LS model, you may want to consider another one. You'll never duplicate the ride, the comfort, and the roominess of the LS, especially with the smaller frame and reduced seating capacity of the IS. The LS has earned the JD Powers 'Luxury Car of the Year' award for thirteen years running. That's a lot of luxury to give up."

A successful salesman for Az/Mex once told me about the concept of SWAT—Sell What's Available Today. He said in a volatile business like fresh produce it was necessary to convince buyers that what they thought they wanted wasn't as good as what he had in stock.

"A wholesale buyer comes in looking for apricots in March?" he'd said. "Not gonna happen. So, you tell him shoppers won't even consider imported tree fruits. 'Everyone's looking for fresh,' I'd say. Then I show the guy some gorgeous navel oranges we just got in."

I thanked Ana for her time and said I'd have to think about it. As I headed back toward my rental she clip-clopped behind me, trying hard to keep up in her tottering wedge heels.

"I can get you a killer deal on that gorgeous Moonglow Pearl LS over there," she said. "It's fully loaded. When it came in I looked over the list of optional equipment and couldn't find one single thing it doesn't have."

"Heated seats?" I said. "Snow and ice traction control?"

She sucked in a breath. "Look, I didn't make my quota last month. I'm willing to forego my commission if you'll buy a car from me today. I hate to pressure you, but my boss is breathing down my neck."

She pulled out a business card and handed it to me. "Seriously, I'd *really* appreciate your business."

We locked eyes. Who was I kidding? I'd been where she was. Not in the strictest sense, since I'd never sold cars for a living. But I knew what it was like to have your boss chewing your backside when no matter how hard you work there's nothing you can do to remedy the situation.

"I loved my LS," I said. "It was Snowflake White, but that Moonglow Pearl is pretty, too."

"It's our most popular color," she said. "Really."

"What the heck? Maybe I'll get it and then order a red IS convertible, too. It wouldn't hurt to have both a cushy car and a fun car."

She put a hand over her mouth and widened her eyes. "Are you serious?"

"As a heart attack."

Ana locked me in a tight hug and then quickly stepped away. "*Mahalo* so, so much, Monica. If you want to take your new car home today I can have one of our guys return your rental for you. You have no idea what a big deal it is to sell two cars on the first day of the month. How can I ever thank you?"

"Tell you what, you go write up the paperwork on the LS, and then let's go to lunch. You get a lunch hour, right?"

"Yes, but I brought a salad from home."

"I'd really appreciate it if you'd let me take you to lunch. I just moved here and I don't have many people my own age I can hang out with."

"Well, now you have me."

🐢 🐢 🐢

I returned to Ka'anapali driving my luxurious new Lexus. I hadn't realized how noisy and bumpy the Altima had been, but now that I'd traded up I was happy to be back in familiar surroundings.

Derek called while I was on the road, but I hadn't figured out how to hook into the Bluetooth yet. After a quick check of the caller ID, I let it go to voicemail. The way my luck was going, I'd end up getting a ticket for using my cell while driving.

I shot through the little tunnel on the Pali Highway and then headed downhill to where the road parallels the shore at Kailili Beach. Would I ever get tired of gazing at the shallow waves sliding onto the beach at Launiupoko? Or watching the half-naked surfers drag their gear out of beat-up Subarus and race into the ocean at Puamana?

The guys sported stunning physiques. Their smooth, tanned pecs and powerfully sculpted biceps were the result of hundreds of hours spent paddling out to catch a wave. Too bad I was scared of water. Surfing was probably a much more enjoyable way to stay in shape than sweating and grunting in an air-conditioned gym.

I chastened myself for ogling strangers. After all, I was finally in a relationship. And it *was* a relationship, wasn't it? Men define these things differently than woman, but Derek's good-bye kiss on Sunday had felt certain, unequivocal. All I had to do was make sure I didn't screw it up.

🐢 🐢 🐢

I got three more calls as I drove back to Ka'anapali. I slipped my new car into a spot in The Jolly Harpooner parking garage. As I headed for the elevator, I couldn't help looking over my shoulder to admire how the shiny Moonglow Pearl finish gleamed against the backdrop of dull gray concrete.

I dug out my phone and checked the recent calls list: another call from Derek, a call from the engineering firm, and then a call from Chloe. I'd call Chloe first, since I didn't want to get cut off from Derek if I lost cell reception in the elevator.

"Hi Chloe, what's up?" I said.

"Miss Gomez, I just tried calling you."

"I know, I'm returning your call. I was on the road and couldn't answer."

"Are you back at the house yet?" she said.

"No, I'm still in Ka'anapali. I think we're going to be living here for a while, but it's okay because I got us a two-bedroom suite. Guess what? I went to Kahului this morning and bought a new car."

"You did? That's great. Did you get that little convertible you were thinking about?"

"No, I ordered one but it won't get here for another month. For now, I bought a car like the one we had at home."

"Miss Gomez, not to be rude or anything, but Maui is your home now. You're done with Arizona."

I smiled. Chloe'd always been a stickler for details. It was one of her many traits that had allowed me to keep my sanity during the past year.

"You're right," I said. "Anyway, it's a Lexus LS like the white car I had shipped over. Only this one's kind of beige."

"Sounds nice," she said. Then she cleared her throat. "Miss Gomez, would you please give me your room number at the hotel again? I need to come talk to you."

"Are you okay? You sound serious."

"It is serious. Can I come over right now?"

When I got to the room Pima was doing her "potty dance" by the door. I took her downstairs for a quick jaunt around the property. By now I was sure the front desk had seen her on at least one occasion, and they weren't pleased. But I'd been given the pity vote since I wasn't there on vacation. My house had been nearly swallowed up by a sinkhole, and everyone working at The Jolly Harpooner had witnessed my misfortune on the local news.

Chloe was crossing the lobby just as I was coming back inside. I called out to her and she turned. Her face looked troubled. The last time I'd seen her look that concerned was the morning a strange woman had thrown an egg at me as I'd arrived at the Phoenix courthouse. I never found out what the egg-tosser's beef was. My lawyer said she'd been written up for attempted assault. I guess it was deemed "attempted" because the egg had missed.

"Is everything okay?" I said when we got in the elevator.

Chloe pressed her lips together and nodded a bit too quickly for me to believe her.

I unlocked the suite and led her out to the lanai. "Gorgeous view, huh? You can see all the way to Black Rock from here."

She was uncharacteristically indifferent. "Do you mind if we go back inside?" she said.

"Sure."

We each took a seat on the L-shaped sofa, Chloe sitting as far from me as humanly possible. Pima's head swiveled, taking in Chloe and then me, as if weighing her options. With a snuff of resolve, she trotted over to Chloe's end and hopped into her lap. At that, Chloe burst out crying.

I got up to go sit next to her. "What's the matter? Are you upset about the house? Don't worry, I'll get it fixed. It's only stuff, Chloe. The three of us are safe and sound."

She kept up the boo-hooing, so I gave up on the pep talk. Best to allow her to work through it and just wait. Lord knows how many times Chloe had been there for me in the past year. Now it was my turn.

I leaned over and put an arm around her shoulder. I must've been lousy at comforting, though, because it only made her cry louder.

When she'd finally been reduced to hiccups and snuffling, I went into the bathroom and got a box of Kleenex.

"No rush," I said, handing over a wad of tissues. "When you're ready to talk, I'll listen. No questions, I promise."

That seemed to help a little. She swiped tissues across each eye and then blew out a big honk. Pima dug at Chloe's hand as if trying to dislodge the tissue wad so they could play "keep away." Chloe got up and threw it in the trash.

I waited.

"Jason got a great job offer in California, and he's gonna take it."

"Well, that's good news," I said. Then I realized that for Chloe it wasn't. "I mean, I'm so sorry. That must be pretty disappointing for you."

"I was hoping he'd ask me to go with him," she said.

She paused, and the tears started up again.

I said, "Ah. But he didn't."

"Nope. He said for the time being, we'll have to be a long-distance couple. He promised to come over and visit if I get lonely."

I thought it best not to weigh in the usual outcome of most long-distance love affairs. So, instead, I shot her my best attempt at my *abuela's* "*Oh, honey, you'll be fine*" look.

"But, he did give me this," Chloe said. "He said it was a Hawaiian custom to give 'parting gifts,' but I think he made that up."

She smiled as she reached into her shoulder bag and pulled out a small white box. She took off the top and shook out a black velvet jeweler's box.

It took me a couple of seconds to realize I was holding my breath.

She snapped the top open on the the box and inside was a white gold or platinum band with a single diamond held by six prongs. The diamond wasn't large, but there was no way it could be mistaken for a "friendship ring."

"Seriously?" I said. I put my hand over my mouth when I realized I'd broken my promise to not ask questions.

She grinned. "As you'd say, Miss Gomez, 'As serious as a heart attack'. Although I almost *had* a heart attack when he asked me."

"And you said, 'Yes'?"

She plucked the ring from the box and put it on, admiring her outstretched left hand.

"Of course I said 'Yes.' I believe in love at first sight, don't you, Miss Gomez?"

I flashed on an image of rolling in the sheets on Derek's multimillion-dollar yacht. It'd been wild and fun. Naked and sexy and over-the-top luxurious. But had it been love? Or even a prelude to love? Probably best for me to not to think about it.

Chloe gave me the full run-down on what'd happened since we'd last talked. A few weeks ago, Jason played a round of golf with a guy from California who'd hired him to give him advice on how to improve his game. Turned out, the guy worked for Pebble Beach Golf Links, a premiere golf course in Northern California.

The golfer had been sent over to covertly audition Jason for an open golf pro position. The two hit it off and the guy went back and told his cronies that Jason's advice had helped him shave two strokes off his game. The head pro did a telephone interview with Jason, and a few days later Pebble Beach offered him the job.

"It's a once-in-a-lifetime opportunity," said Chloe. "He'll be making a lot more money."

"That's great. But why doesn't he want you to move over there with him?"

"He'll be living at the Lodge at Pebble Beach for a little while. He said he needs to completely focus on work. When he finds his own place, he'll send for me."

"And then you'll leave? Chloe, you've only known Jason for, what's it been? Two weeks?"

"Actually, it's been seventeen days," she said. "I hope you'll give me a good reference, so I can find a job there."

"I'll give you an excellent reference," I said. "But I'm going to miss you so much."

"I'm not leaving yet," she said. "And before I go, I'll make sure things are up-to-date. I'll get everything set up so you'll be able to handle it yourself from now on."

"But I don't want to 'handle it myself,'" I said. "I want you to do it. Here, with me."

"Miss Gomez, we both know you don't need me anymore. I'm just sitting around most of the time trying to look busy. You can do this."

"But who'll keep me company?" I whined.

"You've got Pima. And, besides, now you know Bev—and Derek. You'll be fine."

She was right, of course. A healthy twenty-nine-year-old hiring someone to serve as a "companion" was pathetic. It was like something a recluse like Howard Hughes or a tyrant like Leona Helmsley would do.

Chloe went on. "But before I go to California, we need to get this sinkhole thing managed. I feel bad I wasn't there when it happened. Let's make a deal, okay? I promise I won't leave until everything's back to the way it was before, if you'll be the maid of honor at my wedding."

"You got it," I said.

We shook hands like two business wheeler-dealers who'd just put together a wild scheme they hoped would make them both fabulously rich.

Too bad that as things turned out, neither of us would be able to hold up our side of the bargain.

CHAPTER 17

That afternoon I drove Chloe up to the Paradise Ridge house so we could assess the situation. Although it'd been two days since the earth had opened and swallowed my salt water pool, the place was still buzzing with activity. Four vehicles were parked in the driveway: a fire department chief's car, a van marked 'Incident Command', a battered gray Ford pick-up truck, and a red Kawasaki motorcycle.

A firefighter stood at attention at the front of the house like a Marine guarding an American embassy. He was a young hunk wearing a tight navy-blue t-shirt with "Maui Fire" emblazoned across the front and heavy yellow pants held up by red suspenders. As we approached, he left his post and walked toward us.

"This is a restricted area," he said. "I'm going to have to ask you to leave."

I dug out my Arizona driver's license and flashed it at him. "I'm Monica Gomez," I said. "This is my house. I need to go in and get a few things, and my assistant here needs to pack up her belongings."

The guy squinted at my license. "That all the ID you got? I'm supposed to ask for something with this address on it."

"Oh, come on. You've heard my name on the news. How many 'Monica Gomez's' could there possibly be in Kapalua?"

What I didn't let on was that in Arizona no fewer than five "Monica Gomez's" had popped out of the woodwork after I won the money. I guess one of them ran up a pretty impressive tab at some high-end stores in Phoenix before they caught on to her.

The firefighter turned his head and talked into a small walkie-talkie clipped to his suspender at the shoulder. He mumbled something and then a garbled message came back. He nodded and led us to the door.

"Ten minutes, no more than fifteen," he said. "The chief said the ground's still unstable."

Chloe headed for her bedroom. I grabbed a few things out of my closet and went down the hall to help her pack.

She was staring out the window. "I saw the TV coverage of this over at Jason's, but it didn't seem real until now."

"Yeah, and I can't believe that hole is still getting bigger. It looked scary on Tuesday, but now it's almost all the way to the house."

"I hope it stops," she said. "Do you think you'll be able to replace the pool?"

"Probably not. But we never used it anyway. I'll probably just fill it in and expand the lanai. Desert rats like us don't like to get wet anyway."

We finished packing Chloe's things and were out in ten minutes. The fireman at the door offered to help us load the stuff in the car and we accepted. It couldn't have been much fun for a guy like him who's used to action—in more ways than one, I'm sure—to spend hours guarding an empty house.

"Can we go see the hole up close before we leave?" Chloe said. "I want to take a picture."

I looked at the fireman.

He shrugged. "I'll take you back there."

I couldn't believe how big the sinkhole had gotten. The soil had caved in right up to the the house on the near side, and on the far side, the hole had swallowed up a good portion of the lawn.

Six men on the other side of the hole were having an animated conversation. When one of them spotted us, he waved and called out. "No trespassing back here. It's not safe."

"This is my house."

"It's still not safe. You need to leave."

The firefighter who'd accompanied us touched my elbow. "I'm sorry, but he's right. We should go back."

I noticed one of the men in the group didn't look like the rest of the emergency services workers. He was a big man, naked to the waist, wearing a brightly-colored *pareo*, a shawl-like cloth tied around his waist to create a loose skirt. He wore a circle of green leaves on his head and a string of leaves around his neck—sort of like a lei that hadn't been tied together. His dark brown face was grizzled with deep crevices and it looked as if it had been years since his last haircut.

"Who's that?" I said to the firefighter.

"That's the *kahuna*. He showed up this morning, and nobody's got the guts to tell him to leave."

"They told *me* to leave. And I own the place."

"True," he said. "But then, you're no *kahuna*."

Late the next morning, while Chloe took Pima downstairs for a walk, I called Marv at Island Geo to make sure he was still planning to come to Paradise Ridge to check out the sinkhole. I warned him the fire department was still on the scene and I was pretty sure he'd have to get their permission before he'd be allowed to do much of anything.

"I was expecting that," he said. "The fire department doesn't like to hand over jurisdiction. As long as they stay on premises, they maintain command. But that's a good thing for you. There are a lot of looky-loos on this island, and sinkholes are dangerous. They've be known to literally swallow people up."

As before, my driveway was completely filled with vehicles so I had to park outside the gate. I waved at the fireman by the door. He seemed to perk up when he recognized me, and he hurried to fall in step as I walked toward the back.

"Wait 'til you see what's going on," he said.

"What?"

"Just wait."

When we rounded the corner of the house I was rocked back on my heels. There must've been twenty or thirty people gathered into two distinct groups.

"Who are all these people?" I said.

"Follow me."

The fireman led me to where Deputy Chief Cicero was standing with three other fire department officials. I knew they were mucky-mucks since they were all wearing crisp official-looking uniforms, white hard hats, and shiny black leather shoes. You rarely see people wearing shoes like that on Maui.

Chief Cicero turned as we approached. "Gentlemen, will you excuse me for a moment? The property owner is here." He came over and shook my hand.

"What's going on?" I said. I gestured toward the group standing on the opposite side of the hole. "Are those the people from Island Geo?"

They sure didn't look like engineers. There were four men dressed similarly to the *kahuna* I'd seen the day before. They each sported a brightly-colored sarong tied at the waist, and all had leaf garlands hanging around their necks and bare feet. Three women stood a few feet apart from the men. They wore *mu'u mu'us* and their feet were also bare. Everyone looked tense.

"No. Those folks are from the Hawaiian Cultural Affairs office," Chief Cicero said in a low voice. "There's been a development."

"What kind of development? Is the sinkhole getting bigger?"

"No. In fact, that's the one bit of good news," Cicero said. "As far as we can tell, the ground has stabilized. The measurements from yesterday to today indicate no new movement. Did you say you're expecting the engineers today?"

"Yes. Marv, one of the head guys at Island Geo, said he'd come by this afternoon."

"Good. But, unfortunately, I don't think that's going to make much difference."

I waited for him to explain, but instead, he just nodded for me to follow him.

When we got out of earshot of the cultural affairs people, Cicero said, "The Hawaiians are here because this land was hotly contested when this housing development was in the planning stages. They claimed this area was *kapu*— sacred and forbidden. The state allowed them time to prove their claim of cultural significance, but they came up short. So, the developer got his permits. Now, with this sinkhole, they've reopened their investigation. In fact, they're saying the sinkhole is some sort of divine payback for messing with sacred ground."

"Well, that's an amusing story," I said. "And there are probably some people who'd argue that it'd be cool to find some sort of 'sacred sinkhole' on their property, but I'm not one of them. Please tell these people to leave."

"I'm afraid it's not as simple as that," he said.

"Why not? This is my house and my land. I realize I've got a lot of work ahead of me to get it back to what it was, but I'm ready and willing to do it."

Cicero narrowed his eyes. "You see, it's not about who owns the land, Miss Gomez. It's about who *used* to own the land."

"What? Are you saying there may be a problem with the title? I purchased title insurance when I bought this place. They'll back me up. The title to this property was transferred to me free and clear."

"Modern title insurance isn't going to help you, I'm afraid. This is a culturally sensitive issue."

"Huh?"

"They claim this sinkhole has coughed up some *iwi*," he said. "The elders over there are claiming they're *ali'i iwi*. And believe me, those are *not* covered by your title insurance."

"Now you've really lost me."

"*Iwi* are bones," he said. "They found bone fragments which may have come from royal, or *ali'i*, Hawaiian ancestors. This land may once have been an *ali'i* burial ground. Stuff like this is taken very seriously in Hawaii."

The firefighter who'd been guarding the house nodded in agreement. "Yeah," he said. "To put it bluntly, if they find *ali'i* bones here, then you're pretty much royally screwed."

CHAPTER 18

I finally got in touch with Derek in Dubai. I waited to call when it was a decent hour for him since he was working. There's a fourteen hour time difference, so noon for me is two in the morning for him. I can afford to take a call at two in the morning because I can sleep in. He can't.

"Where the hell have you been?" he said.

"I was waiting to call you during your daylight hours," I said. "It's seven at night here."

"I'm quite aware of the time difference." His voice was so cold my cell phone nearly froze to my hand.

"Well, I'm here now," I said. I tried smiling. When I was office manager at Az/Mex I'd taken a customer service seminar. The instructor said if you smile while talking on the phone, it comes through in your voice. "So, how's it going?"

"Monica, this isn't funny. I've been seriously worried about you. I mean, I've called you like, what, ten times? How could you be so rude to not return my calls?"

"I'm calling now."

"Fine. I guess I shouldn't go off on you like that. But, man, I was thinking the worst."

"Well, if it's any consolation, it really has been 'the worst' around here."

I filled him in on my car going in the drink and having to buy a new car. Then I told him about the sinkhole and having to move out of my house. I finished by telling him about the Hawaiian cultural people claiming they found royal bones in my yard.

"What's the deal with that?" he said. "Hawaii's been inhabited for centuries. There are probably human bones buried all over the place."

"I know," I said. "But the fireman at the scene said, and I quote, 'If they're *ali'i* bones, then you're pretty much royally screwed.' I thought that was funny, even though I don't like to think about being permanently evicted from my home."

There was a pause on the line. After a few seconds, I broke the silence, "Derek, are you there?"

"Yeah. Listen, I don't like the idea of a guy talking to you like that. Did you get his name?"

"Who? You mean the fireman?"

"Yeah. I want his name."

"Why?" I said.

"Because I think it's completely unprofessional for a public servant to be talking to a young unmarried woman like that."

"Derek, he was joking," I said. "I'm sorry I mentioned it."

Another big pause. This time I let Derek break the silence.

"Anyway," he said. "I'll be home on Monday. Since you said you aren't allowed to stay at your house, where are you staying?"

I told him about my oceanfront suite at The Jolly Harpooner.

"They're not too thrilled about Pima being there. I'd really like to find somewhere else. I don't know what I'll do if they ask me to leave." I was angling to see if Derek would offer the use of his house.

He cleared his throat. "Say, I'm about to go into a meeting. But it's great to hear from you. Do me a favor, okay?"

"Name it."

"Next time I call, get back to me immediately. I don't care what time it is. Otherwise I worry."

"I promise," I said.

I hung up feeling good that we'd had a chance to connect. I was feeling something else, but I couldn't put my finger on it. What was it? Missed? Cared for? Adored? Whatever it was, I hadn't felt it in a long, long time.

🕃 🕃 🕃

On Saturday morning, I drove up to Paradise Ridge to meet with the people who'd decide the fate of my house. Bev Strong had graciously offered her home as the meeting place. When I got to the door, she clasped me to her bony bosom in a totally uncharacteristic display of emotion.

"I am so, so sorry this has happened to you, Monica," she said. "I know it's ridiculous and unwarranted, but I feel somehow responsible. I would *never* have recommended that house if I'd had even the teensiest, tiniest inkling that something like this might happen."

"I'm not blaming you in the least, Bev," I said. "There was no way you could've known about this. I mean, what are the chances a swimming pool leak would lead to this?"

Bev blew out a breath. It occurred to me that maybe she'd been apprehensive about her potential liability since she'd sold me the house only a month earlier. What Bev didn't know was there was no way I'd sue anyone for anything. I'd spent the last year mired in lawsuits and my lawyer had come over to let me know I was now facing a new one. Even if I lost everything, I'd rather jump off a cliff than use the court system to assign guilt and blame. If the last twelve months had taught me anything, it was that a lot of what life throws at you just comes down to luck—good or bad.

Bev made the introductions. Deputy Chief Cicero was there representing the fire department, a guy named U'uku Ka'akahalanui representing the state agency charged with Hawaiian cultural issues, Stewart Lyons from the Paradise Ridge Homeowner's Association, Marv Van Otteran from Island Geo, and then Bev and myself.

"I'd like to start by offering a chant to honor the ancestors," said Mr. Ka'akahalanui. I later found out his first name, "U'uku," was actually a Hawaiian nickname meaning, "Tiny." As is often true with nicknames, he was anything but. He probably maxed out a bathroom scale at three-hundred-fifty pounds with pounds to spare. I could only marvel at how his heart managed to keep up with the workload.

The chant was mercifully short. This was good, since although I couldn't make heads or tails of any of the words—*mahalo, aloha,* and *malahini* were conspicuously absent—I could tell it was something along the lines of a war chant, with a smattering of guttural outbursts accompanied by fierce facial expressions.

Nobody made eye contact during the chant. I can't speak for the rest of the people there, but I felt awkward and a bit intimidated. In Southern Arizona, most of us were bi-lingual, English and Spanish, so I wasn't used to hearing a foreign language I couldn't understand. When potential customers from states like Utah or Illinois would show up at Az/Mex, I'd speak to our warehouse foreman in Spanish if I wanted to keep it private. I had a feeling that the gist of U'uku Ka'akahalanui's chant was also something he'd rather we didn't understand.

After the chant, Chief Cicero spoke up to say since he'd been Incident Commander, he'd be willing to chair the discussion. No one objected. He then went about asking each person to give an account of how they viewed the situation, and everyone said pretty much what we already knew.

Cicero called on me last.

"It seems everyone agrees my property may contain important and sensitive historical objects," I said. "And I feel bad that the house was built where it was, but I don't think I should be punished for something I didn't know about. After all, I only purchased the property a month ago. I think I should be allowed to fill in the hole, meeting engineering standards, of course, and move back home."

U'uku spoke up. "I understand you had no knowledge. But the wrong must be put right. Sacred ground must be returned to the *kupuna* who rest there." He'd used the word, *kupuna*, before when he'd made his earlier remarks, and he'd explained it meant *ancestors*.

"What are you suggesting?" said Bev.

"The house must be torn down and the ground blessed anew," U'uku said. "That is the only acceptable solution."

"But, that's—" said Stewart Lyons from the homeowner's group.

U'uku interrupted. "*All* the houses on this bluff need to be examined by the proper cultural authorities. And if we find they've been built on sacred ground as well, they *all* must come down."

"What?" Lyons sputtered. "These are multi-million dollar properties."

"Law of the land," U'uku said. "We abide by your laws, you're obliged to abide by ours."

A large vein bulged in Stewart Lyons' temple. It wasn't nice to stare, but I couldn't help myself. I tried to remember the signs of stroke: lopsided smile, slurred speech. So far, he seemed to be maintaining, but his blood pressure was no doubt off the charts.

Deputy Chief Cicero intervened. "Let's all just take a deep breath here. Before we go talking about tearing down houses, we need to see what the experts find. I recommend we get started on it right away."

The meeting broke up soon after. I drove down to The Jolly Harpooner and took Pima out for a long stroll along the Ka'anapali Beach Walk. The day was bright, with light trade winds blowing in from the ocean. I refused to let recent events make me believe that moving to Maui had been a bad idea. But I had to concede that even paradise has its share of hassles.

CHAPTER 19

I woke up on Sunday morning and realized it was April 5th. I didn't need to check a calendar, since the date had been burned into my memory as if it'd been my birthday. One year ago, my life had taken a hard right turn when a grinning David Michael Corcoran and his Prize Posse showed up at my door.

It was slightly amusing that in the past year I'd put thirty million dollars in the bank, yet I'd had to give up everything that reminded me of who I'd been before. Too bad, since if Steve Harrow won his latest lawsuit against me, I'd even lose all the money.

I wallowed in self-pity for only a few minutes before my *abuela's* voice hissed in my ear, "*You've enjoyed outrageous good fortune, Monica. Get off your lazy butt, and be grateful for your good health and the clever head on your shoulders.*" She was right about two things: I'd become the poster child of lazy and I'd always been healthy and smart. Point taken, *abuela*.

I had no idea how long it would take the authorities to examine the sinkhole, so I needed to find a new place to live, just in case. Pima had been an exemplary guest, never once peeing on the carpet or snapping at the ankles of the maids who came in every day, but the people at the front desk were running out of patience. Time to tip generously and be on my way.

Bev showed up at one o'clock that afternoon to take me house hunting. This time I told her I wanted to look at places on the water. Chloe was over at Jason's, spending their final days of bliss together, so it was just Bev and me heading out. That was fine by me. Sooner, rather than later, Chloe would be gone for good and I'd have the new place to myself. So, my opinion was all that mattered.

"Are we talking condo or single family home?" Bev said.

"I don't care. But if it's a condo it has to allow pets."

Bev looked down at Pima, who was giving her "stink eye." The two of them had never bonded. In fact, even after repeated contact, they barely tolerated each other.

"Of course," Bev said. "There's no way you'd want to take this little sweetie-pie to the dog pound at Pu'unene, I'm sure."

Pima raised her upper lip and displayed an incisor. I pretended not to notice.

We drove up and down the West Side, looking at a half-dozen oceanfront properties. None of them worked. It was sort of a Goldilocks situation: this one was old and funky, with avocado green shag carpet, and a kitchen right out of a Winnebago; that one was next to a tourist watering hole advertising bikini-clad waitresses and Wednesday night "all you could chug" Longboard Ale, and so on. In the *The Three Bears* story, Goldilocks finally finds something that's "just right." Sadly, I didn't.

"Don't give up yet," Bev said. "I'm sure something wonderful will pop up on my hot sheet any day now."

In my mind, she sounded even more discouraged than I felt.

"I'm not worried," I said. "I'm an optimist at heart. And besides, Derek's coming home tomorrow. I'd like to have him join us when we go looking next time."

"That sounds promising," Bev said. "Are things getting serious?"

"Not exactly serious. There's no way I'd pull a Chloe after only a few weeks. But I'd like his opinion. After all, he's a self-made millionaire. I value his business sense."

Bev shot me a raised eyebrow as if to say, "*Spare me.*"

I went on, "Okay, he's gorgeous, and fun and all that, but what I really appreciate is he's not after my money. He's got his own, and that's important."

She stared straight ahead.

"But there is something I'd like to ask you," I said. "About Derek."

"You want to ask *me*? From what I hear, you're the one who's seen him naked." She barked a nervous laugh, as if realizing too late she'd betrayed a confidence.

"Derek told you about that?" I said.

"Well, not chapter and verse, exactly. I mean, he said the two of you had been enjoying your time together. He said he'd taken you out on the 'Ah-Love Oyl' and you two had a fun time. I sort of put two and two together, as it were."

I felt heat rise in my cheeks, and I turned to look out the passenger side window. Bev and Derek were friends. I knew that. I had no right to feel upset over him kissing and telling. It's what guys do, right?

"So, what is it you want to know about him?" she said in an impatient voice.

I pushed down my annoyance. "Can you tell me what Derek's job actually is? I mean, what does he really do to make all that money?"

"Why do you ask?"

"Because a friend of mine—well, not a friend exactly, more like an acquaintance—said he's an oil speculator and he's responsible for the ridiculous price of gas these days."

She laughed. "Your friend sounds like one of those 'global conspiracy' types."

She paused as if framing what she was going to say next. "Look, Derek's a very prosperous oil and gas investor. I guess if an uninformed person wants to call him a 'speculator,' then so be it. But America was founded on capitalist ideals, Monica. And capitalism rewards risk and hard work. And Derek is willing to do both in order to get ahead."

"But is he involved in gouging people?" I said. "The high price of gasoline has made it hard for some people to find jobs. They can't afford to drive to work."

"Derek's role in the oil and gas sector is simply an application of the law of supply and demand. As I'm sure you know, Monica, that's the underlying principal that drives our economy. It's what makes America the greatest nation on Earth."

I hadn't gone to college. I'd shied away from hard classes, like economics, in high school and I'd probably been absent from more civics classes than I'd attended. But even so, I was smart enough to sniff out BS wrapped in the American flag when I smelled it.

ধ ধ ধ

Derek's plane was due in at two on Monday afternoon. He'd taken a limo to the airport when he'd left, so I thought it'd be a nice surprise if I drove out to pick him up in my new car.

I parked in short term parking and went inside. While I waited at the bottom of the escalator for the arriving passengers to exit the security area, I spied a middle-aged guy in a faded aloha shirt holding a small whiteboard with the name "Chambers" written in black marker pen. I went up to him.

"Are you waiting for Derek Chambers?"

"Are you him?" he said. It took him a couple of beats to realize his mistake. Then he said, "Uh, I mean, are you traveling with Mr. Chambers?"

"No, I'm a friend of us. I'll give you twenty bucks for your whiteboard. I'll be taking Mr. Chambers home today."

"Make it thirty, and you've got a deal. I usually get at least a thirty dollar tip for a trip to the West Side, and my paperwork says this guy lives in Kapalua."

I doubted he really made that much, but what did I know? He'd need to replace his whiteboard. But, on the other hand, he'd be saving himself a couple gallons of gas.

I agreed, and plucked a twenty and a ten out of my wallet. He pulled a tissue out of his pocket and began erasing the name from the board. I grabbed his wrist, and he jerked back as if about to defend himself.

"Sorry," I said. "But I want it with the name on it. Could you fix it before you go?"

"I'll do better than that. You can do it yourself." He unclipped a black dry erase pen from his front pocket and held it out. Then he ambled away.

Derek came down the escalator looking as if he'd just been awakened from a deep sleep. He yawned as he stepped off the last stair. I held up the sign, waving it around to get his attention.

He walked over and said, "That bad, eh?"

I squinted in confusion.

"I leave for a week and you're reduced to hauling horny businessmen home from the airport."

I laughed a little harder than the comment warranted. I wasn't exactly sure if I should be insulted or not, so I chose not to be.

"Actually, I'm really glad to see you," he said. "You're sweet to come get me." He dropped his carry-on bag and took me in his arms. "You smell like home. And I'm damn glad to be home."

We walked out to the parking lot, and I "peeped" the door locks on my new Lexus with the clicker.

"Huh. Looks like you got an upgrade on your rental," he said.

"Nope, it's mine. I bought it last week." I did a little Vanna White gesture to indicate the lovely lines and shiny "no dings yet" condition of the pearl-colored paint job.

"Huh. Don't you think it's kind of an 'old lady' car?"

"*Old lady*?"

"Yeah, this is a granny car. Like something a Honolulu *tutu* would drive to church on Sunday mornings."

"Are you kidding? It's gorgeous," I said. "And it's a thousand times more comfortable than your Corvette."

He smiled. "Maybe, but it's no Lorinser."

"Is that what this is about?" I said. "A 'mine's bigger than yours' thing? Because I'll quickly concede to the superiority of German engineering over Japanese. But this car cost about ten times less than yours, so—"

"It's more like fifteen times less, sweetheart, but who's counting?"

"Get in, or I'll go find that sweaty limo guy and have him take you home. You'll miss me all the way to Kapalua."

He leaned in and took me in his arms again. He kissed me, long and hard. When he pulled back he glanced down at his beltline. "Can't you tell? I've already been missing you for a week. Now let's get home and do something about it."

CHAPTER 20

There's no denying Derek and I were compatible, and Bev had more than earned her star in the Matchmaker Walk of Fame for introducing us. After all, Derek was in his mid-thirties, and I was just a hair under thirty. He'd moved to Maui from the mainland, and so had I. Looks-wise, we made a cute couple. More importantly, I had an eight-figure balance sheet, and his was that and then some. Neither of us had gone to college, so one couldn't lord that over the other. And, we both avoided the public eye. He had his reasons, I had mine.

I thought Derek would want to go straight home after a week-long business trip and a long trans-Pacific flight, but he surprised me by asking me to take him to The Jolly Harpooner.

"You don't want to go to your house and freshen up?" I said.

"Nope. The Jolly Harpooner is fifteen minutes closer. I want to get out of these clothes I've been wearing for the last twenty-four hours." He leaned over the console and said, "But what I really want is to get *you* out of yours."

I parked and as we walked through the lobby, a bevy of teenaged girls wearing less fabric than a tube sock came giggling past us. Derek's eyes tracked them all the way out the door.

"Hey," I said. "I know it's been a week since you've seen boobs, but you can screw your eyeballs back into your skull now."

He laughed. "I'll take a rain-check on the screwing. Get over here." He pulled me tight against him as we got into the elevator.

A mom dragging a whining, sunburned toddler ran toward the elevator yelling, "Hold it, please."

Derek thumbed the "Close" button, and the doors slid together.

"Hey," I said. "That wasn't nice."

"Sorry, babe, but I just spent twenty hours in the air and crossed more than a dozen time zones. Last thing I need is an elevator ride with a clueless woman and her screaming kid."

We reached the seventh floor. A maid's cart was parked outside my suite and the door was propped open.

"Huh, that's strange," I said. "They already cleaned the room this morning. I wonder why the maid's back?"

"Probably hiding out from her supervisor. I wouldn't be surprised if we find her on your bed with her feet propped up, watching 'Oprah'."

The "Oprah" show wasn't on TV anymore, but I didn't think it necessary to correct him. Besides, I had other concerns.

"Pima?" I called as we came in. "Come here, girl."

Nothing.

Pima's the kind of dog that would love to be surgically attached to my side. She whines when I leave, and just about breaks bones in her scramble to welcome me home when I return. The eerie silence when I called her name poured over me like ice water.

"Where's your dog?" Derek said. "That thing's usually lickety-split to the door."

"I know. I'm worried."

"Probably got locked in the bedroom or something," he said.

We found the maid in the bathroom along with a guy in dark green coveralls. The guy had propped a tool bag on the sink counter, and he was on hands and knees fishing around in the toilet. The maid stood behind him with arms crossed.

"What's going on here?" Derek said. "What're you doing?"

Since this was my suite I thought I should've been asking the questions, but if Derek wanted to take the initiative, it was okay with me.

The coverall guy stood. "Got a jammed-up toilet here. Looks like the lady must've tried to flush some feminine-type products down there."

I shook my head. "Not me."

He pulled his mouth to one side. "Hey, I'm not accusing nobody of nothin'. But what we got here is a major logjam. And usually in situations like this here, it turns out your 'hygiene' items are mostly to blame."

Derek shot me a "sounds about right to me" smile. I wasn't about to argue. I didn't want to eat my words if he managed to pull some disgusting cotton item out of the trap. I hadn't flushed anything other than toilet paper, but who knew if maybe Chloe had? She'd been so distracted, it was possible. Or, more than likely, maybe another guest's indiscretion had been lurking in wait ever since I'd checked in. It wasn't something I wanted to think too much about.

"Have you seen my dog?" I said.

"Your dog?" The guy said. "I didn't think they allowed dogs here."

The maid murmured something to the guy in Spanish.

He shrugged and said, "Sorry, no-speak-o."

I turned to her, "*¿Sabes dónde está mi perro?*"

"*Perro?*" She shook her head. "*Lo siento, pero no sé. ¿Qué hace su perro?*"

"*Ella es pequeña, con pelaje gris,*" I said. I'd described Pima as small, with gray fur. I thought that was more than enough description for her to recollect whether she'd seen the only dog currently in residence at The Jolly Harpooner.

Derek broke in. "If you girls are finished with your little private conversation, I'd like to take a shower, preferably *now*. Tell your friend 'Maria' here to vamoose. How do they say it in Spanish? Am-scray?"

"Derek, there's no need to be rude. And her name isn't 'Maria;' it's Dolores. It's right there on her name badge."

"Maria, Dolores, whatever. They're all 'Marias' to me."

The coverall guy spoke up. "I've done all I can from this end. We're gonna need to bring in a plumber. Don't use this toilet until he shows up." He threw his tools in his bag and stomped out.

Dolores bent down to wipe up a puddle of water on the floor.

"Tell her to leave," Derek said. "But, don't forget to say 'please' and 'thank you.'" He gave me a peck on the cheek. "I'll be waiting in the living room."

In Spanish, I told Dolores not to worry about cleaning up, I'd do it later. I explained my friend had just come in from a long plane ride and he needed to take a shower right away. She offered to come back in an hour, but I assured her it wouldn't be necessary.

As she gathered up her rags and mop, I pulled a ten-dollar bill from my purse and folded it into fourths. I slipped it to her as we crossed through the living room on the way to the door. Her eyes widened and she glanced over at Derek like a Chihuahua who'd been given a juicy bone in front of a vigilant Doberman. She slipped the bill into her pocket with a quiet "*Grácias*."

"What just happened there?" said Derek.

"I tipped the maid."

"Why?" he said. "She's just doing her job. And the toilet's still plugged up. If you want to tip someone, it should be the plumber who shows up to actually fix the thing."

"Do you know how much plumbers make?"

"Spare me the socialist sermon," he said. "That girl's probably an illegal anyway. They're like feral cats. If you feed them they'll never go away."

I picked up the ice bucket from the counter near the door. "I'm going to get some ice," I said.

I speed-walked down the hall, quietly calling for Pima. I checked in the vending machine room and the alcove near the elevators. Where could she have gone? It wasn't like her to take off without me.

I filled the ice bucket and went back to the suite. I heard water running in the shower, so I used the bucket to prop the door open for Pima. Then I went into my bedroom.

ꗉ ꗉ ꗉ

At seven o'clock Derek suggested we call for take-out from the Hula Grill. I ordered the Kula tomato and Maui onion salad, followed by *kiawe* wood-grilled *ono*. Derek chose the charred short ribs appetizer and the fire-grilled *ahi* steak for his entrée.

"How much for delivery?" he said to the guy on the line.

There was a pause.

"Okay, let me put it another way. I'm willing to pay fifty bucks to have someone ride the elevator up to the seventh floor of The Jolly Harpooner. It's right next door to your restaurant. I'm sure you've got a waiter there who's willing to make a quick McGarrett for slipping away for ten minutes."

"McGarrett?" I said after he'd hung up.

"Yeah. Fifty bucks. You know, like Hawaii Five-O?"

It took me a couple of seconds, but then I smiled.

A half-hour later there was a knock at the suite door. Derek slipped on a white waffle-weave robe with "Jolly Harpooner" embroidered over the breast pocket. The short spa robe hit him just above the knee.

"You look cute," I said, pulling the bedsheet up to my chin. "Are you going to have them bring it in here, like room service?"

"Whatever you'd like."

"Let's have them leave it in the kitchen. I'm not decent."

"Oh, sweetheart. You're a good three notches above 'decent,'" he said with a wink. "But I won't hold it against you."

What the hell did *that* mean?

The person at the door knocked again, more forceful this time.

"I better get the door before the guy scarfs down my *ahi* and runs back to work claiming I stiffed him."

I waited in bed until I heard the outside door close. Then I got up and went into the kitchen, naked.

"Did you leave the door propped open?" he said.

"Yeah, I was hoping Pima would come back."

"The dog will come back when it gets hungry. Until then, I want you to keep your door closed and bolted." He crossed his arms. "Especially if you're going to walk around naked."

"I've always wanted to eat fancy food naked," I said.

"Huh. How about we *feed* each other fancy food naked?"

The next hour was a languorous back and forth of Derek slipping bites of my food to me and me doing the same back to him. By the time we'd finished, I had bits of *ono* lodged between my breasts and a smear of salad dressing on my cheek. Seems it's harder to get food into another person's mouth than your own.

"Let's take a shower together," I said.

"I just took one a couple of hours ago," he said.

"Not with me, you didn't."

At the rate I was going, I was on target to make up for my past year of celibacy in record time.

CHAPTER 21

John Dease called at eight o'clock the next morning. I considered not taking the call, but I'd promised I wouldn't ignore him anymore. Derek had gotten up very early and taken a cab to his house to get to work, and Pima was still missing. John had a good head for solving problems. Maybe he'd have an idea of what I should do.

"Hello, Mr. Dease. So, what's the good news?"

That had become my signature greeting with John. After a few months of working with him, I'd joked that he never called me unless he had bad news. So, each time after that, he'd tried desperately to start the call with good news: the University of Arizona Wildcats were in first place in Pac-12 basketball, or the weatherman had predicted less than hundred-degree temperatures for the next few days of summer. I think it made John feel bad to always be the bearing of bad tidings.

"You're not gonna believe this, but I actually *do* have some good news for you. Unfortunately, it's wrapped in lousy news for someone else," he said.

"Sounds like the Riddle of the Sphinx."

"Look at you with the mythological metaphors," he said. "A woman like you doesn't need college to be smarter than most everyone else around."

"Flattery will get you love, but it won't pay the bills, John. What's up?"

"Seems our friend, Mr. Harrow, has received some very discouraging news."

"Again? What now?" I said. "They dig up a dozen more illegals in his warehouse?"

"Worse. Much worse," he said. "Seems the guy's been diagnosed with pancreatic cancer. Stage four. According to his attorney, they've only given him weeks, a couple of months at the most. He wants to spend whatever time he has left with his family so he's agreed to settle with you according to the deal we drafted before you left."

"What about the federal suit? The undocumented workers?"

"Seems he's agreed to take that off the table. He admitted to his lawyer he'd trumped up the whole thing. Said he'd called in the feds himself, and the so-called illegals actually had green cards, after all."

"What an ass," I said.

"Yeah, but he's a soon-to-be-dying ass."

"So, he's still going to take half of my winnings?"

"Half of *the* winnings, Monica. Remember, Harrow believes he should've gotten it all."

"Yeah, right. So, that leaves me with, what? Fifteen million?"

"I haven't talked with your CPA lately, but after you buying that place over there in Hawaii, it's probably closer to ten."

"Yeah. That's another story."

I told John about the sinkhole, the royal bones, and me looking for a new place to live.

"Well, just keep in mind you've got half of what you had yesterday," he said.

I thanked John for the call and hung up. A blast of emotions roared through me with such force I had to sit down. Steve was dying? Of cancer? What a horrible way to go.

And he'd dropped the lawsuit? No more depositions, no more legal bills? But what about him falsely accusing me of a federal crime? I could've done jail time for that one. How bitter does a person have to be to go that far for revenge?

With the shock of John's news I'd forgotten to ask his advice on finding Pima. I got dressed and went down to the front desk.

"We don't allow animals on the premises," said the pale guy at the front desk.

How does a guy stay that pasty-faced on Maui? It must take SPF One Million to avoid getting even a hint of tan.

He went on. "I certainly can't allow you to put up a flyer, nor could you expect us to mention it to our registered guests."

"But it was your housekeeping staff who let her out," I said. "Don't you think that makes The Jolly Harpooner at least partly responsible?"

"Miss, we're responsible for assuring our guests a wonderful vacation. And that doesn't include pestering them about lost dogs. Especially dogs that shouldn't have been here in the first place. Think about it, if we tell our guests to be on the lookout for a missing pet, the next thing you know we'll be besieged by requests to allow all kinds of pets on premises. Iguanas, cockatiels, pit bulls..." He rolled his eyes upward in horror.

"Look, I'm only trying to find my little dog. Would you please at least notify your staff to be watching out for her? I'm offering a substantial reward."

"Substantial?"

"Yes," I said. I calculated in my head what that word might mean to a guy making fifteen bucks an hour. "A hundred dollars."

He snorted. "We have bellboys who make twice that in tips every day."

"Okay. Five hundred."

He gave me a one-shoulder shrug. "As you wish."

I figured Mr. Pale Face may or may not pass along my request to the housekeeping staff. Pima was out there somewhere. It looked like it was going to be up to me to find her.

I walked along Ka'anapali Parkway looking under parked cars and peeking through bushes. It didn't make sense to call her name because I could see everything for a block around. Aside from being under a car or tucked inside a bush, there was no place to hide. I wondered if she'd try to make her way back to Paradise Ridge, but that seemed ridiculous. She'd only lived there a month and, besides, it was miles up a busy highway. But where else would she go?

I circled back to my hotel, stopping at a few shops in Whaler's Village to ask if anyone had seen a dog. At the ABC Store a nice clerk asked if I had a photo and I showed her a picture on my phone. She clucked about how cute Pima was, and how sorry she was, and then said she'd keep an eye out.

By the time I'd gotten back to the lobby I was beating myself up pretty bad about fooling around with Derek yesterday afternoon instead of immediately starting the search for Pima. I justified my actions by telling myself I thought she'd just nose around the hallways for a while and then come back when she felt like it. Pima had a mind of her own. If she wasn't ready to come when I called, she didn't. She was more like a cat than a dog in a lot of ways.

As I waited for the elevator, I looked out at the beach and saw a darkly-tanned girl of about four or five with long black hair lugging something wrapped in a beach towel. The *something* was about the size of a baby. It surprised me that a mother would let a kid that young carry her baby.

Especially since the kid was struggling with the weight of it. Hopefully, the mom was nearby.

The elevator pinged and the doors slid open. I took one step inside and then I hopped back out again as if I'd encountered a swarm of bees. That baby. I hadn't gotten a good look at it. Maybe it wasn't a baby, after all.

I pushed through the glass doors that led out to the beach. By now the little girl was twenty or thirty yards away. I jogged to catch up. When I got alongside, I said "Hi," but she ignored me and clutched the bundle tighter to her body.

I asked if I could please see her baby and the kid started screaming bloody murder.

🜁 🜁 🜁

It's never fun to talk to the police, even if you haven't done anything wrong. The two guys who showed up quickly after the kid starting yelling had obviously been trained in good community policing tactics. Don't threaten, don't yell, and don't slap the cuffs on 'til you're pretty sure you've got the right perp.

The little girl's mom turned out to be a local woman who'd taken her two kids to the beach on her day off. The "baby" in the beach towel turned out to be a two-liter bottle of pop the little girl had pilfered off someone else's beach mat. I had a feeling the mom had put her child up to the thievery, but nobody asked so I didn't tell. From my perspective, I wasn't guilty of anything except maybe foiling a robbery.

Still, I apologized to the mother for scaring her kid. She gathered up her stuff, along with her two little accomplices, and left—muttering under her breath the whole time about "rich *haoles* think they own the place" and other choice comments, some more colorful than others.

When she'd gone, I told the cops my story about losing my dog and how I'd thought maybe the kid was carrying it in the towel. The two of them gave me the look you'd give a crazy cat lady who claims she'd personally given birth to each of the thirty-seven cats on her property. But, thankfully, they managed to play it straight when I finished my story.

"So, your dog's gone missing?" said the first cop.

His name badge said "Wilcox." I can't decipher police insignia, so I didn't know if the guy was a foot patrolman, a sergeant, a lieutenant or whatever, so I stuck with just calling him "Officer."

"Yes, Officer. She's been missing for more than a day now."

"Where'd you last see the dog?"

The second cop seemed anxious to get out of there and go find some real criminal activity to break up, but he stood by, nevertheless.

I explained I was staying at The Jolly Harpooner and it appeared my dog had run off when the maid left the door open.

"Huh," he said. "I didn't know they allowed pets in there."

He looked over at the gleaming oceanfront tower of The Jolly Harpooner, and I wondered if there was an ordinance prohibiting dogs in Hawaii hotels.

"They don't," I said. Then I filled him in on my sad tale about the sinkhole and losing my house. For good measure, I also threw in how my car had gone into the harbor at Kahului.

He caught his partner's eye. "You sound like one unlucky *wahine*."

I smiled, but didn't argue the point.

"I supposed you've already checked the animal shelter," he said.

"No, I don't even know where the animal shelter is."

"The big one's in Pu'unene, on the other side," he said. "But there's a lady down in Lahaina who also takes in lost dogs. Her place is pretty close to my folks' house. Now and then we get a noise complaint about the barking, but mostly everyone's cool."

"Why would she do that?"

"What? Take in stray dogs? Because at the animal shelter they only hold a lost dog for one day. After that, it goes up for adoption. By the time you realize your dog's gone, someone else could've adopted it—or worse."

"They kill them?"

"I'm sure they don't want to. But if they get too many…"

Panic rose like bile in my throat. Pima had been gone for a day. If she'd been taken to the Pu'unene shelter her sweet face could already be featured in a "Pet of the Week" line-up. She was a purebred and darn cute. I may be biased, but I figured anyone looking for a little rescue dog would snatch her right up.

"Can you give me the address of the Lahaina dog lady?"

"Sure," the cop said. He pulled out a business card and flipped it over. In slanting left-handed printing he wrote on the back.

He handed me the card. It said, "Yellow house by garage sale/ Shaw St." Underneath, he'd printed the name "Nancy."

"Garage sale?" I said.

"Yeah. There's an *'ohana*—that's a family—down there got a garage sale goin' like every day of the year. It's like a neighborhood landmark."

"I really appreciate this," I said. "*Mahalo*."

Officer Wilcox's walkie-talkie squawked. It sounded like garbled gibberish to me, but a look passed between the two cops.

"We gotta go," said the second cop.

"Sorry about your dog," said Officer Wilcox. "We hope you find it."

♻ ♻ ♻

I pulled up at the yellow house on Shaw Street fifteen minutes later. I parallel parked as far over as possible, but the side of my car still stuck out into the narrow roadway. There was a guy weeding a flower bed by the side fence. He wore an old blue ball cap which made it hard to see his face, but something about him seemed vaguely familiar. But, since I didn't know anyone in Lahaina, I shrugged it off.

A chorus of barking greeted me as I walked up to the tiny bungalow. A pack of about seven or eight dogs had flung themselves against the chain-link fence and were leaping and yipping in an apparent attempt to see if their owner had shown up to liberate them. I tried to see if Pima was among them, but four big dogs had secured the front spots; the smaller dogs were hidden behind.

The baseball cap guy stood up and began walking toward me. It was Max, the volunteer who'd helped me sort produce at the Maui Food Bank.

"Whoa," he said. "Look what the tide washed in."

He flipped off his cap and wiped his hands down the sides of his cargo shorts. Since the shorts were already streaked with red dirt, it didn't appear to make much difference.

He stuck out a hand. "Sorry, I'm kind of grubby. But it's great to see you again."

We shook hands.

"I'm surprised to see you here," I said.

"You are?" He scrunched his forehead, a stack of furrows pleating his forehead from his eyebrows to the scalp of his bald head. "I thought you'd come to visit."

"I did. Or more honestly, I've come to visit Nancy."

"How do you know my wife?"

"I lost my dog. A cop in Ka'anapali told me to check here first."

"Ah, then we better take a look out back. Nancy's gone to Makawao to pick up dog food. She buys it in bulk at the feed store up there. It's a lot cheaper than the grocery store."

"I really hope my dog's here," I said. "She's a miniature Schnauzer, dark gray with a sweet face. She would've been brought in yesterday or today. Do you remember seeing her?"

He laughed. "Nancy doesn't get involved in my volunteer stuff and I don't know much about hers. I'm pretty sure someone brought a dog in yesterday, but I couldn't for the life of me tell you what it looked like."

He walked me around the side of the house and unfastened the gate. The pack of dogs rushed us as if they hadn't eaten in a week and we smelled like steak. There were a lot more dogs than I'd first thought. They appeared to be mostly mixed breeds, especially lab and terrier conglomerations. Most were brown or black, with few white ones thrown in.

As the dogs leapt and snuffled around us, I frantically searched for a flash of gray fur and a pair of familiar brown eyes. No luck.

"Any of these your dog?" Max said.

"No, I'm afraid not."

"Why don't we go inside and you can fill out one of Nancy's BOLO forms," he said. "She posts them around town at places where locals hang out. You know, grocery store bulletin boards, the free clinic, churches. It helps if you have a picture. And it *really* helps if you offer a reward."

"I'll get a photo made and bring it back. And I'm thinking of offering a five-hundred dollar reward."

"Whew, that more'n ought to do the trick." He laughed. "You know, I don't mean to sound judgmental or anything, but it always amazes me how people get more sentimental about hearing about somebody losing a pet than hearing about a guy who lost his job, or a family who lost their home to foreclosure. And when it comes to money, it's nuts. The public will open their wallets if a stray dog's in trouble, but they get real stingy when it comes to helping their fellow man."

"Does your wife know you feel this way?"

"Sure, but her argument is pets are like kids. They're powerless. People aren't comfortable watching an animal suffer. But they figure poor people got that way by their own doing. Like, they chose drugs over schooling, or drinking over going to work every day."

"But what about poor kids? Hungry kids?"

"Yeah, well they're sort of what the military calls 'collateral damage,' I guess. That's why the food bank uses pictures of kids in their public service ads. No argument there about 'making bad choices.' Unless you believe a kid cosmically picks his parents. And that's a train of thought way more 'woo-woo' than I'm willing to take."

I filled out Nancy's Be On the Lookout, or BOLO, form and promised I'd come back later with a photo.

As I was leaving, Max said, "I take it you've already checked with the shelter in Pu'unene."

"Not yet."

He tapped the face of his black plastic watch with a grimy fingernail.

"Tick-tock if you're dog's over there," he said. "They don't mess around. Twenty-four hours, that's all they hold 'em for you. Nancy started taking in West Side dogs because a lot of times if a family over here lost a dog, it was pretty much a sure thing they'd never see it again."

Max walked me outside and a shiny blue pick-up truck pulled into his driveway. The windows were darkly tinted.

"Looks like your wife's home," I said.

"Nope, that's not her."

"Oh? Well then, it looks like you may have somebody else who's lost a dog."

"Nope. Not that, either."

"You know who it is?" I said.

"Yep. And so do you."

I squinted at the windshield, but still couldn't make out the shadowy face in the driver's seat.

"Who is it?"

Max crossed his arms and smiled. "Give it a minute. You'll see."

A few seconds later, the engine shut off and a door popped open. When the driver got out, I thought, "Oh great. Just what I need."

CHAPTER 22

Keo Kekane sauntered over and stuck out a hand to Max. Instead of a normal handshake, they did a series of fist bumps and forearm grabs that looked more like a couple of South Tucson gang members "signifying" than two adult men with liberal political leanings greeting each other.

When they'd finished with the hand jive, Keo turned to me.

"Nice to see you again," he said. His benign smile masked any embarrassment he might've felt over how we'd left things a week earlier in my suite at The Jolly Harpooner.

"You too," I said. "How're things at the food bank?"

"Great. We've received some nice cash donations in the past couple of days," he said. "It's really helped. But we never know if it will continue. That's always the challenge."

I shot him a weak smile. I wasn't sure if he was hitting me up for a continuing pledge or just making small talk. I hoped it was small talk because there was no way I was going to reward his churlish diatribe against Derek.

He went on, "We had hopes you might become a regular volunteer. But I guess with everything going on, you know, the sinkhole and now the cultural people looking for bones, it's understandable. Sounds like you've got your hands full."

The sinkhole and the possible finding of the *ali'i* bones had been prime media fodder for the past week. Anyone pining for their fifteen minutes of fame ought to walk in my Manolo Blahniks for a mile. What I'd learned is that just like the toe-squishing stiletto-heeled shoes, notoriety can be painful.

"Yeah, I've been pretty tied up. And now my dog's gone missing."

"Ah, I was wondering what you were doing here," he said.

Max spoke up. "I told her she should check the animal shelter at Pu'unene."

"Give me a few minutes and I'll take you," said Keo. "It's not a trip a person should make alone."

"Why's that?"

"Because if it turns out to be bad news, you'd have to handle it on your own."

"Keo, I've been handling bad news on my own since I was twelve years old."

"Suit yourself, but I'm willing to take you."

"*Mahalo*, but I'll be fine. In fact, I'm sort of looking forward to the drive over there."

I said my good-byes and headed out to my car.

Truthfully, I wasn't looking forward to any part of the trip to the Pu'unene Animal Shelter. I pictured forlorn furry faces beseeching me to take them home when there was no way I could. And, what if I found out Pima had been adopted, or worse, that she'd been brought there injured or even dead? But I'd be damned if I was going to allow Keo to play the knight-in-shining-armor to my damsel in distress. Nope, no way. If Pima wasn't there, he'd probably get all high and mighty about how it was my duty to bring home some flea-infested mongrel to take her place.

I got in my car and watched the two men go inside Max and Nancy's bungalow. I sniffed the new car smell and gazed at the familiar Lexus dashboard. I allowed my body to relax into the comfy leather seats.

I started the engine and pulled out onto the street. But before I even made it to the Honoapi'ilani Highway intersection, tears blurred my vision. I turned left, instead of right, and headed back to The Jolly Harpooner. I wasn't ready to face the animal shelter. And besides, Pima had been micro-chipped. I'd kept my same cell phone number from Arizona, so if she got taken to the animal shelter they'd read her chip and call me. Since I hadn't gotten a call there was no reason to rush over there.

My cell phone went off as I was unlocking the door to my suite. I dug the phone out of my purse and checked the caller ID. It was Derek.

"Did you find your dog?" he said.

"No, but not for lack of trying," I said. "I've spent the whole day looking for her."

"Give it time. When the dog's ready to come back it will. It's probably at a doggie singles' bar trying to score a canine booty call." He laughed.

"I don't think so. I had Pima spade at four months old."

"Harsh."

I blew out a breath. "It was the right thing to do, Derek."

"Maybe right for you, but think about your dog. No hook-ups for the dude, ever. Seems you should've let the little guy sample the goods at least once."

I wasn't about to discuss proper pet parenting with a man who refused to even keep my dog's gender straight.

"Did you just call to talk about my dog?" I said.

"No, actually, I wanted to see if you'd like to hop over to Lana'i with me on Saturday. I have about a half hour of work to do and then we'll have the rest of the day to ourselves."

"Sounds fun."

"Good. Then it's a date. Let's plan to leave about ten. I'm going to be in Honolulu for the rest of this week, but I'll be back Friday night."

"I'll look forward to it," I said.

"Great," he said.

There was a beat, and I thought he'd hung up. But as I was about to click off the call, he added, "Oh, and I hope you find your dog, Monica. But if you don't, I'll buy you a new one after we get back from Lana'i."

ॐ ॐ ॐ

With Derek out of town, Chloe at Jason's, and Pima still missing, I was going stir crazy at The Jolly Harpooner. On Wednesday morning I tried reading a book out on the lanai but my mind kept wandering. I couldn't imagine where Pima could be and why I hadn't heard anything from either Nancy or the shelter.

Finally, around noon, the phone rang.

"Monica? It's me, Max. Are you in a place where you can talk?"

"Did you find my dog? Do you have Pima?" My voice cracked, like he'd caught me crying.

"No, sorry. I'm calling about something else. I guess your little Schnauzer's still missing?"

I nodded; then realized Max couldn't see my reaction. "Uh, yeah, she's still gone."

"How about the shelter? What'd you find out there?"

"Max, please tell me why you called."

"We'd like to offer you a seat on the board."

"What board?"

"The Advisory Board at the Maui Food Bank. We've got an open position, and your name came up as a possible candidate. It's not a lot of work. We have a meeting once a month and then we do a couple of fund-raisers during the year. But we thought you might enjoy it. And you'd be bringing a much-needed new perspective to the group."

"Who's 'we', Max?"

"Everybody. I thought about it when you were over here yesterday and so I mentioned it to Keo. He talked with Makaila this morning and she agreed. I think you already know one of our other board members—Beverly Strong from the Realtor's Association?"

"Yeah, I know Bev. She's on your board?"

"Yes, and she does a great job. What do you say?"

"I don't know, Max. I don't have the best relationship with Keo. He said some pretty rude things about the guy I'm dating."

"Look, I just want you to think about it. Talk to Beverly and see what she thinks. It's a great way to meet people. And, hopefully, it would get your mind off some of the stuff you've been dealing with."

I paused. No harm in considering it, I guess.

"Okay," I said. "I'll think about it. But don't take that as a 'yes.' It's a 'maybe,' nothing more."

"That's good enough for me."

I hung up feeling strangely pleased with myself. I'd been hit up for so much in the past year it wasn't like I hadn't been asked to support a cause before. But I'd never been asked to actually help out. I'd simply been the girl with the fat wallet and the bottomless checkbook, never the grown-up who was asked to contribute something mean-ingful.

I screwed up my courage and called the Pu'unene Animal Shelter. As much as I wanted to avoid it, I couldn't put it off any longer.

The shelter worker told me the only way to be certain Pima wasn't at the shelter was to come to Pu'unene and see for myself. She said they had so many dogs and cats coming and going sometimes the volunteers get overwhelmed.

I headed out. I knew if I hesitated, I'd end up making excuses to not go. I'd done that when my mother died: I came up with a million reasons why I couldn't go pick out her casket, and then I pretended to be busy with homework on the day I was supposed to meet with our priest to discuss the service. I attended her funeral mass, but slipped out the back before the "casserole ladies" laid out their spread in the community room. My *abuela* had picked up the slack for me, picking out a casket and meeting with the priest. She offered excuses for my dismal behavior just as she had for my mother after my father died.

I pulled into the shelter's gravel parking lot and parked. As soon as I opened my door I heard frantic barking and whining. If Pima was in there, she'd be too freaked out to bark. She didn't like to be around other dogs. She trembled and whined when I took her to the vet. Once, after an especially agitated visit to get shots, I'd talked the vet into coming out to my house, after hours, to treat her. It cost a lot more, but it was well worth it to avoid the aggravation.

A smiling older woman in a dark green apron with a big white paw print on the bib greeted me as I came through the door. Her name badge identified her as "Marilyn," a volunteer.

"Are you here to adopt a new family member?" she said. She no doubt noticed I wasn't carrying a sad new detainee, so she probably assumed I was there to make a withdrawal rather than a deposit.

"No, I've already adopted," I said. "I'm looking for my dog."

It wasn't technically true that I'd "adopted" Pima. I'd actually paid a small fortune to a Phoenix breeder for Pima, because after I'd won the money I wanted everything shiny and new. The thought of going to a shelter to rescue a "used" dog seemed like going to Goodwill to shop for shoes. I didn't need to do stuff like that anymore.

As Marilyn escorted me down the concrete aisles of the dog cages, I found myself unwilling to look any of the dogs in the eye. I felt ashamed I'd insisted on a pure-bred puppy. Who'd allow the sweet-faced Pomeranian-mix in cell block three, or the doe-eyed Water Spaniel at the end of the row, to be euthanized simply because their owners either couldn't, or wouldn't, take care of them anymore?

"Do you know if you've gotten in any miniature Schnauzers in the past couple of days?" I said. "My dog's name is Pima, and she's about a year old."

"No, but then I don't see every animal that comes in," Marilyn said. "As you can see, we're at capacity."

I remembered what the cop at Ka'anapali Beach had said about them being forced to euthanize leftover pets *when they get too many*. I sucked in a breath and said, "Did you have to put any dogs to sleep today?"

"Not me, personally," she said.

Her tone was snippy, but I didn't take offense. I couldn't imagine it was easy working the front desk of an animal shelter when you knew all too well what was going on in the back.

We continued to check each of the cages, but it was clear Pima wasn't there. I thanked her for helping me look and then I filled out a missing pet form. I told her about Pima's microchip.

She brightened. "Oh, well then, no worries. The first thing we do when a new animal comes in is to check for a chip. If your dog shows up here, we'll call you."

She cleared her throat. "If you can, we'd really appreciate a donation. Even though we're mostly volunteer-run, it still costs approximately thirty dollars a day to feed and shelter each animal."

She held up a coffee can wrapped in Con-Tac paper festooned with cartoon faces of smiling dogs and cats. It had a plastic lid with a slit to push the money through.

I pulled out my wallet and took out two fifties and shoved them through the slit. After all, it wasn't as if I could plead lack of funds.

"*Mahalo* for checking with us today," she said. "And I hope you find your Pima. But if you don't, please come back and consider taking home a new friend. Oh, and even if you do find her, you may want to think about getting her a companion."

I smiled but refrained from explaining that Pima didn't play well with others.

🐾 🐾 🐾

Since I was on the far side of the island I figured it wouldn't hurt to at least drop by the food bank to let them know I was still considering the board position. I parked on the street and walked around to the office door.

When I came inside, Makaila got up from her desk and came over and gave me a big hug. Once again, I was reminded of the safe feeling I'd felt when I'd been hugged by my *abuela*.

"*Aloha*, Monica," she said. "How you doin'? Take a seat, girl."

We sat nearly knee to knee in the cramped outer office. I could hear Keo's voice, but his office was on a few doors down a narrow hallway so I couldn't see him. The good news was he couldn't see me either.

"You here for your new board member orientation?" Makaila said.

"I haven't decided yet. I'm not sure if I'm the best candidate."

"Why's that? You're smart, and a hard worker."

"Oh, come on, Makaila, we both know that isn't why they offered me the position."

She leaned back and crossed ample arms over her even more generous bosom. "No? Well, we don't need no more slackers or divas around here, tha's for sure. It's true you gave a big donation, but from where I'm sittin,' that just shows you're serious."

"Max told me Bev Strong's on the board."

"That's right. She's not as active as some of our other board members, but when we need her, she always comes through."

She leaned in and lightly tapped my forearm. "C'mon, I'll buy you a cup of the worst coffee on the island."

She led me down the hall. As we passed Keo's office, I saw him hunched over a stack of papers on his desk. He didn't look up. I was pretty certain he wasn't a hundred-percent behind my board nomination, but he was probably reluctant to say he couldn't support me because of my poor choice of boyfriend.

Since it was a Wednesday, the warehouse was alive with workers briskly sorting canned food into cardboard boxes. Everyone looked up as we passed and then they went right back to work. I spotted Starshine at the end of one of the long tables. She was standing behind a stick-thin female worker who was frantically sifting through cans.

"I said, 'tomatoes'," said Starshine. "Each box gets *one* can of tomatoes. What's the matter with you? Can't you read?"

The woman mumbled something and kept picking through the cans.

"Then look at the picture! They mostly have pictures on them. Jeez, if you don't keep up, I'm not gonna sign your timecard. Then you'll have to find somewhere else to get your hours."

The woman's shoulders slumped, and she turned and looked at Starshine with pleading eyes.

"Oh, don't give me that," said Starshine. "You think if you mess up I'll find something easier for you to do? Maybe get you a job where you can sit down? Well, it don't work that way. This is as good as it gets, sister."

Makaila shot me a sideways glance but kept moving toward the coffee room. When we got inside I smelled the unmistakable odor of a scorched pot. Sure enough, a nearly empty glass coffee carafe had been left on the burner. The dark brown crust on the bottom was smoking and popping.

"I've tol' these folks a million times to turn off the machine when the coffee's gone. Now look at this mess." Makaila picked up the carafe and headed for the sink.

"You should probably let it cool before you clean it," I said. "The glass will break."

I walked over to the sink and folded a paper towel in fourths. "Set it on this for a while."

Makaila smiled. "See? I said you were smart. That's why they want you on the board."

I laughed. "You played me! You weren't gonna put cold water in that thing."

"You can't never know what I might do. But I know we could use someone around here who's got a good head on their shoulders. Some of these board members are so out of touch with real life I gotta wonder how they manage to wipe their own ass."

I was surprised by her rough talk, but it got the point across.

"Seriously, Monica, we need you. To be fair, I should let you know Keo's nursing a little beef with you comin' on. But he'll get over it. He's a big boy."

And I was a big girl. Besides, I kind of liked the idea of making pretty-boy Keo Kekane squirm a little.

CHAPTER 23

I drove back to the food bank on Thursday morning. My orientation wasn't scheduled until two-thirty that afternoon, but I left the Jolly Harpooner at ten hoping Makaila could fit me in sooner. I didn't have anything else to do, and I wanted to see if I could finish up before Keo and his merry band returned from making deliveries at the pantries.

I'd gone from a shower cap-clad worker bee to a board member queen bee in less than a month. Rags to riches, the story of my life. But aside from Keo, there was no telling how the rest of the great unwashed would take the news of my appointment, especially Starshine.

Makaila wasn't at her desk when I got there. I heard voices in the back, so I slipped quietly down the hall to see if I could find her. I was a few feet shy of Keo's office when the door flew open and Starshine came barreling out into the hall.

"Yeah?" she yelled back into the room. "Well, joke's on you, asshole. I'm outta here."

She whirled around and plowed right into me. I'd managed to put up an arm in defense, and my elbow caught her tattooed shoulder.

"Yow!" she shrieked. "That hurt."

She rubbed her upper arm.

"Sorry," I said, more out of habit than truth.

"You should be," she said. "What're you doing sneaking around here? It's Thursday, everybody's at the pantries on Thursdays. I already told you that like a million times."

"I'm looking for Makaila."

Why did I feel the need to explain myself? It was none of Starshine's business why I was there.

Keo came out of his office looking placid and serene, a regular Buddha of a man. He took in the two of us like Daddy preparing to referee a sisterly quarrel.

"I thought I heard you, Monica," he said. "Can I help?"

Comparing Starshine's flushed face and angry expression with Keo's calm, smiling countenance was like watching the masks of drama come to life. For a moment, I was envious of his composure. It was a skill I could have really used over the past twelve months.

"I came to see Makaila."

"About the board position?" he said.

I nodded.

Starshine jerked back. "Board position? Don't *even* tell me you're thinking of putting *her* on the board," she hissed.

"It's not something you need to worry about," he said.

"And *don't* tell me what to worry about, neither. I'm the freakin' volunteer coordinator around here. Every volunteer works for *me*. Since when don't I get a say about who's gonna be put on the board?"

Keo eyes narrowed, but he kept the composure thing going. In a low voice he said, "Would you excuse us a minute, Monica?"

He draped an arm around Starshine's shoulder and steered her back into his office. As soon as they cleared the doorway, he pulled the door shut.

I stood there not knowing whether to stay or leave. I didn't want to make the forty-five minute drive back to Kapalua, only to have Makaila call an hour later to ask if I was on my way. But I didn't want to hang around while Keo attempted to sweet-talk Starshine out of her foul mood, either.

I should've never agreed to do this.

I headed back to Makaila's desk and then remembered I'd brought five pounds of 100% Kona coffee for the break room. Compared to the swill they'd been drinking, the Kona would taste like heaven. I went out to my car to get it. I pulled the bag of beans and a new coffee grinder out of my trunk. When I looked up, Makaila was hoofing across the parking lot carrying a giant white paper bag with the McDonald's logo on it.

When she got within earshot, I said, "You know that stuff can kill you."

"Maybe yeah, but I'll go with a greasy smile on my face."

She pulled a fistful of fries out of the bag and folded them into her mouth. "*Ono.* That means 'yum.' You want some, girl?"

I didn't usually allow myself to eat fast food, but I'd been stressed more than usual the past couple of weeks, so I made an exception. The fries were hot out of the fryer and shamefully salty. She'd been right about the greasy smile.

"I got an extra burger in here, too," said Makaila. "But aren't you early? I thought your orientation wasn't 'til two-thirty."

"It is, but I'm having second thoughts."

"What second thoughts? You need me to beg you?"

"Keo and Starshine were in his office, and I guess I interrupted something. She wasn't at all happy to hear I'd be joining the board."

"*Pfft.* Who cares? Making that girl happy is a full-time job with lousy benefits. Don't even think about it."

"Well, the problem is, I *am* thinking about it. You said yourself that Keo doesn't want me here. And now Starshine doesn't either. Seems maybe I should do everyone a favor and just bow out."

By then we were at the front door. Instead of going inside, Makaila pointed to a splintery picnic table at the side of the building.

"Let's eat out here in the shade," she said.

She sat down heavily on one side, and I walked around and took the bench facing her.

"I'm probably talkin' outta line here," she said. "But let me bring you up to speed on how I see it. Keo's not used to having someone around who doesn't treat him like a rock star. That's why he's sportin' attitude about you." In her lilting, sing-song voice, the "you" came out sounding more like "chew."

"But don' let that get to you. It's good for him to get a little push-back now and again." She made a fist and thumped her chest a couple of times. "You know, it builds *ikaika*—character."

"Well, I may offer a character-building opportunity for Keo, but Starshine *really* doesn't want me around. And you said yourself, she's a scary girl."

She laughed. "Oh *ipo*, don' worry about her. She's all bark and no teeth. The reason she don' want you around here is 'cuz she's scared maybe Keo really does."

🙂 🙂 🙂

When my orientation was over I knew a lot more about how the food bank operated, but I was as clueless as ever about why Keo had gone along with offering me the position. When I'd finished with Makaila, she dropped me off outside his office.

"He always likes to give a little speech to new board members," she said. "You know, welcome them aboard, thank them for their service, that kinda thing. But don' worry, it won't take long."

She went back to her desk, leaving me to knock on his door.

Keo glanced up from his ancient computer when I came in, and for a second he looked annoyed. Then he seemed to reboot. He stood to shake my hand and flashed me his red carpet smile.

"Ah, so you're finished with orientation," he said. "Any questions?"

I asked him a couple of soft-ball questions and he responded with one-sentence answers. When I got up to leave, he looked relieved our time together was over. But then, so was I.

I said my good-byes to Makaila and thanked her again for lunch. I walked out to the parking area and found Starshine leaning against the driver door of my Lexus.

"I know somethin' you don't know," she said.

Her eyes glinted with malice. I'd seen those eyes before, at school, when the ringleader of the "mean girls" would taunt me about my mother's latest public indiscretion. I willed my face to appear indifferent.

"Excuse me," I said. "I need to get in my car."

"Find your dog yet?" she said.

I didn't catch myself in time, and I'm pretty sure she noticed the involuntary flash of distress in my eyes. "How do you know about my dog?"

"Duh. Max told everybody your dog ran away. He said you were offering a reward."

"I am."

"So, like if I found it, you'd give me the money?"

"Yes."

"Dead or alive?" she said.

I hesitated. Again, memories of hurt and humiliation came flooding back.

"I'm just sayin'," she went on. "Maybe he got runned over or something."

"My dog's a 'she.' And I don't think she got hit by a car because I've searched everywhere. I filled out a missing dog form with Max's wife, and then another one at the animal shelter."

"Your dog got a name?"

"It's Pima."

"What kinda dumbass name is that?"

"It's from where I used to live, in Arizona. It's an old name for one of the Indian tribes. It's actually a funny story. The white people came and asked the local Native Americans all sorts of questions, but the Indians couldn't understand them, so they answered, '*pi mac,*' to everything. The white guys figured the Indians were saying the name of their tribe, but actually '*pi mac*' means, 'I don't know.' Anyway, the name stuck, and the tribe got called the "Pima.""

"What are you, some kind of know-it-all school teacher or somethin'?"

"No."

Starshine trailed a hand along the rear door panel of my car. "You know you got a bad scratch here?" she said. "Looks like somebody keyed your pretty new car."

She was right. A meandering scratch extended from the driver door to the back quarter panel. The five-foot-long mark had gouged the paint all the way down to the metal.

"Tough luck," she said. "I guess that's what you get for slumming."

I wanted to reach out and slap her. Instead, I knotted my hands into fists and dug my knuckles into my thighs.

She sauntered away. "I'll be sure and let Keo know if I find your dog," she said over her shoulder. "Maybe he'll want to bring you some flowers again to celebrate."

CHAPTER 24

My fury over Starshine's vandalism got pushed aside when my Bluetooth went off on the ride back home. I glanced at the dashboard display and it showed the caller was "County of Maui." I took the call.

"Hello, this is Monica Gomez," I said.

"Ms. Gomez, this is Deputy Chief Cicero from Maui Fire and Rescue. How are you doing today?"

"Fine, and you?"

"Good, thanks," he said. "It's been nice to have the trade winds back these past couple of days, don't you think? Gets kind of sticky around here when we don't have a breeze."

Had the guy simply called to chat about the weather? Seemed like a poor use of taxpayer dollars.

After what seemed like an unnaturally long pause, he went on. "Anyway, I'm calling with somewhat mixed news. Your home was cleared for temporary occupancy today."

"That sounds like *good* news to me," I said.

"Yes, but there's a catch. You need to agree to allow geologists and archeologists from the University of Hawaii to enter your property, at will, to conduct on-going research regarding the cultural issue."

"They won't be taking the property? What about the royal bones?"

"The cultural commission's still claiming your property may contain human remains, but so far they haven't been able to prove it. That's why you're being offered temporary occupancy. You can move back in, but final approval will be pending the outcome of the investigation. While the cultural investigation is on-going, we agreed that you should be allowed to stay there as long as you abide by their conditions."

"And what are those conditions?" I said.

"They're pretty straight-forward. You allow the scientists to come on your property whenever they show up. And, you agree to stay out of the marked boundaries of the site whether the researchers are there or not."

"Sounds reasonable," I said. "But at the meeting at Bev Strong's house I thought the cultural commission said they'd already found bones."

"They did. But those bones turned out to be animal bones, not human. Your house may be sitting on an old dump site, not a burial ground. Actually, that's a more likely scenario for creating a sinkhole. Large quantities of rotting organic matter creates trapped gases and unstable soil conditions. Add in a leaking swimming pool and you've got the recipe for a collapse."

"Well, that is good news," I said. "I'm not thrilled about the possibility of living over a landfill, but it sure beats the alternative."

"You can move back in as soon as tomorrow. The people from UH are probably already out there. And remember, if they find anything significant, you'll probably be required to move out permanently."

"Got it."

I drove to the hotel and started packing to move back home. As I added Pima's bed and food dish to the bellman's trolley I hesitated. Maybe I should stay. What if she came back on her own and I wasn't there?

But that was ridiculous. Even if she managed to make her way back to the building, she wasn't going to be punching the "seven" button on the elevator and then trotting down the hall looking for the right number on the door. And anyway, her ID chip had my cell number on it. Anyone who found her could easily track me down.

As I checked out, I made a final plea to the desk clerk.

"I'd really appreciate it if you'd call me if anyone finds my dog," I said.

I handed him one of my calling cards with my contact information. Underneath, I'd folded a twenty-dollar bill. He took the card and slipped the twenty in his pocket in one fluid motion, as if performing a magic trick. He never broke eye contact.

"I doubt if anyone would notify the front desk if they found your pet," he said. "But if by some chance coincidence I hear of a loose dog, I'll call."

"She's gray, a miniature Schnauzer," I said.

He whipped out my flyer from a shelf under the desk and held it up. "Yes, we know. *Mahalo* for choosing The Jolly Harpooner. We hope you enjoyed your stay."

His eyes darted to a guy waiting in line behind me. "Now, is there anything else I can help you with?"

I went out to the portico where the valet had brought my car around. The bellman was busy transferring all my stuff into the trunk and the lid was still open. The valet whipped open my driver door as if I'd told him I was in a big hurry to get out of there. I slipped a tip to the bellman and then tipped the valet as I slid into the seat.

"*Mahalo*, Ms. Gomez," the valet said.

I was taken aback that he knew my name, but then I realized I'd been staying there for a week and a half. The sinkhole at my house had been all over the news and my lost dog flyer was at the front desk. The guy would've had to be sniffing glue for the past ten days to not recognize me.

"I want to point out some damage I noticed on your vehicle," he said. "I'm pretty sure it didn't happen here in our parking facility, but if you think it did, I can get you a damage report form to fill out."

"*Mahalo*," I said. I peered at the name on his badge and added, "Edwin. But I got the scratch when I was in Wailuku. It didn't happen here."

He ducked his head in acknowledgment and went around back to slam the trunk shut. I pulled out of the portico and into the brilliant sunlight of another perfect Maui day.

The drive to Kapalua was bittersweet. I was finally going home, but I was all alone. No Chloe, no Pima. It was a good thing I'd be seeing Derek tomorrow night or I might've actually felt sorry for myself.

⌬ ⌬ ⌬

Derek didn't call on Friday night, but he called early Saturday morning. He made excuses about getting the last plane out of O'ahu and then he complained that the airport limo driver at Kahului hadn't shown up to meet him. He said by the time he made it back home it was too late to call.

"No worries," I said.

"What does that mean?" he said. "Weren't you concerned when I didn't call?"

"No, I didn't mean it like that. I'm just saying I was allowed to move back into my house yesterday, so I was busy getting resettled. I knew you'd call when you got a chance."

"Huh," he said. "Well, you sound pretty chipper about the whole thing. Maybe you had 'help' moving back in. You hire some brawny local boys?'"

"No, Derek, I was completely alone. I don't even have Chloe and Pima here anymore."

"But you still didn't miss me? What is it with you? Are you telling me you'd rather be alone?"

The conversation was going down a road I didn't want to take.

"So," I said. "Are you still planning to go over to Lana'i this morning?"

"Yeah. Like I said, I've got a little business to conduct over there. You still want to come, right?"

"Definitely."

"We need to leave in an hour," he said. "Do you mind picking me up? I don't like to park any of my cars at the airport."

"We're flying over?" I said. "I thought you'd take your boat."

"It's a rough crossing, Monica. And a lot less hassle to go by air. It's only a fifteen minute flight."

Derek arrived in the Corvette. He got out and gave me a soulful kiss. I gave him a short tour of the backyard, showing him how close the sinkhole had come to the house.

"That's some kind of mess you got here," he said.

"Yeah, and it's just the beginning," I said. "I had to give access to people from the University of Hawaii to dig around here for as long as they want."

"What? That's nuts. Why didn't you tell them 'No way'?"

"Because that's the deal. I was only allowed to move back if I agreed to let them poke around. Otherwise, I'd still be at the hotel."

"That's another thing. You should talk to a lawyer. You shouldn't be expected to bear the full expense for this. You haven't lived in this house that long. I can think of about six people who need to step up and accept liability, starting with Bev Strong."

"I thought Bev was a friend of yours," I said.

"She is, more or less. But she's also a licensed Realtor. They carry liability insurance. This isn't personal, Monica. It's business. Bev's well aware of her accountability. She's just hoping you're too dumb to realize it."

We drove across the island and were soon at the congested area of Kahului near the Costco store. When I stopped at the traffic light at Dairy Road and the Hana Highway, Derek said, "You need to make a right here."

"You know a shortcut to the airport?"

"In a way. We're not flying out of the big airport. I've got a little plane I keep at general aviation."

I flashed back to my arrival on Maui on the small chartered jet. Had it only been a month ago? It felt like years. I'd had Chloe and Pima by my side then as I'd arrived for my new unfettered life in Hawaii. Now I had a demanding boyfriend, a crazy tattooed girl determined to make my life miserable, and a house about to fall into a sinkhole. The word "unfettered" didn't seem so applicable anymore.

I pulled into the parking lot at the private terminal. I had to blink to clear my blurry vision as I remembered my first glimpse of Maui and my dream of paradise. I dabbed a knuckle at the side of each eye to make sure I wasn't leaking.

"Are you crying?" Derek said.

"No, I'm good. I think the humidity's making me perspire."

🕉 🕉 🕉

Derek led me out to a sleek single-engine plane parked at the edge of the tarmac. He opened the passenger-side door and helped me up into the cabin. He walked around the plane, stopping to peer closely at something on the wing. Then he climbed into the pilot's seat.

"This is just a toy," he said as he strapped himself in. He reached over to check if my seat belt was properly buckled and he handed me a set of bulky headphones.

"Do you read me?" he said into the headphones. His voice sounded far away, like he was calling from down a long hallway.

"Yes. How about me? Can you hear me?"

"Whoa," he said. "You're coming in hot. We need to take you down a notch."

He reached over and adjusted a knob. "Try it again."

"Hello Derek," I said in a somewhat softer voice. "How's this?" I felt self-conscious about yelling in his ear.

He gave me a thumbs-up and turned his attention to the panel of gauges and levers in front of him. He started the engine and the prop began turning, faster and faster, until it became an invisible blur. He radioed the tower, identifying our plane as "November Nine-Seven-Seven Whiskey."

The guy in the tower mumbled something I couldn't make out, but obviously Derek could, because soon we were picking up speed as we rolled down the tarmac. I felt a quickening in my chest as the engine whine rose to an almost deafening sound.

"Hang on," Derek said. Before I had a chance to grab something solid, the little plane bumped twice, the nose lifted, and we were airborne.

Within seconds, the glittering ocean loomed on the horizon. I leaned over and looked out my side window.

Enormous green patches of sugar cane shimmered and rolled beneath us, like a pool of water ruffled by the wind.

"Wow," I said. "I didn't realize how big the cane fields were."

"Not even close to what they used to be," he said. "It's a dying industry."

Before long, we were over Ma'alaea Harbor with tidy rows of white catamarans lined up along the gray docks like teeth on a comb.

He pointed to an island dead ahead. "See how close it is?"

He was right. Lana'i looked like a golden-brown hump in the vast expanse of blue-black water.

He tapped his watch. "We'll be on the ground and heading for Lana'i City in fifteen minutes."

Derek hadn't told me the nature of his business, but I didn't think it could amount to much if he could finish in a half-hour. I didn't know a thing about Lana'i, but hoped after he was finished we'd be able to find a secluded beach and be able to linger for a while before heading back to Maui. I'd brought my new bikini along. After Derek's snide comments about my old swimsuit I'd tossed it in the back of my closet, vowing to never wear it again.

We approached the Lana'i airstrip and Derek radioed for clearance. The tires chirped as we made a couple of low bounces along the tarmac, then Derek throttled back the engine and we glided to a smooth stop.

I pulled off my headphones and shook out my hair.

Derek touched my arm. "I didn't instruct you to do that."

"Do what?"

"Take off your headset."

I held out the headphones to him like an offering. "Sorry."

"When you're the passenger, you're required to wait for commands from the pilot," he said.

I checked his expression. Was he serious? Apparently so.

He got out and went around the plane to assist me in getting out. There were no stairs like on the private jet, so I had to hop down. No small feat in my four-inch wedge espadrilles.

"Are we going to have time to go to the beach over here?" I said.

"Hard to tell. We'll see how it goes."

A shiny black Hummer was parked just outside the airport gate. The driver greeted Derek by name, and said, "As you wish, sir,' after Derek told him where we were going. The driver held the door for us as we climbed into the back seat, then he hopped into the driver seat and we were on our way to Lana'i City.

After a few minutes, Derek leaned forward to talk to the driver. "I want to make a quick stop at Dole Park," he said. "Let me off over by the Blue Ginger."

Derek turned to me, "You don't mind, do you? I have something I need to handle at the park before we go up to the Lodge at Koele."

I assured him I was just along for the ride, so whatever he needed to do was fine with me. I watched outside the window as the road wound its way past vast taupe-brown fields of scrubby vegetation.

"All that land used to be under cultivation," Derek said. "Hundreds of acres of pineapples. Now it's just going to waste."

Dole Park turned out to be a wide open space in the middle of a minuscule town. Towering pine trees outlined the perimeter and a sign pointed to a public swimming pool and community center. About halfway down the park, on the far side, a group of thirty or forty people were carrying signs and chanting. I couldn't make out what they were saying, or clearly read the messages on the signs.

"What's happening?" I said, loud enough that both Derek and the driver could hear. "Is there a festival going on today?"

The driver glanced in the rear-view mirror, his brow creased with concern. "Not sure, miss. Mr. Chambers, are you sure you don't want me to take you on up to the lodge? I think stopping here may not be such a good idea."

"You're not paid to think, Archie," said Derek. "Just pull up a little closer. We'll only be a couple of minutes."

Derek turned to me and said, "I need you to come with me, okay?"

I nodded.

He took my hand as we got out of the car. Then he led me over to where the crowd had gathered. A guy in the center of the group was perched halfway up a six-foot A-frame ladder holding a bullhorn. With his height advantage, he was able to spot us before the rest of the people did.

"He's here!" he yelled into the bullhorn.

He pointed at Derek with his free hand and nearly lost his balance on the ladder. "You've got some nerve showing up here, Chambers."

The rest of the group turned, and now I could read the homemade placards they carried. One sign said, "Save Our Island." Another read, "Don't Californicate Lana'i." A badly printed sign, lettered with red paint that dripped down the poster-board like fresh blood, said, "Big Wind = Bad Kapu."

"What is this, Derek?" I said.

He didn't answer. Instead, he grasped my hand tighter as we plunged into the crowd. I tried to pull free, but he was too strong. His grip was so fierce my knuckles ached.

As we plowed through the group, the protesters made way until we were at the base of the ladder. Derek took a thick white envelope from an inner pocket of his jacket and passed it to me. "Give this to Mr. Big Mouth."

I looked down at the envelope, trying to figure out what it was, but Derek gave me a nudge. "Go. Now. Hand it to him so we can get the hell out of here."

I held up the envelope for the guy on the ladder. He seemed puzzled, but he leaned down and took it.

"You've been served," bellowed Derek. Then he jerked my arm and we began making our way back through the crowd to the idling Hummer. Archie stood by the open back door, looking apprehensive.

The crowd was quiet for a moment while the guy ripped open the envelope and pulled out the papers inside. Then he yelled into the bullhorn, "Asshole Chambers is evicting me! And not just me. He's kicking out everyone who's leasing a place from him. That's most of you here. If there's anyone left on Lana'i who still thinks this project is good for our island, wake up! Chambers thinks getting rid of us will shut down the opposition, but it won't. We'll stand united until..."

We got in the Hummer and Derek said, "Take us back to the airport, Archie."

Archie looked into the rearview mirror, an inscrutable look on his face.

"Don't give me that," Derek said, catching his eye. "If it wasn't for me, this place would be as worthless as Kaho'olawe, and you know it."

I didn't say anything during the short ride back to the terminal. My stomach grumbled. I thought about how great it would've felt to cradle a glass of well-chilled chardonnay while strolling the lush grounds of the five-star Koele Lodge before going in for lunch. But from the grim set of Derek's jaw, it was clear that lunch and beach-time afterward were no longer on the agenda.

CHAPTER 25

By Monday morning, my yard was swarming with workers and equipment. One of the more notable guys seemed to be channeling his inner Indiana Jones, wearing a pith helmet and a khaki safari shorts outfit.

There was also a small contingent of tanned, barechested guys wearing nothing but billowy sarongs tied at the waist. The rest of the group looked pretty much like the University of Arizona students I used to see headed south to Mexico for Spring Break. Young, smiling, and half-naked. In any other situation I would've been humming "It's Raining Men," and dancing around my kitchen thanking God for the blazing display of testosterone, but even the male eye candy in my back yard couldn't pull me out of my slump.

I'd made the local news again. And, as usual, it wasn't because I'd been crowned Radish Festival Queen or made the high school honor roll.

For nearly a year, the media had portrayed me as a greedy bitch who'd stolen millions of dollars that should have rightfully gone to my hardworking boss. Then a few weeks ago, I'd been featured on page one of the *Maui News* as the pitiful owner of the only car that had ever fallen off a barge in Kahului Harbor. A week after that, I'd been interviewed on TV when my swimming pool caved in creating a massive sinkhole. My name had come up again when the cultural commission claimed my house had been built over the sacred bones of Hawaiian ancestors.

As if I hadn't already garnered a hundred times more than my fifteen minutes of fame, on Sunday it happened again. After my quick trip to Lana'i with Derek, I once again graced the front page of the *Maui News*. This time the story was below the fold, but it featured a photo of me handing the eviction notice to the guy with the bullhorn. Luckily, my name wasn't mentioned in the photo caption, but I'd have to wear a blond wig and fake glasses with a plastic nose and mustache to get away with not being recognized.

"I saw you in the paper yesterday," said the guy who'd come over to fix a spouting sprinkler head in my front flower bed. "You want them to put those big wind machines on Lana'i and kick those people out of their houses? Tha's too bad. Those families be living over there for generations, eh?"

I didn't want to discuss politics, especially politics that weren't even mine, with a wiry guy in a jumpsuit with "Maui Tree & Floral" embroidered on the pocket. But I found myself doing it anyway.

"The wind farm will bring jobs to the island," I said. "And since the pineapples left, there aren't any jobs over there."

"Eh, putting in all those wind machines will bring a few jobs for a short time. But once it's done, the jobs will be done too. And the beauty of the island is gone. Besides, they gonna send the power to Honolulu. I say, if Honolulu wants power, let them put wind machines on O'ahu. Leave Maui County alone."

I'd forgotten that Bev had mentioned that the islands of Lana'i and Moloka'i were part of Maui County. She'd said people on Maui were protective of their less-populated "*ohana* islands." Sort of a *you mess with them, you mess with me attitude,* I guess. It was admirable, in a Big Broth-er kind of way, but I wondered how the people of Lana'i and Moloka'i viewed the arrangement.

🐢 🐢 🐢

Although the bare-chested guys out back were fun to look at, they soon became a pain in the ass. Every half-hour or so, someone would tap on the lanai door and ask if they could fill up a water bottle or use my bathroom. I thought about renting a Port-a-Potty, but I was pretty sure the homeowners' association would have something to say about that. Not to mention the potential aroma that might waft into my house.

The most annoying thing about having strangers traips-ing through my yard all day was the uneasy feeling that some of them might be there under false pretenses. I didn't want to seem paranoid, but Derek had warned me that since there'd been no effort to secure the site, I had no idea who was, and wasn't, a legitimate research worker. Some of them looked more like high school kids who'd skipped school to come over and smoke pot behind my hibiscus bushes than college-age archeology students. Others were so grubby I couldn't help but think they were simply beach bums casing my house for a potential burglary.

I called U'uku Ka'akahalanui at the Cultural Affairs Of-fice to voice my concerns.

"Chill out, Monica," he said. "This isn't Los Angeles or New York. We know everyone working at the site. This is a small island, eh? And if you're worried about loss or dam-age to your possessions, you should lock 'em up. That gate you got out front isn't gonna stop anybody if they got bad *mana'o* on their minds. And after what went down on La-na'i, you betta be glad to have people around to look out for you."

He was right, of course. But it didn't quell my apprehension.

That afternoon I got a call from Bev Strong.

"Monica," she said. "I'm really, really sorry I've been so thoughtless. I should have called sooner to congratulate you on your appointment to the Maui Food Bank Advisory Board."

"No problem, Bev," I said. "I know you're busy."

"So, I guess your dear, dear puppy is still missing. Any word on that?"

I felt a catch in my throat. "Not yet. I haven't given up hope, but I'm afraid it's fading."

"Oh my. I can't imagine your anguish. You know what? I'm thinking we need to get you a new doggie right away. I'll buy you any kind you want. If you'd like, I'll go online and find a perfect match to your first one."

"Thanks, Bev, but like I said, I haven't given up hope of finding Pima. And I think if I ever do get another dog, I'll get one from the animal shelter. There are so many there that need to be rescued."

There was a pause on the line.

Then Bev said, "That's admirable. Certainly admirable. But who knows where those dogs have been? I have a friend who's a shiatsu breeder on O'ahu. She claims those poor shelter dogs are train wrecks with brown eyes. Diseased, abused, and the fleas! The thought of your beautiful home overrun with heaven-knows-what...it makes me sick to my stomach to even think about it."

"Well, then don't come down here any time soon," I said. "My place is already overrun."

"What?"

I explained about the motley crew working in the backyard.

"Oh, I wouldn't worry," she said. "But if you want, I'll put in a call to my contact in the Public Affairs Office at the University of Hawaii. They're very concerned about their image. The university has had a few, shall we say, *challenges* in the past couple of months and they can't afford another public relations snafu."

"That's okay," I said. "I'm probably just over-reacting. I've lived so privately for the past year it's just weird to look out my window and see strangers milling around. But I must say I do feel a bit put upon when they ask to use my bathroom."

"What?! You allow those people in your home? That's unacceptable, Monica. Totally unacceptable. I will absolutely make that call."

I calmed her down and explained they only used the guest powder room in the foyer. I felt odd defending the workers when I'd been the one who'd complained about them in the first place, but I couldn't have Bev making me out to look like more of a selfish bitch than I already appeared to be.

"Let me tell you why I called," she said. "You know I'm chairing the Maui Food Bank fund raiser in two weeks. It's coming along nicely, but I'd really appreciate your help."

"Sure. What can I do?"

"There's a press get-together this Wednesday at the fund raiser venue. We'll serve a few *pu'pus*, drink a little wine, and talk up the event. We've invited the social scene reporters from all the island papers, but we're especially hoping that at least one of the Honolulu television stations will send a team out. TV always trumps print when it comes to publicity."

"Sounds great. The fund raiser's being held at the King Kamehameha Golf Club, right?"

"Correct. I simply love, love, love the King Kam. Such a gorgeous setting. And all the Frank Lloyd Wright touches are so special. The architecture, the furniture, the stained glass, simply all of it. Wait! You're from Arizona. Did you ever tour FLW's fabulous estate up in Phoenix? You know, Taliesin West?"

"No, as a little girl, architecture wasn't exactly my thing."

"I've been there twice. I can't imagine why people from Hawaii will fly six and a half hours to go to Las Vegas every year, but they totally ignore the spectacular home of America's premiere design genius, Frank Lloyd Wright. It's a pity how far our civilization has fallen."

We agreed to meet an hour before the event at the King Kamehameha Golf Club in Waikapu. If the food bank wanted to bring out the über rich, they couldn't have picked a better setting. The King Kamehameha is the only private eighteen-hole golf course on all of Maui. And, for the well-heeled, nothing spells "must go" like exclusivity.

🍥 🍥 🍥

On Wednesday, I drove up to Waikapu at eleven. I'd asked Bev if she wanted to carpool, but she'd declined. She said she was working from her Kahului office that day and would have to get back there by three, so she'd take her own car.

A valet took my Lexus at the portico, and I stood outside marveling at the architecture of the clubhouse. The place was gigantic. It was a round building, painted an adobe-clay color. Many of the windows were round, and the entire structure was topped by an enormous mushroom-cap roof. Bev had described it as "mid-century," but as I pulled up I wondered, which century? The next one?

Inside, the foyer ceiling sported an expansive stained glass skylight in jewel-tone colors. Everything in the place was bigger and more ornate than any golf club I'd ever seen. Even the swanky Kapalua Golf Course up near my house paled in comparison.

"May I assist you?" An older man in a pale green aloha shirt had come up behind me so stealthily I hadn't heard him approach, even though the place was deathly quiet.

"Oh, yes. I'm Monica Gomez. I'm here for the press event for the food bank fund-raiser."

"Will you be serving or hostessing for us?" he said.

I suppose some Latina women would've been insulted. I was merely amused. "I'm a member of the food bank's advisory board, so I guess that makes me a hostess."

"Oh, please forgive my error, Miss Gomez," he said. He looked so flustered, I was sure if there'd been a sword within arm's reach he would've committed *hari kari* on the spot.

"No problem. I'm a new member of the community. I'm sure I look a lot more like a tourist than a local."

Actually, I probably looked more like every hard-working maid from their cleaning crew, but there was no way either of us would admit that.

"Well, *aloha* and welcome to the King Kamehameha. We've got your party set up in here," he said.

He led me to a beautiful round room with wrap-around windows. The windows looked out on a jaw-dropping view of an emerald-green valley below. At the far end of the valley was the base of Mt. Haleakala. And, at both sides of the vista were tiny glints of ocean from both the east and west shores of Maui.

"Wow, I've never been up here before," I said. "The view is spectacular."

"It is. Do you know how we came to be here?"

I looked over at him. Was he questioning whether I knew about the birds and the bees? I smiled, recalling my *abuela's* short, yet to-the-point explanation. *A man and a woman get excited in love. They rub together. When they do, some stuff comes out of the man and gets inside the woman. That makes a baby. Now you know. But don't let yourself get excited for a man too soon or you'll end up with a baby before you want one. Okay?*

I didn't respond to his question, so the guy went on. "This entire seventy-four thousand square foot clubhouse was designed by Mr. Frank Lloyd Wright. You know who he is, right?"

I nodded. "An architect from Arizona."

"Well, not technically. Mr. Lloyd Wright was from the Midwest—Wisconsin, I believe. But he had a winter home in Phoenix, and he built an architecture school there in the desert."

I kept up the nodding.

"Anyway, do you know who this building was initially designed for?"

I wasn't even going to venture a guess. If I was playing *Jeopardy!* and one of the categories was 'Famous American Architects,' it would've been the last category I picked.

"Marilyn Monroe," he said. He narrowed his eyes. "You *do* know who she was, right?"

Again, I nodded.

"Her husband, Arthur Miller, was going to give the house to her as a gift. But before the home could be built, they divorced. The plan went into the archives of the Frank Lloyd Wright Foundation. When the owners of this golf club were deciding what kind of clubhouse to build, they contacted the foundation and learned this plan was available."

"Marilyn Monroe was going to live in a seventy-four *thousand* square foot house?"

"No, no. Of course not. It's *based* on the house design. This clubhouse is much bigger. They added numerous banquet rooms, expanded the kitchen, added a pro shop and so on."

By now Bev had arrived. She strode into the banquet room like it was home turf.

"*Aloha*, Lee. Good to see you again." She kissed him on both cheeks as if proving the point that she might be a high society matron, but she wasn't above getting cozy with the help.

She turned to me. "And *aloha* to you, too, Monica," she said. I got a hand squeeze instead of the cheek kissing. "I trust Lee has regaled you with all the remarkable history behind this wonderful place."

"He has."

"I always feel I can sense a bit of Marilyn's spirit in this building," she said.

"*I vant to be alone...*" I said it with a slight German accent. It was the only Marilyn Monroe quote I could think of.

"No," said Bev, sounding a bit exasperated. She looked at Lee. "See how fleeting fame can be? The younger generation doesn't know the difference between Greta Garbo and Marilyn Monroe."

"Oh," I said. "It was Greta Garbo who *vanted* to be alone?"

"Yes. Marilyn Monroe came along later."

"Wait!" I said. "Is she the one who sang, 'Happy *birth*day, Mr. President'?"

"That's the one," Lee chimed in. "I actually saw it on TV when it happened."

"Speaking of TV," Bev checked her watch. "Where are those reporters?"

Bev and I walked out to the foyer where about two dozen people were chatting and laughing. No one seemed in a big hurry to head into the banquet room.

"*Aloha*," said Bev in her *I'm in charge* voice. "So wonderful to see all of you joining us today." She gestured toward the banquet room. "We have *pupu's* and a bit of refreshment set up in the Lewa Room. Right this way."

"*Aloha*, Bev," said one of the reporters.

Then he turned his gaze to me and the rest followed suit. "But it looks as if the real story is right here."

CHAPTER 26

They surrounded me so quickly I had no opportunity to flee. The reporters pushed in, all talking at the same time. Hadn't their *abuelas* taught them to wait their turn?

"Is it true you're in a relationship with power broker Derek Chambers?"

"Why does Chambers want to ruin the island of Lana'i for personal gain?"

"What does Chambers hope to accomplish by evicting the members of the 'Save Lana'i' group from their homes?"

One of the female reporters tugged at the sleeve of my dress. I reached up and flicked her hand away like you'd brush off a stink bug. I tried to take a step back to get away from the onslaught, but I was wedged in tight.

"Excuse me, ladies and gentlemen," Bev shouted over the din. "But we're here today to talk about a fabulous evening of food and entertainment for a worthy cause. Please follow me."

I'd never witnessed anyone be so completely ignored. It looked like the only way we'd get the vultures into the banquet room was to throw them a little meat.

"Yes, I'm in a relationship with Derek Chambers," I said. "And yes, he's building a wind farm on Lana'i. It will bring jobs and prosperity to an island that desperately needs it. The eviction was perfectly legal. Every property owner has the right to evict tenants who don't abide by the agreed-upon terms of their lease."

I was channeling the kind of "lawyer-talk" I'd overheard from John Dease during the past year. Since I hadn't had a chance to ask Derek why he'd evicted the people, I was pretty much making it all up. But my explanation sounded reasonable to me.

"But Ke'ali Wilson, the head of the opposition group, claims they've followed their leases to the letter. He says Chambers is kicking everyone out solely based on their opposition to his wind farm."

"I'm afraid I'm not privy to Mr. Chamber's business decisions," I said.

"But you were the one who served the eviction notices. Surely Chambers let you in on why he was doing it."

I smiled and a dozen strobe flashes went off. I wasn't smiling to be coy. I was smiling because it was how I'd learned to cope. If someone throws crap at you—and believe me, I'd had a lot of crap heaved my way—the best way to handle it is to plaster a fake smile on your face and keep walking.

🜚 🜚 🜚

It turned out to be a lackluster press event where the reporters were a hundred times less enthusiastic about the upcoming fundraiser than they'd been about harassing me over the Lana'i evictions. When it was over, Bev and I took a seat at a back table and commiserated.

"I should being getting back to the office, but I probably won't get anything done," she said. "Let me buy you a glass of wine. You've earned it. I can't believe those jackals would have the nerve to attack you like that and then gobble up every last *pupu* and suck down an entire case of overpriced chardonnay."

"They're just doing their job," I said. "But I'm sure Derek isn't going to be pleased when I tell him what happened."

Bev barked a laugh. "Tell him? Oh honey, I think that'll be totally unnecessary. Those reporters burned through about a million data bytes before they took their first sip of wine. Watch the news tonight. You'll see what I mean."

Unfortunately, Bev was right. That night, I was not only the lead story on the local news, but I even made the promos. Again and again.

"*Derek Chambers' latest girlfriend defends Lana'i evictions. Watch 'News Five' at six. News Five: Island wide, island strong.*"

The story that ran at six o'clock had been edited to make me look like a Machiavellian shrew. It started with me saying, "Every property owner has the right to evict tenants," and ended with me smiling like Cruella de Ville eying a litter of new-born Dalmatians.

Derek called at six-thirty. "Looks like you had an interesting day," he said.

"Yeah."

"Sorry about that," he went on. "How about you let me buy you dinner at the Lahaina Grill to make amends?"

"I don't think going out to a fancy restaurant tonight is the best course of action," I said. "It'll look like we're celebrating."

"We are."

I waited for him to explain. I wasn't feeling very celebratory, and couldn't figure out why he was.

"Look, Monica. I'm sorry your fundraiser thing got waylaid this afternoon. But Bev's already lit into me about that, so point taken. But we can't grovel to the crazies about the Lana'i project. It's gonna happen, tree huggers or no tree huggers. The sooner everyone stops pissing and moaning, the sooner we can break ground. Your 'get over it' speech to the press was pitch perfect and I want to show my appreciation."

"You ambushed me," I said.

"What do you mean?"

"You took me to Lana'i to serve those eviction notices, but you didn't tell me that's why we were going."

He chuckled. "Well, tell me something, would you have gone if I'd told you?"

"No."

"Damn straight. So you see, I did us both a favor by keeping it to myself. Wear something low-cut tonight. I'll pick you up in half-an-hour."

I started to object, but he cut me off. "Look Monica, I'm not the bad guy here. I'll answer any questions you have at dinner."

He picked me up in the Lorinser. I had to admit Derek had balls. It appeared he wasn't feeling one bit contrite about the evictions.

The Lahaina Grill didn't turn out to be the best place to speak openly about a touchy local subject. It's a small space, and the tables are close together. The wait staff is so attentive we were never more than a sip of water away from having someone reaching in to add another ounce or two to our glass.

"I take it you don't want to explain your side of things," I said after I'd tried a couple times to bring it up.

He nodded in the direction of the hovering waiter. "Probably not the best time and place."

When he took me home, he ran around to my door and helped me out. But he left the engine running.

"Aren't you coming in?" I said.

"I need to get home and get some work done. I've got a big conference call at oh-dark-thirty tomorrow morning."

We kissed, but it was one of those "see ya later" pecks on the lips. Not the kind of kiss I was used to from Derek, where the flick of his tongue could make my knees to collapse.

"I'll call you," he said, sliding into the driver's seat.

And then he was gone.

🐢 🐢 🐢

The next morning, I was once again in the *Maui News*. This time I didn't make the front page, I was on page five. But the newspaper's so thin everyone reads it front to back. The article echoed the previous night's TV news coverage, essentially painting me as Maui's answer to Marie Antoinette. Supposedly I'd revised her "Let them eat cake" to something along the lines of, "Let them move to a Honolulu high-rise."

Keo called at nine.

"Did I fail to mention during your orientation that we encourage our board members to refrain from pissing off the entire community?" he said.

"I was misquoted," I said.

"Misquoted? How's that? Did you, or did you not, personally serve eviction notices on eleven members of the 'Save Lana'i' group?"

"I did. But I didn't mean to."

There was a pause. He probably wanted me to explain myself, but since I was still unclear about whether Derek's wind farm was a job-creator or merely a shameless get-rich scheme, I kept quiet.

"Can you come in to the food bank later?" Keo said. "We need to talk about damage control."

"Oh, please. My picture's on page five. Big deal. I'm sure it'll blow over."

"Hang on," he said.

I heard muffled noise on the call as if he was juggling the phone while walking. The next thing I heard was traffic noise and a low rhythmic chant in the background.

"Hear that?" he said, when he came back on. "We've got protestors out front. When you come you may want to consider wearing a disguise. I'd suggest something along the lines of a paper bag over your head."

The call went dead.

☙ ☙ ☙

At ten-thirty, Bev and I carpooled to the food bank. I could tell from her terse answers to my attempts at conversation that she was fighting back the urge to give me a piece of her mind. In the past few days I'd demolished four months of hard work on the fund raiser.

We turned the corner to the food bank. A crowd filled the street, blocking access to the parking area.

"Wow, there must be forty or fifty people here," I said.

Bev slowly shook her head. "Unbelievable. We didn't get this many people to the press event, and I was serving free food and booze."

"I'm really sorry about this, Bev. I never meant to ruin things."

"Not your fault, just bad timing. But now let's get in there and figure out what we're going to do about it."

We parked on the street. The crowd didn't seem to notice as we got out, they were too busy chanting. An especially loudmouth guy started yelling "death to the one-percent" and the crowd picked up the mantra. We kept our heads down as we sprinted to the front door.

When we got to Keo's office most of the other board members were already present. The air in the room pulsed with resentment and irritation.

"Nice of you to finally show up," said one of the board members.

Keo put up a hand to quell any piling on.

"We've been reviewing our options," he said. "We've had thirty-two cancellations for next weekend's fund-raiser and I'm afraid there will be more on the answering machine. I sent Makaila home when the protesters showed up. She said she felt threatened."

"What?" said Bev. "This is ridiculous. This is like cutting off your nose to spite your face. The food bank isn't responsible for what happened on Lana'i. In fact, it's quite the opposite. We're trying to help people. Why the cancellations?"

"I didn't talk to everyone," Keo said. "But the ones I did speak with seemed concerned about possible PR problems. They said if they showed up at an expensive gala while one of our board members is throwing people out of their homes on Lana'i, it looks like they approve of the evictions. And, let's face it, most of our wealthy supporters are very concerned about their public image."

"I should resign," I said.

"Thanks for the offer," said Keo. "But the damage is done. We need to find a way to put this behind us in the next couple of days or cancel the fund raiser."

By now the protesters were beating drums and blasting air horns. The board members agreed to go home and come up with ideas for saving the fund raiser, or if that couldn't be done, suggest alternate solutions for raising the money needed to keep the food bank operating.

"Come on, folks," said Keo. "We aren't just raising money for something trivial, like sponsoring a hula show or a music festival."

One of the board members, who was also on the Maui Community Arts Guild, cleared her throat—loudly.

Keo quickly went on. "Okay, those are worthy causes, sure. But what we're doing here is keeping parents from scavenging dumpsters to feed their kids. This food bank is life and death, people. Plain and simple."

If I lived to be a hundred, it was hard to imagine I'd ever feel more ashamed.

CHAPTER 27

Bev dropped me off at home and I called Derek. I asked him to come for dinner that night and I promised to cook Mexican. He loved green chili enchiladas and claimed there was no decent place in all of Hawaii to get them.

I'd found a small *tienda*—a Mexican store—in Honokowai that sold all manner of foodstuffs: spices, fresh tortillas, even homemade *tamales* made fresh every morning. I went shopping and got home around two.

As I puttered around my vast kitchen, I watched the swarm of university students milling around the edge of the sinkhole. It looked like maybe someone had found something of interest; lots of pointing and smiles and back-slapping going on. I ignored them and focused on my enchiladas.

Derek arrived at seven with a bottle of wine that probably cost nearly as much as my latest pair of ostrich Christian Louboutins. The shoes were crazy-looking flats—yellow, with pointy bumps all over the leather and, of course, they had the signature red soles. Whenever I had to slip them off to go inside, island-style, I'd wonder if a thief with an eye for fashion would swipe them. After all, they went for nearly a thousand bucks a pair.

"I hope red wine's okay," Derek said. He didn't wait for my reply before taking me in his arms and giving me a kiss that made me glad my housekeeper had put fresh sheets on my bed that morning. But something was off. He smelled strange. Not his usual citrus and sandlewood scent.

"Did you change aftershaves?" I said.

"Uh, no. Why do you ask?"

I sniffed his shirt. "You smell different. Kind of like hippie oil."

"Hippie oil" was what we'd called patchouli oil in high school. The stoners doused themselves with it to mask the smell of the pot they'd been smoking out behind the bleachers.

"Huh. I can't imagine what it'd be," he said. "Maybe my maid changed the soap in my shower or something. I don't keep track of stuff like that."

I led him into the kitchen and he opened the wine. His hands shook a bit as he struggled with the corkscrew. I pulled two balloon red wine glasses from the cupboard.

"Are you okay?" I said. "You seem preoccupied."

"Never better. I've got some work stuff that's weighing on me, but I'll get it straightened out. How about you? When you called you seemed upset about something."

"I am. It seems our little jaunt to Lana'i is really making a mess out of things at the food bank."

"Try this," he said. He poured a small splash of wine into each of the glasses. We both took a sip.

Derek grimaced as if he'd bit into a persimmon. "I think this tastes 'off,' don't you?"

The wine was exquisite. Fruity, heady, with notes of chocolate and berries. I'd learned all that mumbo-jumbo from my lawyer, John Dease. He'd often take me to dinner after a day-long court session. Since I'd moved to Maui, I never once missed the hours I'd spent on those hard wooden courthouse chairs, but I did miss my dinners with John.

"It's lovely," I said.

"Nah, it tastes kind of metallic to me." He headed for the sink and began pouring the rest of the bottle down the drain.

"Stop! I'll drink it."

"No way. There are two things in life I can't stomach. The first is bad wine and the second is disloyalty."

He eyed me suspiciously.

"What's going on?" I said.

"You've been spending a lot of time with your buddy over there at the food bank."

"Bev?"

"No, not Bev. That local guy, Keto or Keno or whatever."

"It's Keo Kekane."

"Yeah, well, whatever. Seems every time I turn around you're heading over there."

"Derek, we're in the middle of a crisis. And it's a crisis *I* caused. If you'd told me about serving those eviction notices on the wind project protestors I'd have told you I couldn't do it. It's ruining our fund raiser at the food bank."

Derek looked annoyed. "What's the problem?"

I explained about the donors feeling uncomfortable about coming to the gala after I'd been photographed kicking people out of their homes.

"That's ridiculous," Derek said. "So, a few bleeding hearts aren't coming. What's the big deal?"

"No. It looks as if most *all* of the people aren't going to attend now."

He walked over to the built-in kitchen desk and plucked a pen from the pencil cup. "How much we talkin' about here?"

"How much for what?"

"How much to buy all the tickets for your little get-together?"

"We were expecting a hundred-fifty people at the dinner. And the seats are a hundred dollars each. Plus, we'll be having a live auction. The auction items are valued at, I don't know, probably another seventy-five thousand."

"So, if you do the math," he said, "It sounds like you need fifteen-thousand for the dinner and another seventy-five for the auction. Ninety total. That sound about right?"

"Well, yeah. Bev told me her budget for putting on the dinner and hiring the entertainment was around ten thousand. So, we were hoping to net about eighty thousand, give or take."

"So, if you were to sell me all the dinner tickets and I gave you the asking price on all the auction items, the fund raiser would be considered a success, right?"

"Actually, we'd make an additional ten thousand, since there wouldn't be any expenses." My heart rate was quickening. But it was only fair. Derek had created the PR mess; it was only right that he clean it up.

"No, you'll have expenses. Because I want them to go ahead and hold the event. You and I are going to be there, eating, drinking, and dancing."

I shot him a confused look.

"My event, my rules." He laughed.

Then he leaned in and whispered. "I want the show to go on. I want to remind your pal Kekane whose bitch he's been sniffing around."

To say I was shocked by his rude remark would be an understatement. But I didn't want to risk having him rescind his offer by demanding an apology. I pulled the enchiladas out of the oven and poured him a shot of Patrón Silver tequila. Then we sat down to eat.

🪔 🪔 🪔

During the next week I was more distant with Keo than I'd previously been, and that's saying something. I avoided being alone with him at the food bank, and I kept all conversations short when he'd call to ask how things were going.

He seemed unimpressed with Derek's generous act of charity. In fact, I'd been present when Bev handed him the check for ninety-thousand dollars and Keo merely nodded. I had the feeling if Derek had paid in gold pieces, Keo would've bitten one of the coins to see if they were real.

I convinced Derek we'd have a lot more fun if he'd allow me to invite a few people to join us at the gala.

"Invite away," he said. "I'm thinking of offering tickets to a few of my business associates."

The fund raiser committee agreed it would be best to not hold the live auction since Derek had already paid for all of the items. But Bev insisted on displaying everything since she was hoping the press would show up and she didn't want a bare table. I thought it looked weird that every item had Derek's name already posted as the winning bidder, but Bev seemed pleased with the arrangement.

The entertainment was originally slated to be a five-piece Maui-based group that specialized in Hawaiian versions of popular mainland tunes. The group, which had won a few local Grammys, begged off claiming one of the guys had laryngitis. We hustled around and hired an aging "lounge lizard" from a Waikiki piano bar who probably couldn't care less about Maui County politics. He said he'd bring along a friend who played guitar and invite his nephew, a drummer with a Waianae garage band, to make it a trio.

Bev ordered a white baby grand piano to be set up in a corner of the ballroom. She'd asked the singer if he'd take requests and he'd agreed. I hoped no one would ask for anything from Katy Perry or Kanye West, since although the drummer could probably handle it, I doubted the piano man could. His publicity shot showed a guy sporting a stiff blond pompadour and a white dinner jacket. From the looks of it, the photo had been taken not long after Hawaii became a state in 1959.

🐢 🐢 🐢

On Tuesday, Bev and I went shopping for dresses. It was fun flying to Honolulu for the day and cruising the huge shopping center at Ala Moana. I'd never enjoyed shopping before I won the money because I could never afford anything I liked. And after winning, I'd avoided it because it was lonely and stressful dodging the press and worrying whether my latest purchases would be introduced in court as evidence of my grand larceny.

By contrast, shopping with Bev was relaxing and enjoyable. We each found a dress at the Chanel Boutique. Derek probably would've preferred I wore something a bit slinkier than the red floor-length gown with the modest U-shaped neckline I selected, but Bev warned me that food bank fund raisers were not the place for plunging necklines and slits up to there.

🐢 🐢 🐢

The night of the gala Derek arrived ten minutes early but I was ready.

"You look fabulous," he said. "Bev told me you'd be wearing red, so I brought you a little something to go with it."

He handed me a black velvet box about the size of a slim book. I tipped the lid open and my eyes caught a glimpse of gold and sparkly red.

"It's beautiful," I said in a voice usually reserved for the Lord's Prayer.

Nestled in the satin lining was a spectacular necklace. Matching earrings were positioned in the upper corners of the box. The necklace was made of gold links, featuring a red-colored center stone about the size of a man's thumbprint, with two flashing white triangular stones on each side. The earrings had a red center stone surrounded by a ring of smaller white stones. When I lifted the necklace from the box it felt heavy for its size.

"It goes great with your dress, don't you think?" Derek said. "Here. Let me help you fasten it."

"It's my birthstone, isn't it?"

"I don't know. When's your birthday?"

"January. My birthstone is garnet."

He shrugged. "Then sorry, it's not your birthstone."

"Oh. Do you know what type of stones these are?"

"The center jewel is a six-carat ruby and the side stones are prism-cut diamonds. The earrings each have a three-carat ruby along with diamonds. I picked this set up on my last trip to Dubai. I figured it was kismet when Bev said you'd be wearing red."

I hugged him. "Thank you so much. I absolutely love them."

When we got outside, I saw the Lorinser parked in my driveway. I told Derek that Bev had arranged for free limousine service for everyone attending.

"Aren't you concerned about leaving this car with a valet?"

"Not really. If anything happens, I'll make sure someone gets fired." He said it laughingly, but I could tell he wasn't kidding.

We pulled up at the clubhouse and Derek ordered the valet to go inside and get a cloth napkin. When the valet returned, Derek got out and told the guy to spread the white cloth on the driver's side floor board.

"You see, I'm very particular about my car," Derek said, handing the guy the keys. "And in case you're wondering, I've checked the odometer, so don't even think about it."

The young valet looked petrified as he slipped into the driver seat. He inched the car into a parking space only a few feet from the front door.

"I believe forewarned is forearmed," Derek explained to the silver-haired doorman who was holding the door open for us. "Don't you agree?"

"Absolutely, sir. I'll make sure everything's just as you left it."

"Thanks." Derek deftly pulled a bill from his wallet and tightly folded it before holding it out to the doorman.

The older man held up a palm. "Not necessary, sir."

"I insist. Please don't make me look bad."

The guy took the money. When he sneaked a peek at the denomination, his eyes widened.

"*Mahalo nui*, sir."

"Yeah, whatever. Just make sure nobody touches that car."

The spacious banquet room had been transformed into an underwater wonderland of silver, white and turquoise. A parquet wood dance floor had been set up on the far side along with the white piano and drum set. The tables glistened with so much crystal and china there was barely enough room for the centerpieces: round glass aquariums with white and turquoise sand, little silvery castles, and silver and black angelfish darting in and out of white plastic seaweed. The chairs had been wrapped in white skirting with wide turquoise satin bows tied around the backs.

"This is gorgeous," I said.

Bev hustled over as soon as she saw Derek. The three of us stood together, taking in the spectacular room.

"For ninety grand it'd better be gorgeous," said Derek. "How many people are we expecting?"

"We've had twenty-two confirmed and eight 'maybes,'" Bev said. "I can't for the life of me understand why so few people RSVP'd. I mean, I called everyone on your list and told them the tickets were *gratis*, thanks to you. All they had to do was show up. Oh well, *c'est la vie*."

There was a small commotion behind us and I turned to see what had caused it. There stood Starshine. She was arguing with a hostess who'd asked to see her ticket. Starshine was sporting her usual head-to-toe black in a shapeless calf-length dress, ripped fishnet stockings, and clunky black Doc Martens. She'd accessorized for the evening with a brass snake arm ornament encircling one colorfully-tattooed bicep.

"Shut up!" she yelled. "I told you. I'm one of the VIP's. I don't need no damn ticket."

I was surprised when Derek excused himself and went over to deal with the situation. He touched Starshine's arm in greeting. The two of them chatted briefly, then Derek turned and spoke quietly to the hostess. The woman bobbed her head and retreated.

Starshine sashayed into the room, grinning in triumph.

I went over to Derek. "I'm so sorry about that. That girl's the volunteer coordinator for the food bank. She can be—"

"I'm well-acquainted with Starshine," said Derek. He didn't sound pleased to admit it.

"How do you know her?"

"She's a friend of a friend. Hey, let me get us a glass of champagne. Bev, you want some?"

Bev declined. Derek crossed the room to a waiter carrying a tray of drinks and plucked two champagne flutes off the tray. The staff at the King Kamehameha appeared puzzled that there were so few people in the enormous room, but they hid it behind well-rehearsed smiles.

Derek handed me my champagne. "Starshine will be joining us at our table," he said.

"What?"

"Yeah, she said her date's going to be late and she asked to join us."

"Derek, I'd rather not sit next to her."

"Then don't. I'll seat her next to me, on my other side. Funny, I didn't take you for such a snob." He smiled and leaned in to give me a peck on the cheek.

I don't remember much about the dinner. I'm sure the food was fantastic, but all I recall was Starshine's appalling behavior. There were eight of us at our table and she repeatedly interrupted conversations, especially those between Derek and me.

When the lightly-seared *ahi* appetizer was served, she pushed her plate away with a loud, '*Yuck, raw fish. That's pukey.*'

She got up and left the table at least four times, making all the men stand in courtesy. She seemed to revel in disrupting the other diners with her arrivals and departures so much that I wondered if she really needed to leave, or she was just being ornery.

"Nobody has a bladder that tiny," I muttered.

"Maybe she's taking phone calls," Derek sad. "You know, it's rude to use a cell phone at the table. She's being considerate by leaving."

Keo showed up at about the time dessert was served. He came over and congratulated Bev on a job well done. He and Derek traded a truck-load of "stink eye," but neither greeted the other.

Then Keo began working our table, stopping to chat briefly with everyone. I was frankly surprised Keo hadn't started with Derek, since it was common knowledge that Derek had single-handedly saved the fund raiser from being cancelled. But regardless of Keo's initial snub, I was sure it was only a matter of time before he'd have to "man up" and publically thank him for his support.

When he finally made his way around to Derek, Keo presented him with a white business envelope.

"This is for your tax preparer," Keo said. "Obviously, this qualifies as a write-off."

"Good," said Derek. "I'll have my tax accountant call you for the pertinent details."

"No need to call," Keo said. "It's all there."

"Well, maybe it is, and maybe it isn't. In any case, I'll have him call to make sure everything's legit."

Keo turned his back and moved on without so much as a *"Mahalo for your ninety grand."* I felt my cheeks flame in fury.

But that wasn't the last bit of puzzling behavior. When Keo moved on to Starshine, I expected her to leap from her seat and throw her arms around him in her usual over-the-top "my boyfriend's back" embrace. Instead, she flinched and looked annoyed when he touched her shoulder.

"How come you're so late?" she said in a flat voice. Her eyes smoldered beneath her thick black eyeliner. "We ate without you."

Keo didn't respond. Instead, he moved on to the other tables, smiling and shaking hands as if he'd written the big check instead of Derek. I watched Derek's face but he appeared indifferent to the snub.

By now, the ruby earrings were beginning to pinch. I had pierced ears, but these were clip-ons. I took them off and slipped them into my tiny satin clutch, carefully snapping the clasp to make sure they were safely stowed. I put the clutch bag under my chair and finished my dessert.

After coffee, Mr. Lounge Lizard cranked up his microphone and invited everyone to the dance floor. He asked for requests and one of the guests trotted over to the piano. I hoped we'd be spared a medley of Barry Manilow tunes, but judging from the age of the attendees, I braced myself for an evening of golden oldies.

Derek scooted his chair over and put an arm around me as three couples stepped onto the dance floor. He didn't ask me to dance, but the requested songs were too dreary to dance to anyway, so I didn't mind sitting them out. After a couple of tunes, Starshine got up and left one more time.

I watched as an especially skillful couple whirled around the tiny parquet dance floor. From the moves they were bustin' it looked as if they'd spent their kid's college tuition money at Arthur Murray. When the musicians took a break, Derek excused himself and got up.

"Hurry back," I said.

He lifted my hand to his lips and kissed it.

A few minutes later, Keo came over.

"May I join you?" he said.

I glanced around for Derek, and not seeing him, nodded. Keo sat in Derek's now empty chair.

"Are you enjoying yourself?" Keo said.

"Yes, it really turned out great."

I pondered whether I should voice my concern over Keo not thanking Derek, but Bev showed up before I could figure out how to say it without sounding snarky and demanding.

"I'm so, so glad this is almost over," she said. "Keo, I think perhaps you should use this break time to make an announcement thanking Derek Chambers for his support. I think he should be publically acknowledged, don't you?"

I could've kissed her. Much better that it come from her than me.

"C'mon, Bev," Keo said with a laugh. "We both know Chambers wouldn't have given us a dime if he wasn't bedding one of our board members. And besides, he caused the whole mess in the first place."

Bev's eyes narrowed and her voice turned brittle. "Derek Chambers is a good friend of mine," she said. "And he pulled my fat out of the fire when this thing was about to make the food bank the laughingstock of the island. I don't give a rip what his motives were. If you won't make the announcement, I will."

Keo turned to me with a slight smile and said, "Would you excuse me a minute, Monica? It seems I have a chore to attend to."

Derek still hadn't returned.

"Hold off a bit, will you, Keo?" I said. "Derek's stepped away for a minute. I'll go find him."

I went down the hall toward the rest rooms but didn't see Derek. I pulled my cellphone out of my clutch and called his number. No answer.

I needed to use the ladies' room. I entered the hushed, lavishly-appointed rest room and I was the only one in there. I did my business, washed up, and opened my purse for my lipstick. As I looked for the lipstick, I came across only one ruby earring. I emptied my purse on the sink counter but still came up one earring short. I dashed back into the toilet stall. Not there. I looked under the sink. Not there, either.

I pushed the restroom door open, and there stood Bev. She reached out and put her hand on my arm in a sympathetic way. Had she found my earring?

"I'm so sorry to hear about Derek," she said. "And Keo didn't even get a chance to thank him."

My concern over the missing earring vanished. "What's happened to Derek?"

"I ran into him a second ago and he said he wasn't feeling well. He said he was leaving and asked if I'd take you home."

"That's strange," I said. "He was fine a little while ago. By the way, I seem to have misplaced an earring. Have you seen it?" I reached up and touched my naked earlobes.

"No, but it's probably back at the table." She then said, "Oh my goodness, Monica. I hope Derek didn't get food poisoning from the *ahi*. That's all we need after everything else that's happened."

"I'm sure he'll be fine. He told me earlier he's been stressed about work."

"Would you mind helping me pack up the things from the auction table? I want to make sure Derek gets all his goodies."

"Sure, if you'll help me look for my earring while we work."

"Of course."

We still hadn't located the earring as we crammed the last of the fancy wine baskets, art pieces, and boxed gift certificates into Bev's car. I was thinking about how I was going to break the news to Derek that I'd lost the valuable ruby, when Keo came out to the portico.

"It's too bad Chambers had to leave before I could slather him with praise," he said. "I was looking forward to it."

"No, you weren't," I said.

"Can I speak with you for a moment, Monica?" He glanced at Bev. "Alone."

I excused myself and Keo led me back inside the foyer.

"I wanted to say I'm sorry about what I said about Derek's motive for saving the fund raiser," he said. "I hope I didn't offend you."

I wasn't about to tell him it was okay. Because it wasn't.

"Listen, Keo. Derek wrote the food bank a check for ninety thousand dollars, which will keep us going until the United Way money shows up. I know you don't approve of how Derek Chambers makes his living, but when will it dawn on you that it takes money—not noble intentions—to make things happen?"

"You're right, money makes things happen. But many times, it's *bad* things that happen, Monica. Not good things."

We locked eyes like a couple of arm wrestlers right before the takedown.

"Excuse me," I said. "I need to get back out there and help Bev."

For a split second I wondered if I should mention my lost ruby earring, then reconsidered. I didn't need any more grief about being shallow and self-indulgent from Keo Kekane.

"Before you go," Keo said. "Have you seen Starshine? She hitched a ride over here with one of the board members but I promised I'd take her home."

"She left our table a while ago," I said. "I haven't seen her since."

Keo folded his arms across his chest. "Huh. Remember what I said about money and bad things? If I'm right, I think you're soon gonna understand just what I mean."

"What are you talking about?"

"It's just a hunch," he said. "Let's leave it at that."

I gave him a pitying look. "It must suck to be you."

"How's that?"

"Always finding the glass half empty."

He shot me a rueful smile, then pulled the door open. "Maybe, but at least I'm able to face the truth. Now, let's help Bev finish up."

On the ride home, Bev oohed and awed over my jewelry. Her fussing made me feel even more guilt-ridden about losing the earring.

"Do you have any idea how much a ruby necklace like that would cost?" she said.

"I'm sure it was expensive."

"Rubies of that quality are the most expensive colored stones there are," she said. "It's a good thing you went with the red dress. If you'd worn blue you probably would've ended up with something less valuable, like sapphires or even topaz."

We laughed, but I was concerned about Derek finding out about the earring. I was also worried about him leaving without saying anything.

"Bev, do you think Derek's the kind of guy who'll settle down someday?"

Even though we were winding through the curves of the Pali Highway, Bev took her eyes off the road. Her look was dead serious.

"Monica, if you'd asked me that six months ago I'd have given a different answer. But the truth is, since he's met you he's a changed man. When he came over to ask what you'd be wearing tonight I swear I've never seen him so excited. He even said he thought you might be 'the one.'"

"Really?" I wanted to believe her, but Derek had sent some mixed signals lately, not the least of which was his tricking me into serving the eviction notices, and now his disappearing act after dinner.

"Seriously," she said. "He told me he's never been happier. He swore me to secrecy, so don't say anything, but I think he's in love."

She dropped me off at my house and I thanked her for the ride. The evening hadn't gone as expected, but all in all it had been a success. As I unclasped the ruby necklace and returned it to its case, I felt a surge of emotion. I looked up and smiled at my reflection in the mirror.

Love. At last.

CHAPTER 28

I awoke Sunday morning and stayed in bed for more than an hour basking in the glow of Bev's parting words. I wanted to call Derek right away, but held off. I was anxious to know if he was feeling better, but I didn't want to wake him up. If he was sick, he'd need rest.

Around ten-thirty, I gave in to my curiosity and called his cell. It rang and rang. I left a message saying I hoped he was feeling better and to call when he woke up.

After flipping through TV channels for half-an-hour, I decided to bake cookies. If Derek was feeling better later I'd take some up to him. Everyone likes fresh homemade cookies, and bringing him cookies would give me a chance to check out if Bev had heard him correctly when he'd called me "the one." I was dying to know.

The cookies were cooling on a rack when my doorbell rang. My heart rate bumped up a notch. Ah, it seemed Derek had come over instead of calling.

I looked out the sidelight window before opening the door. The vehicle in my driveway wasn't one of Derek's many luxury cars, it was a blue truck. A rather familiar-looking blue truck. And the guy standing on my doorstep wasn't Derek.

"Hello, Keo," I said.

He was holding a cardboard box like the ones used for canned goods at the food bank.

"*Aloha,* Monica. I wanted to thank you again for your help with the fund raiser. I brought you something I think you'll like."

Whatever was in the box was scratching at the sides. Oh, no. Had Keo gone and gotten me a new puppy? How could I politely refuse something I really didn't want?

"Oh, don't thank me," I said. "Bev's the one who did—"

By that point, whatever was in the box sounded frantic, whining and scratching in what sounded like a desperate attempt to escape. Keo bent down and put the box on the ground. A filthy gray miniature Schnauzer leapt out, its tail and ears tucked tight to its body. It was scrawny, with fur matted into clumps, but it looked so much like Pima my hand flew to my mouth.

"Aren't you going to welcome your friend home?" Keo said. He picked up the skinny little thing and held it out to me.

"Oh, no. Is it?" I looked in the dog's terrified eyes, "Are you?"

"I'm pretty sure it is," he said.

"Pima?"

The emaciated dog wagged its stump of a tail. I threw my arms around Keo, crushing Pima between us in the hug.

"Thank you, thank you, thank you," I whispered into his brawny chest.

"So, I guess this means we're back to being friends?" he said.

"Friends, for sure. How can I ever thank you?"

He smiled the smile I recalled from the first time I met him at the grocery store.

"Seeing you happy again is thanks enough for me," he said.

Pima smelled awful, like a mixture of hippie oil, urine, and musty closet. I couldn't believe how bony she felt.

"Where did you find her?" I said.

"In the break room at the food bank. I went in this morning to pack up some things from the fund raiser and there she was."

"And you don't know how she got there?"

"Nope."

"Come inside. I just made cookies. Let's have a few to celebrate."

"*Mahalo*, but I think your dog needs nourishment more than I do. Do you still have dog food in the house, or would you like me to run to the store? I'm not a big fan of hunger, as you know."

"Thanks, but I've still got all her stuff." It was hard to talk since I was half-crying and half-laughing. "Come inside anyway."

I snuggled Pima close. "I can't believe this. You're finally home, sweetheart."

I put her down on the kitchen floor and went to the pantry to get her bowls and food. She sniffed around tentatively, as if—like me— she was hoping this wasn't a dream. Where had she been the past three weeks? Wherever it was, she sure hadn't eaten much. She was down to just fur and bones.

"How did you know it was Pima?" I said.

"Remember? I was there when you went to Max and Nancy's to fill out the missing dog report. I took her over there first to make sure. Nancy ran Pima's ID chip and your name came up."

"How'd she do that? The chip's embedded in Pima's neck."

"There's a phone app that reads those chips. Nancy's had one since they first came out."

By now Pima was snarfing through kibble like a Hoover in a roomful of feathers.

I picked up the bowl. "I better not let her eat too much at once or she'll get sick."

"Speaking of sick, how's your friend Chambers doing this morning?"

"I don't know. I called, but I had to leave a message."

"Huh. That's interesting."

"What's that mean?"

"Doesn't mean anything. I just thought it was weird, you know, him taking off like that."

"Look Keo, I really appreciate you bringing my dog home. But I've got a few things I need to get done, and—"

"And you want me to clear out before Chambers finds out I'm here."

"Too late," said a deep voice from the foyer. It was Derek.

He came into the kitchen and Keo turned and stuck out his hand. Derek ignored it. He looked ghastly. His red-rimmed eyes and ashen skin tone reminded me of my mom's face after a night of especially hard partying. There was a sheen of sweat above his lip and he hadn't bothered to shave.

"What're you doing here?" Derek said to Keo.

"I brought Monica's dog home. It showed up at the food bank this morning."

"Oh, did it? Or maybe it's been there the whole time."

"No chance," said Keo. "We've got an army of community service workers who love nothing more than squealing on each other. Trust me, the dog just turned up."

"And you felt the need to rush right over here and play the hero." Derek fisted his hands. Was he actually thinking of throwing a punch? I felt both appalled and a little thrilled.

"I really should get going—" Keo turned to me. He extended an arm as if he were going to give me a hug.

Derek stepped between us. "Yeah, you should."

"Thank you again," I said. "I am *so* grateful."

"Don't be getting too grateful, there," said Derek. "He probably had the dog all along."

Keo shook his head and left.

When he'd gone, I turned to Derek. "What was that all about? The guy brought my dog home. Nothing more."

"How can I be sure your pal Kekane wasn't here all night?"

"Are you nuts? You're the one who left without even saying 'goodbye.'"

"I got sick. It happens. But that doesn't give you permission to sleep with the guy who drove you home."

That did it. I wanted him to leave. I started to speak, but Derek interrupted.

"I just came down here to get my freakin' jewelry."

"You mean the ruby necklace?"

"Yeah, the damn ruby necklace and the earrings, too." His voice had become a hoarse growl. "What? Did you tell lover boy the stuff was yours?"

"I already told you Keo brought Pima back, nothing more. He got here less than fifteen minutes before you did. I really resent your insinuations."

He grabbed my arm, hard. "Then why don't I see your damn dog around here anywhere? If that's why he was here, where's the dog?"

I looked around. He was right. Pima had skittered away to some back area of the house. It wasn't like her to leave me when someone else was in the house, but who knows what had happened to her in the past couple of weeks.

"You scared her. She's probably hiding."

He narrowed his eyes. "Go get the freakin' rubies. Now!"

I pulled away and headed to my bedroom. My heart was pounding. What had happened since he'd disappeared last night? I snatched up the velvet box from my dresser and when I turned, Derek was standing in the doorway. His eyes were slits of fury.

"Here's the jewelry. I didn't realize it wasn't mine to keep," I said.

"Yeah? Well, here's what's mine," he said in a steely voice. He strode into the room and shoved me onto the bed. Then he climbed on top, gripping me by both shoulders.

By now I was seriously scared.

"Derek, you need to leave," I said in the calmest voice I could muster. It came out a little squeaky, so I cleared my throat and went on. "Right now. You leave and we can part as friends."

"Friends?" he roared. "You think I want to be your *friend*? I cared for you, Monica. I thought we had a good thing going. And you screw me over like this?"

I struggled to pull free.

He leaned down to within inches of my face. His breath smelled like roadkill. "You're playing with fire. You understand? You have no idea what I'm capable of."

He gave me a final squeeze, as if trying to leave a bruise. Then he swung a leg over and leapt up. He grabbed the velvet box and strode out of the room. I struggled to sit, grateful when I heard the front door slam.

I blew out a breath and fell back down on the bed. After a few minutes Pima poked her head out of the closet. She looked left and right, and then raced across the carpet and hopped up next to me.

"That was unbelievable," I said.

She nuzzled into the crook of my arm. "Know what? You're lucky you're a dog because people are nuts."

She looked at me as if in complete agreement.

I got up and went to work cleaning her up. I ran a few inches of warm water in the kitchen sink. When I carefully lifted her in, she was shaking so hard I was worried she might be having a seizure. The stench of her wet fur brought tears to my eyes.

"Where have you been?" I said.

Her deep brown stare seemed to beg me to read her mind. I petted her bony skull.

"I'm so sorry. I looked everywhere for you."

She calmed a bit, letting out a doggie sigh.

I was grateful to whoever designed the app Nancy had used to read Pima's ID chip. Too bad there wasn't an app to read a dog's mind.

CHAPTER 29

B ev called around five on Sunday night but I didn't take the call. I still hadn't fully recovered from Derek's tantrum and the last thing I needed was to try to explain it to her. When my cell pinged that she'd left a voicemail, I listened to it.

'Hey, Monica. Just calling to see if you want to grab a little dinner. Derek just left and he said he had to work tonight, so I thought you might be alone.' She laughed. *'Maybe he changed his mind. Anyway, if he did, have fun you two!'*

I went to bed early. I was exhausted from the adrenaline dump over Pima showing up and then Derek's snit and I just wanted the day to be over. Sooner or later I'd have to talk to Bev, but I wanted to let some time pass before dealing with it.

The next morning my phone chimed. I checked the caller ID: Chambers, D

"Hello," I said. I tried to make my voice positively flat. Like I was answering a telemarketing call.

"Hey, Monica. Say, I wanted to call and apologize."

I waited.

"I shouldn't have left like that without saying a proper good-bye. But I just needed to get out of there."

I said nothing.

After a couple of seconds, he went on, "How about I take you to lunch this afternoon? If you want, we could fly over to Lana'i and grab a nice lunch at the Koele Lodge. If I'm not mistaken, I owe you one."

"Uh, Derek?"

"Yeah."

"I don't think that's a good idea."

"Why not? Too last minute?"

"No."

"Seriously, I've got a few hours between conference calls. I feel bad I had to leave so abruptly from the fundraiser the other night. Let me make it up to you."

I'd heard about people with mental problems who did bad things and then had no memory of it. Was Derek one of them?

"Derek, when you came over here yesterday you really scared me."

"Oh that. Yeah, well, sorry. I shoot my mouth off like that sometimes. I hope you don't think I meant it."

"I don't know what to think."

"Look, let me pick you up around noon. We'll fly over and grab some lunch and I'll fly you right back."

"Uh, if you don't mind, could we have lunch somewhere closer? I'd rather not be gone so long since I just got Pima back. I don't want to leave her here alone."

"Sure, no problem," he said. "How about you pick the place? I'll be down there at noon."

I clicked off the call. Time to call Bev.

I asked if she had time to come by my house for a cup of coffee before going in to work. "Sure," she said. "I don't have an especially busy morning."

She arrived a half-hour later. I told her about Derek's tirade on Sunday afternoon and then him acting as if nothing had happened when he'd called to invite me to lunch.

She eyed me suspiciously. "Have you been sleeping well, Monica? You seem kind of 'off.' Are you remembering to take a multi-vitamin every day?"

"What does that have to do with Derek hurting me and then acting as if it's no big deal? If anyone needs a pill, it's him."

"Look," she said. "He came by my house yesterday afternoon and apologized for leaving the gala. He said when he got up to go to the restroom he got a call from a client halfway around the world. It seems a huge deal he'd been working on for months was about a half-inch from falling off the cliff. He had to get home and deal with it."

"I thought he was sick."

"That was my mistake. The night of the gala I must've misunderstood him. Anyway, as we were talking he told me he'd just been at your house and he'd picked up the rubies. He said he told you he needed to borrow them so he could get them appraised. You can't get jewelry insured without a certified appraisal, you know."

"Bev, that's not what happened at all."

"Monica, I have no reason to doubt what he told me. Maybe you misunderstood. By the way, did you tell him about the missing earring? I mean, that was probably a five-thousand dollar boo-boo you made by losing it, right?"

I was so stunned I had to pause to get my bearings.

"Bev, you have to believe me. It wasn't like that at all. He was angry over Keo being at my house, and he threw me down on the bed and bruised my arm. Look." I lifted the sleeve on my designer t-shirt. Sadly, there was only a faint bluish haze. Seems it was going to take a few days for the full bruise to bloom.

She laid a hand gently on my forearm. "I've got to get to work, Monica, but I'm so happy you found your little dog. You've been under a lot of stress these past few weeks. First your car, then that darn sinkhole, and then your dog getting lost and your assistant taking off with her boyfriend like that. You've got a steady stream of strangers trooping through your yard and even using your toilet! It's a miracle you're not half crazy."

The way she said it sounded as if she thought I was somewhere beyond *half* crazy.

Bev left and I sat down to reconsider. Maybe I had over-reacted to Derek's bizarre behavior. He'd warned me he valued loyalty above all else, so maybe it was understandable he'd flip out if he thought I was cheating on him. I owed it to him to hear him out. But he'd have to listen to me, too. My hard-scrabble roots had given me a thick skin. Derek needed to know I'd come too far from the mean streets of Rio Blanco to put up with a bullying boyfriend.

ତ ତ ତ

Derek arrived in the Corvette. He'd put the top down and it was a gorgeous afternoon with light winds and a sky so brilliant blue it seemed like a photo from a travel brochure.

I waited for Derek to come to the door and knock. After his last visit I didn't want to appear overly eager.

He came inside and wrapped his arms around me. I stiffened a bit out of reflex, but he didn't comment. He gave me a quick kiss and stepped back.

"Ready to go? Where do you want to eat?"

"How about the Sea House?" I said.

The Sea House is one of my favorite West Maui restaurants. It's on the beach at the Napili Kai Resort, just down the road from Kapalua. I actually like it better for lunch than dinner because during the day you can see the perfect crescent beach of Napili Bay, with little kids trying out their new boogie boards and old guys stand-up paddle boarding in the protected waters of the bay.

Derek took my hand as we strolled through the manicured grounds of the resort. We were seated at an oceanfront table with an unobstructed view of the glittering bay.

"I want to say how sorry I am about yesterday," he said. "I wasn't myself. I was looking forward to seeing you and then when I saw you with that guy. I just...I don't know. It just set me off."

"You have nothing to worry about, Derek. Keo and I are—"

"Do me a favor, okay? Let's not talk about him. I'd rather focus on us. Anyway, I'm sorry and I want to give you something to show I mean it."

He pulled out a small velvet box from his pants pocket and placed it on the table. My breath stalled. It was the size of a ring box. I still hadn't fully recovered from his meltdown so I was in no way prepared for a proposal. He must've seen my reaction because he pushed the box toward me.

"Don't worry," he said. "It's not serious."

I popped the lid open. Inside was a ruby earring. It looked exactly like the one I'd lost on Saturday night.

"I, uh." I struggled to come up with an appropriate remark. My mind was racing. Where had he found the earring? Had he seen me lose it and hadn't said anything? Or, had the staff at the King Kamehameha found it and returned it to him? I was flummoxed as to how to respond.

"Bev told me you'd lost it. I found it in my car."

But hadn't I been wearing the earrings when we arrived at the fund raiser? I clearly remembered putting both earrings in my clutch purse when I was at the dinner table.

"And since I'm in such a generous mood..." He reached into his jacket and pulled out the black velvet necklace box. "I want you to have the whole set. To keep."

"They're beautiful, but..." I was becoming more confused by the minute.

"In fact, why don't you put them on?"

"Here? Derek we're in a restaurant. I'll put them on later. It'll be easier with a mirror."

His face registered annoyance but in a flash it was gone. He took my hand and gave it a light squeeze.

"Just as long as you'll wear them for me the next time you wear red. You look amazing in red."

We enjoyed a leisurely lunch and Derek took me back home at around two. Since it was a Monday, the sinkhole workers were back in force.

"Mind if I come in?" Derek said.

"It's such a zoo here. Why don't we go up to your house?"

"Ah, today's not a good day. I've got the cleaning people there."

"Do you realize I've never been to your place?" I said.

"Really? I could've sworn we had drinks on my lanai. You remember—it was after we first met."

"No, I've never been to your house, Derek."

"Huh. Well, I'll have to have you over sometime. We'll make it a date."

҉ ҉ ҉

That night Bev and I went to the Pineapple Grill for dinner. She'd wanted to invite Derek but I said he'd told me he had back-to-back conference calls scheduled far into the night.

"That poor boy works harder than anyone I know. I hope you two got things straightened out today at lunch."

I got home after dark and my driveway gate was standing open. From the first day the university workers had shown up I'd repeatedly asked them to please close the gate behind them at the end of the day. At least half the time they forgot. I pulled into the garage and went into the house through the laundry room. Pima came running to greet me as usual, but when the initial glee was over, she raced to the foyer and began furiously barking at the front door.

"Take it easy, girl."

I flicked on the porch light and peeked out the side window. "There's no one out there, Pima. I suppose you're gonna see bogeymen for a while so I don't blame you, but—" I stopped short.

There *was* something on the front mat. And it definitely wasn't another velvet jeweler's box.

🐢 🐢 🐢

When I opened the door, the fish stink hit me like a wet towel to the face. I went into the kitchen and grabbed a thirty-gallon plastic garbage bag and dropped the entire mess: rotting fish, door mat and wet piece of white paper, into it.

I twisted it shut. The smell abated a bit, but the damage was done. No amount of Febreze was going to be able to offset the reek of what stank like three-day-old off-brand cat food.

I threw the bag in the garage can and clamped the lid down tight. Then I called my landscaper and asked him to come pick it up. He said he'd come by in the morning, but I told him I'd give him a hundred bucks cash if he'd come within the hour.

As soon as I'd finished the call my curiosity kicked in. Had the slimy piece of paper held a clue as to who'd leave a putrid fish on my doorstep? And was there some hidden meaning behind the dead fish, like a pot dealer chopping off a debtor's forefinger to make it tough for him to roll his own joints? Rio Blanco had a handful of rival gangs with weird initiation rites and revenge rituals. Maybe the decaying fish at my door was more significant than simply an olfactory assault.

I doused a Hermès scarf with Tommy Bahama cologne and wrapped it, bandit-style, over my nose and mouth. Then I snapped on a pair of rubber gloves the cleaning ladies had left under the kitchen sink.

Before I'd put the bag in the garbage can, I'd knotted it tight so it took me a minute to get it undone, but at least it was right on top of all the other stuff.

The stink cut right through Mr. Bahama's best fragrance efforts and I came darn close to stuffing the mess back in the can to avoid hurling my dinner on top of it. But my *abuela* always said that sucking it up in the short-term usually resulted in less misery long-term, so I kept digging through the bag until I found the soggy piece of paper, now splotched with brown and yellow ooze.

In the dim light of the garage I made out four handprinted words. One was misspelled. GO OR DIE BICH.

CHAPTER 30

The next morning I drove to The Bakery on Limahana Place in Lahaina and bought four fresh-from-the-oven cinnamon rolls. I brought them home and found a hamper-style picnic basket that had been a housewarming gift from Bev. I lined it with a cheery palm tree print kitchen towel, then added the rolls, a thermos of fresh Kona coffee, and a plastic container of cut-up pineapple. On top of all of it I tossed in two cloth napkins.

It was time to see Derek's house. Bringing a picnic breakfast offered me a great excuse to surprise him.

As I passed by Bev's house, I noticed her car was parked in her driveway. I checked my watch. Ten o'clock. Pretty late for her to still be at home.

The security gate to Derek's driveway was locked so I used the speaker box to call him. One of the downsides of gated homes is it makes it tough to surprise the residents. It's one of the upsides if you don't like surprises. The speaker buzzed, and I waited for Derek to answer.

Nothing.

I buzzed again. Where could he be at ten o'clock on a Tuesday morning? Then it dawned on me. Maybe he was on the phone and couldn't get away.

If Derek's security fence was like mine, there'd be a walk-in opening somewhere along the side perimeter. I got out of my car and headed down the right side of the property. Sure enough, there it was, about halfway down. I tried the access gate and found it unlocked.

Once inside, I doubled back to the front of the house. I knocked on the front door. I waited a minute and then rang the bell.

After nearly a minute, the door swung open and there stood Derek. He looked like he'd been roused from a deep sleep. He wore the same clothes he'd had on when we'd gone to lunch the day before and his hair was matted on one side.

"Hey," I said. I held out the picnic basket like Little Red Riding Hood making overtures to the wolf. "I brought you breakfast."

He stood silent for about three beats and then he scowled and pushed the door closed in my face. I was astonished. I knocked again.

This time he only opened the door wide enough for his head to peek out.

"What's going on?" I said. I pronounced each word slowly, as if I were talking to a sleepwalker.

He cleared his throat. "What is it about 'go away' you don't understand?"

He started to shut the door again, but I reached out and pressed my palm against it. Then I wedged a foot in the sill.

"Did you leave a dead fish at my house last night?" I said.

He barked a short laugh and pushed harder against his side of the door. I pulled my foot back just in time to avoid it being crushed. This time when he shut the door I heard the bolt click in the lock.

I dropped the basket on the porch and jogged back to my car. Okay, I'd had enough. The guy was clearly suffering from some type of mental defect.

Of course when I talked to Bev, she didn't agree.

"Derek's lights have been on 'til all hours of the night," she said. "I think you woke him up. You know some folks just aren't morning people, Monica."

"Something's wrong with him, Bev. Are you sure you haven't seen or heard anything weird going on over there?"

"Nothing more than the usual comings and goings. You know Derek's got all kinds of household help, and then there are his work colleagues and the landscapers and all. But I haven't noticed anything I'd consider unusual. He's a busy man, that's all."

About ten years earlier I'd read the highly-rated dating advice book, "He's Just Not That Into You." As I pulled out of Bev's driveway, I looked over at Derek's house.

"Don't worry, Derek. I'm not that into you anymore, either."

🐢 🐢 🐢

Instead of returning home, I drove to the Maui Food Bank. It was a Tuesday, which meant it was food sorting day. I hoped I could catch Keo alone for a few minutes without attracting a lot of attention.

"Makaila drove the truck to Makawao to pick up more produce," said Keo. He was standing at Makaila's desk, impatiently rifling through a stack of files. "She should be back any minute now."

"Is Starshine here?"

He looked up, perturbed. "What? I don't know. Haven't seen her."

"Can I ask you something? It's about Hawaiian culture."

He stopped fiddling with the files. "Sure, what's up?"

"What does it mean when someone leaves a dead fish at your door?"

He scrunched up his face "Did someone leave you a dead fish?"

I nodded.

"When?"

"Last night. I got home after dinner and a really rank fish was on my door mat. Along with a nasty note."

"What'd the note say?"

"It said 'Go or die, bitch.' Actually, the word 'bitch' was spelled wrong. I was wondering if the dead fish might have some cultural meaning. You know, the sinkhole thing."

"It doesn't have any meaning that I know of. But the note sounds threatening. Can I see it?"

"I tossed it away with the fish. It stunk beyond belief. I had my landscaper come and take the whole mess away last night."

He rubbed his chin. "You should report this to the police."

"Since I didn't keep the note, I have nothing to show them. And, besides, with all that's happened lately, I'm reluctant to draw any more attention to myself."

He gestured for me to follow him to his office. He shut the door. "So tell me, are you having problems with Chambers? I feel bad about messing things up for you when I brought your dog back."

I gave him a quick rundown on what had transpired with Derek since Keo left my house on Sunday morning.

"As you can imagine, I think either he's nuts or I am," I said.

"You probably already know my opinion on that." He looked out the window. "Makaila's back. You want to talk to her?"

"Not really. I just came to see if there was any significance to the fish. I'd appreciate it if you'd keep my love life troubles to yourself."

"No worries. If you'd like, you can use my side door."

He pointed to an exterior door which led from his office to the parking lot. I came outside just as Starshine was getting out of a dark green VW Beetle that looked like it'd gone a few rounds in a demolition derby. She looked at me and her eyes narrowed.

"You're disgusting," she snarled.

I looked around to make sure she was talking to me. She trotted over and got right up in my face.

"Sneaking out of Keo's private door like some 'ho' after a ten-dollar blow job."

She was wearing her signature black baggy tunic, so it was hard to tell whether her rumpled clothes were clean or days old, but I recognized the ridiculous fishnet stockings from Saturday night. Same gaping hole in a spot just above her right ankle.

"Watch your mouth, sister," I said.

"Or what? You wanna fight?" As if she suddenly remembered something, her demeanor quickly changed. "Oh, I heard you got a present."

"Are you talking about the dead fish?"

She laughed. "No, I heard you got back something you lost."

"Where'd you hear that?"

"Wouldn't you like to know? Don't forget, this is a small island. People talk."

As I moved to step around her to go to my car, she reached out and grabbed a handful of my hair. It startled me and I instinctively tried to pull away. She yanked harder.

"Since you brought up the fish," she hissed. "Maybe you should take the hint."

She released her grip on my hair. I pulled free and speed-walked toward my car. I thought I may have heard

Makaila call my name, but I was bent on getting out of there so I didn't look back.

As I drove back down the Honoapi'ilani Highway, I assessed my situation. Ever since I'd won the money I'd received threats by email, snail mail, and voicemail. One time a note had been tied around a rock and tossed over the seven-foot privacy wall surrounding my ranchette outside of Rio Blanco.

I'd had to close down my Facebook page, change my email address and stop Tweeting. I'd avoided Reddit and cut myself off from Instagram. The few unpleasant messages that did manage to sneak through were usually lame blackmail attempts or dire metaphysical warnings, but some were bona fide threats as ominous as the fish note. Chloe had always handled the situation. She'd contacted the authorities and made copies of the evidence. She'd filed them in a pink folder she'd wryly labeled 'Love Letters.'

When I got home, my phone pinged. It was a text message from Derek. Just two words, *Call me.*

I wasn't looking forward to the break-up, but it had to be done. In three short days I'd gone from being "the one" to being "the one who gets the door slammed in her face." This time I wasn't going to take the blame with the "it's not you, it's me" speech because it was clearly *not* me.

"What's up, sweetheart?" Derek said brightly when I called him back.

He'd played this game before, so I was prepared.

"Did you find the picnic basket I left on your front porch this morning?" I tried to keep my voice light, but it sounded phony, even to me.

"Yeah, that was nice of you. Sorry I couldn't invite you in, but I wasn't expecting company. The house is a mess."

"I thought your cleaning people were there yesterday."

"Oh, yeah. I guess they were. I must be a real messy guy."

You could say that again. I no longer felt compelled to get to the bottom of his inconsistencies, contradictions and erratic behavior. I felt I owed it to him to meet face-to-face to end our relationship since we'd dated for more than a month, but I felt no obligation to explain why.

I was prepared for how it might go. He'd hand me some song-and-dance about how sorry he was and how much stress he'd been under with work and he'd ask me to reconsider. But I'd already decided no more chances. Probably ten minutes after I'd bid him farewell he'd be over at Bev's calling me names and filling her in on what a lousy lay I'd been. I didn't care. No matter what, I'd be relieved to be done with him.

"How about dinner tonight?" he said.

"I had a late lunch and I didn't sleep well last night. Would you mind if we just went for *pu pu's* and a drink?" Making him buy me a drink would probably be added to his list of grievances, but I wanted to part ways in a public place to insure he kept his temper in check.

"Then let's go to Momi's," he said. "You love that place."

I did love the sunset views from Momi's Place in Lahaina. I hoped the memory of dumping Derek there wouldn't spoil it for me in the future.

"Sounds good."

"Great. I'll pick you up at seven."

"I, uh…" I desperately tried to come up with a good reason to take my own car. But there was limited parking at Momi's and I couldn't think of anything even remotely feasible to offer as an excuse.

Derek arrived right on time carrying a small bottle of port. "I thought we could come back here and enjoy a little nightcap," he said. He seemed jumpy and his eyes were nearly as bloodshot as they'd been when I'd gone up to his house that morning.

"Or we could go to your place. I still haven't seen your house."

What was I saying? I had no intention of going to his house after telling him we were through. But then, I had even less intention of letting him come back in to my house, so I didn't want him leaving his fancy port wine sitting on my kitchen counter.

He looked out at the sink hole. "Do those university guys always leave their tools lying around like that?" He pointed to a shovel propped against my back slider door.

"Not usually. I can't believe this thing is still dragging on."

"You get a gust of wind and, next thing you know, that thing will come right through the glass."

I went outside and dragged the shovel to a temporary tool shed the workers had set up, but the shed door was locked. I leaned it against the shed and promised myself I'd chastise them in the morning for leaving my yard a mess.

We drove to Lahaina and Derek parallel-parked the Corvette outside the restaurant. We went inside and up the stairs to the lanai bar. After we'd been served drinks and a plate of crispy calamari, I began my spiel.

"Derek, I'm afraid this isn't working for me," I said.

"What? Your cosmo? Didn't they make it right? I'll get you another." He looked around for our waitress, but I laid a hand on his arm.

He turned and looked at me.

"The drink's fine. What's not working for me is *us*."

"What are you talking about? We're great. No complaints here." His smile seemed sort of contrived, like he knew what was coming but he refused to make it easy for me.

"The past couple of days have made me rethink my situation," I said. "I'd like to take a break from seeing you for a while."

"Take a break? What is this, a *job*?" His voice had risen to a level above the general din of the bar and the couple at the next table looked over.

"Please lower your voice. I've been doing some thinking and things between us are moving a bit too fast for me. I want to—"

"Don't even say it, sweetheart. I know exactly what you want." He was bellowing now. "You want me to back off so you can screw that mango-muncher from the food bank. Hell, you've probably screwed him already and you're just scared of what I'll do when I find out."

He swept his arm across the table. Our drinks and the dish of calamari went crashing onto the hardwood floor. The couple next to us leapt up as liquor, broken glass, and deep-fried seafood flew in all directions.

"Screw you, bitch," Derek said. "I'm outta here."

He got up and staggered away from the table as if he was already drunk, leaving me to field the pitying looks of the others in the bar. Then he disappeared down the stairs.

I pulled out all the cash I had in my purse, about fifty dollars, and left it on the table.

🍤 🍤 🍤

Derek was waiting just outside the restaurant door. He grabbed my upper arm tightly, right where the bruise from Sunday was beginning to bloom.

"Don't you *ever* pull something like that in public again," he snarled.

"I won't, Derek, because there won't *be* a next time," I said. "Public or private."

His eyes were glassy; his pupils so dilated they looked like shiny black buttons. He'd sweated through his shirt, dark rings encircling his armpits.

For some reason, my mind flashed back to the night two solemn-faced border patrol agents came to our house to inform my mother that my father wasn't going to be coming home. My mother's body shook as she screamed, "No, no, no, no."

"Derek, you shouldn't drive," I said.

He didn't loosen his grip as he dragged me toward the car.

I kept my voice low and calm. "Let me call a cab."

"Shut up, whore! Look what you've done. You and that damn food bank. I was doing good. I'd made amends, and...."

He opened the passenger door and shoved me inside. He locked the door with the remote after slamming it shut, and then he jogged around to the other side. I was trying to decide what to do when he unlocked his side, hopped in and pressed the ignition.

It was now or never. I thumbed the button to unlock my door just as the car lurched into reverse. Derek slammed his foot on the accelerator as I pushed the door open. Gray asphalt flew by like water under a jet ski. I set my jaw and rolled out, keeping my sights on getting beyond Derek's grasp so he couldn't reach over and pull me back in.

He didn't try. The Corvette rocketed away from the curb, narrowly missing a white sedan.

I staggered to my feet and began digging through my purse for my phone. I ignored the white-hot sting of my scraped elbow and my aching twisted knee. It felt as if I had half-a-pound of gravel embedded in my right arm, but I managed to pull out my phone and type "taxi lahaina maui" into the Google toolbar. While I waited for the link to connect, my elbow began to bleed.

"You need a ride?" said a male voice behind me.

I spun around. Keo was leaning against a corner of the building, arms folded across his chest.

"Sorry if it looks like I'm stalking you, but I'm here picking up a food donation. Nola Lawson's a big supporter. C'mon, the truck's right over there."

I looked where he was pointing and saw the familiar Maui Food Bank logo emblazoned on the side of a panel truck.

"I bet you're dying to say 'I told you so'," I said.

"Not really. But even if I was, you still need a ride. And the sooner you clean those rocks out of your arm, the less chance you'll get an infection."

🐢 🐢 🐢

The ride up to my house was quiet. Keo didn't say much or ask any questions. He must've figured there was no need to discuss the obvious. It was a good thing I wasn't expected to hold up my side of the conversation because I felt myself slipping into shock, both from injury and humiliation.

He pulled up at the closed gate to my driveway and said, "Do you still leave it unlocked?"

I nodded and shot him a thin smile. He got out and dragged the gate open. When we got to the house, I thanked him for the ride and began to climb out.

"Hang on," he said. "I want to make sure you get inside okay."

He helped me down from the cab of the truck, which was no easy task given my right arm was pulsing with pain.

"Hand me your keys and I'll unlock the front door," he said.

I started to object, but my arm hurt so much I nearly passed out just fishing through my purse to find the keys.

As expected, Pima put up a racket when we came in. No amount of shushing could get her to settle down. Ever since she'd come back home she'd been more hyper-vigilant than ever. Since Schnauzers tend to be manic anyway, her recent behavior bordered on downright schizo.

Keo reached down and picked her up. She licked his face with gusto.

"If you need to talk later, give me a call," he said. "I'll be home all night."

"Do you have to leave so soon? I think you getting me out of there is at least worth a glass of wine, maybe a whole bottle." As soon as I'd said it, I inwardly winced. How pathetic. He probably thought I must be enjoying playing the damsel in distress and didn't want it to end.

"Okay, I'll stick around a bit. But I'll just have water. I still have to drive over to the other side. But first, I want to make sure you get all the dirt out of that arm."

It hurt a lot to scrub the grime and bits of rock from my elbow, but I didn't let on. Keo helped me bandage the wound.

"You okay to sit up or do you need to lie down?"

"I'm fine. Look, take a seat in the living room and I'll bring us something to drink."

I got out two brand-new Riedel crystal goblets from my cupboard and poured myself a glass of red wine and a glass of Perrier for him.

When I handed Keo his water, he inspected it and said, "Nice glasses. They're Riedel?"

"Actually, yes. I've never used them before."

"They're beautiful. Just like their hostess."

And so it began. We ended up kissing and caressing like two hormone-charged teenagers when the parents are out of town. Every now and then my bandaged elbow got in the way, but I managed to keep the gasps and ouches to a minimum.

"What about Starshine?" I said when I came up for air about a half hour later.

"What about her?"

"Aren't you a couple?"

"Oh, we're a couple all right," he said with a laugh.

When he saw my horrified expression, he went on. "No, seriously, it's not like that. We're more like brother and sister. Maybe even father and daughter. She got herself in some trouble a while back and I took her under my wing."

"What kind of trouble?"

"I'm not at liberty to give details," he said. "But like a lot of the folks out at the food bank, Starshine went through a rough patch and she needed help. I was that help."

"But she acts like the two of you are dating," I said.

"No. We're close, but not in that way." He ran a fingertip lightly down my cheek and gently tapped my lips which were starting to get puffy from all the making out. "Believe me, it's strictly platonic."

After another half-hour of what essentially amounted to foreplay, Keo whispered, "I better get going. I've got meat that's getting into the danger zone."

He waggled his eyebrows.

We both laughed, but I knew what he meant. The frozen meat and seafood he'd picked up at Momi's Place was out in the food bank truck getting warmer by the minute. If it completely thawed, it'd have to be thrown out.

"Rain check?" he said.

"I'll be praying for rain," I said, pleased with my clever come-back.

We kissed one last long tender kiss in the foyer. After I finally closed the door I wanted to fling it back open and beg him to let me go home with him, or better yet, convince him to stay. I could write a check for whatever food would have to be tossed out.

Luckily, he'd already started the engine and was heading down the driveway. I went into my bedroom and got ready for bed. When I flicked off the light, I was surprised to see the glowing red numbers on my clock showed it was nearly eleven.

I'd hoped the ordeal with Derek and all the smooching with Keo would've sent me right off to sleep but no such luck. I was still awake at midnight. I'd spent the hour replaying every minute of the messy break-up with Derek, along with worrying about how my budding relationship with Keo might play out with Starshine and the other workers at the food bank.

Like everyone else, I'd always imagined that if I had a million dollars I'd be guaranteed a fun, carefree life with no worries. But here I was with a busted-up arm, a humongous hole in my backyard, and the hots for a guy with a viciously jealous woman in his life.

If I'd learned anything in the past year it was this: gobs of money can pretty much buy you anything, but it can't buy a single thing that matters.

CHAPTER 31

The next morning the sound of the doorbell made Pima go downright apoplectic. I rolled over and checked the clock next to my bed. Nine-thirty? It seemed after I'd finally dozed off, I'd slept pretty well after all.

I staggered out of bed and slipped my bathrobe over my shoulders. It had to be Derek. He'd probably come to try to win me back while denying any memory of his outrageous behavior the night before. I considered not answering the door, but figured if I was going to stand my ground, I might as well get it over with. And, since I saw university workers out in the backyard when I passed through the kitchen, I knew I wasn't there alone.

I looked out the sidelight window. It wasn't Derek. It was two police officers. A few yards behind them stood a disheveled-looking guy I thought I recognized from the archeology crew. He looked troubled as he ran a hand nervously through his greasy locks and kicked the heel of his hiking boot into my recently power-washed driveway.

"Good morning, officers," I said. "Can I help you?"

"Good morning, miss," the first policeman said.

I wondered at what point strangers would stop calling me "miss" and switch to "ma'am." I hoped it wouldn't be anytime soon.

"We're here to alert you to a problem that's come up. And we'd like to ask you a few questions."

"Please. Come in."

Once they got inside, Pima snuffled their pants cuffs like a drug-sniffing dog at the Nogales border crossing, but she didn't put up a fuss.

"What's this about, officers?"

"It's about the body we found in your backyard," said the second cop.

"The *what*?"

"There's a deceased person in your yard, and we'd like to know what you can tell us about it."

I worked my jaw up and down as if trying to speak, but I couldn't seem to get any words to come out. Finally, when coherent thought kicked in, I said, "I have no idea what you're talking about."

"We received a call from a gentleman who said he's out here doing archeological work for the U of H. He reported finding a deceased female on the property."

"In the sinkhole?" I spluttered.

"As a matter of fact, ma'am, that's correct."

There it was, the dreaded "ma'am." I guess when you've got some 'splainin' to do, you suddenly look a whole lot older.

The first cop spoke again. "So, what can you tell us about it?"

"Nothing. I had no idea..."

I was too stunned to finish. I wanted to ask them if they knew who it was, or how she died, but I thought that might make me sound guilty. Like I was playing guessing games with them or something.

"We've called in detectives, and the medical examiner's people will be removing the body, but if there's anything you want to say before they get here, now's your chance."

My chance for what? To implicate myself in a possible crime I'd only learned of thirty seconds earlier? No, *grácias.*

"Sorry," I said. "I don't know a thing about it."

They went outside to put up crime tape and I called Bev. No one had better professional contacts than Bev, and I had a hunch that in the next few hours I was gonna need all the contacts I could get my hands on.

☙ ☙ ☙

Bev got down to my house so fast I thought she'd teleported herself. I was out front as I watched her shake a finger at the cop guarding the driveway and then push right past him. She race-walked over to me.

"How'd you get by the cops?" I said.

"Don't you worry about a thing," she said, ignoring the question. "I've got the best attorney on the island on her way over here right now. She'll set these clowns straight in no time."

"I bet you told them you were my attorney, didn't you?" I said.

Once again she ignored the question. She leaned in.

"Have they figured out who it is?" she said in a conspiratorial voice. "On the phone you said it was a woman. Is it someone from the neighborhood? Someone we know?"

"When they retrieved the body out of the sinkhole they'd already put her in a body bag," I said. "So, I have no idea who it is."

"Or *was,*" said Bev. She looked expectant, as if hoping maybe a death in the neighborhood would mean a new listing for her.

Bev's attorney, Lisa Neville, showed up ten minutes later. She was a painfully thin, light-skinned young woman who appeared to be only a few years older than me. As Lisa made her approach, Pima took off down the driveway, barking and growling as if pleased to be finally facing someone small and skinny enough to perhaps be afraid of her.

I called to Pima to knock it off.

"Don't let Lisa's youthful appearance fool you," said Bev, as if reading the expression on my face. "A lot of old guys—both judges and district attorneys—have underestimated Lisa and lived to rue their disrespect later. Believe me, juries simply *love* her."

How did Bev know so much about judges and juries? I had a hunch Bev had a bit of interesting history she hadn't yet shared with me.

Bev introduced me to her lawyer and Lisa and I shook hands. Her eyes took me in as if trying to determine my guilt or innocence, but of course it really didn't matter what she thought.

We went inside.

"Tell me everything," she said as the three of us got settled in the living room.

I told her I'd gone to Momi's Place for drinks with Derek and I'd broken up with him while we were there. Upon hearing this, Bev let out a little chirp of dismay. I ignored her and went on to say I'd had to leap from his moving car because he began acting crazy. I underscored this by rolling up my shirt sleeve and displaying my bandaged elbow. Then I said a friend had driven me home.

"What time was this?" said Lisa. She made notes in a little notebook she'd taken out of her purse.

"Around seven-thirty or eight. My friend brought me home, and he left just before eleven."

"He?" said Bev.

Lisa shot her an annoyed look.

"Sorry," said Bev. "Just trying to help."

"Yes, it was a 'he,'" I said. "It was Keo Kekane. He's the manager at the Maui Food Bank. He was at Momi's picking up some donations. I know him because I'm on the food bank's advisory board."

"As am I," said Bev. "Why didn't you call me, Monica? I would've been happy to come get you."

Lisa put a put a hand on Bev's arm. "Beverly, maybe it would be best if you waited for us outside."

"Sorry. I won't say another word." Bev crossed her heart with a finger. "I promise."

Lisa turned back to me.

"Go on," she said.

"Anyway, Keo and I, uh well, we talked until nearly eleven. After that, I went to bed. When I woke up this morning, the police were at my door."

"And you didn't hear anything during the night? No sounds of struggle or footsteps?"

Lisa said it the way a prosecutor might on cross-examination, as if not hearing anything in my own back-yard made me guilty of gross negligence or something.

"Not a thing."

"How about your dog? Do you recall your dog acting as if it might've heard someone?"

We all looked at Pima, who appeared to enjoy the attention. She trotted in a little circle and then jumped up on Bev's leg. Bev promptly pushed her back down.

"No, she sleeps with me. And she was quiet all night."

"So, let me see if I've got this right: you broke up with your boyfriend at Momi's and then talked until nearly eleven with another man here at the house. After that, you were alone until the police showed up this morning. And you didn't hear anything out of the ordinary the entire night."

"That's correct."

"I'm having a little difficulty with one thing," she said. "Your dog."

"What about her?"

"When I came to the house the dog put up quite a fuss."

"Yeah, so?"

"But you said it made no noise at all, even though a human body showed up just a few yards from where you were sleeping?"

"Actually that's quite typical of Pima. She only cares about me. If she thinks I'm okay, she pretty much ignores everything else."

"So, you're saying it's not much of a guard dog." Her tone was condescending.

Pima looked at Lisa as if she'd grasped the underlying disrespect. She blew out a snort and hopped up next to me.

We talked a few more minutes and then someone knocked on the back slider door. Pima flew off the sofa, skidded across the kitchen floor, and unleashed a torrent of ninety-decibel barks as she made her way to the door.

"Not much of a guard dog, my ass," I mumbled as I slid the door open.

"Is this your shovel, ma'am?" said a guy in civilian clothes. He wore rubber gloves and a dour expression.

"I don't know. It probably belongs to the university people working on the sinkhole."

"Well, it appears to have blood on it so we're going to be taking it in for testing."

"Fine by me."

As I turned to go back to the living room, Bev sang out, "Who was that at the door, dear?"

"Just the police. They found a shovel they think has blood on it."

"Oh, great," said Lisa. "A shovel of yours?"

"No, all the stuff out there belongs to the university people."

Then I remembered dragging a shovel away from my lanai door the night before when Derek had pointed it out.

"What's the matter?" said Lisa. "You look concerned."

"It's nothing. I was just thinking of how sad it is that someone died right here in my own back yard."

"Yes," said Bev. "And we still don't know who it is."

Lisa left soon afterward, but Bev stuck around for moral support. I offered to make her a cup of tea, and she accepted. She sat at the counter while I put a tea kettle on the massive cooktop surface. One of the great features of high-end appliances is everything's speeded up. Convection ovens, halogen burners, and a whisper-quiet dishwasher made short work of kitchen chores. The tea water boiled in less than a minute. I dropped herbal tea bags into cups and sat down next to Bev.

"It sounds as if you and Derek have hit a rough patch," she said.

I rolled my eyes. She was as bad as he was at accepting reality.

"Bev, we broke up," I said. "For good."

"He really cares for you, Monica. No matter what he might've said or done, I know underneath it all he's a great guy and he'd do anything to make you happy."

I said nothing. I wasn't about to argue or plead my case. I didn't care what Derek was like *underneath it all*. I'd had more than I was willing to stomach of what he was like on the surface. And besides, things with Keo were getting interesting.

She went on. "He called me last night...late. He told me he'd been called to the Middle East on business and he wanted me to keep an eye on the house while he was away. He never said a peep about a break-up."

I nodded but kept quiet.

"Here's where it gets kind of interesting," she said. "He said he's thinking of selling his house and wanted me to tell him what I thought it's worth. I assumed he was considering getting something bigger. For the two of you."

"Well, I'm afraid that's not the case," I said. "But hey, at least it's a good listing for you."

I shot her a quick smile but she didn't return it.

We finished our tea in silence.

"I need to get to work," said Bev. "I'm going to do Derek's CMA this morning. I wish it was under happier circumstances."

"CMA? What's that?" I didn't want to dwell on the break-up.

"A comparable market analysis. I'm a bit worried because with this sinkhole business going on and now a dead body in the neighborhood, it will probably impact the value of Derek's property. And not in a good way."

Was she seriously trying to guilt-trip me?

"I'm sure Derek's balance sheet can withstand a small hit in the real estate area," I said.

"Yes, I'm sure he'll be fine. But still, it's a pity he's going to be bearing the brunt of all this, don't you think?"

She gestured to the backyard, where the university workers had been replaced by CSI-types. Crime scene tape had been looped completely around the sinkhole.

I thanked her again for calling Lisa Neville for me, and then I wordlessly walked her to the door.

CHAPTER 32

I was hoping Keo might call me that morning, but he didn't. At noon I turned on the TV news, and lo and behold, there I was again. "Murder On Maui" was the lead story, and the sinkhole in my backyard was once again featured.

A male reporter was saying, "...at the home of Monica Gomez, in Kapalua. The female body has been identified, but the name is being withheld pending notification of family." Looking at the scene, I could tell the guy was standing in the street right outside my driveway. It was eerie to realize the broadcast had been taped only a few hundred feet from where I was sitting.

The afternoon passed slowly, as if I was slogging through deep mud. I wanted to get out of the house, but I wasn't willing to battle my way through the media vans and police vehicles blocking the way, so I remained vegged out in front of the TV. I recalled how I used to resent that I had to record my soaps and Spanish-language *novellas* while I worked at the produce warehouse in Rio Blanco. I'd binge watch them on weekends while I tidied up or ironed, but now that I had nothing to do, I could see how tedious and repetitive they were.

At three-thirty, a breaking news bulletin interrupted to say the body found in Kapalua had been identified as a Lindsey Elizabeth Durrell of Wailuku. It also said new evidence found at the scene indicated "foul play." "Play" seemed like an odd word to describe killing someone, but then, people had said my dad had "passed on" when he'd been brutally murdered. I thought it sounded dismissive, as if my father had just decided life wasn't that great, so he'd taken a pass and moved on.

I didn't know anyone named Lindsey Durrell, and I had no idea why someone had dumped her body in my yard. Maybe they were just too lazy to dig a grave and figured why not dispose of her in an existing hole. Seems the cultural people got their human bones, after all.

At four o'clock, my phone rang. I leapt up to get it, but it wasn't Keo. It was Makaila.

"How you doin'?" she said.

"I'm okay. I can't believe this is happening," I said.

"Yeah, and to one of our own."

"I appreciate you saying that, Makaila. Especially since I only joined the board a few weeks ago."

"No, I mean, you're one of us too, sure. But I was talking about Starshine."

"What about Starshine?"

"That was her that got killed up at your place."

"The TV said the woman's name was Lindsey Durrell."

"Oh yeah, that's her *keiki* name, the name she was given by her *'ohana* when she was little. But she tol' us to call her Starshine. What was she was doin' over on that side of the island? And how'd she end up at your place?"

Good question, Makaila. Good question.

🔁 🔁 🔁

After I hung up from Makaila's call, I cried. I cranked up my Israel Kamakawiwo'ole "In Dis Life" CD and bawled almost as hard as when my *abuela* died. Pima stuck by me, her soft brown eyes watching my every move.

I cried for every sad thing that had ever happened to

me: my dad being murdered, my mom killing herself, my asshole boss accusing me of theft, and my friends abandoning me. I cried over my stupid car falling off the ferry and the bizarre sinkhole in my backyard. I cried because someone had abused Pima and I hadn't been able to stop it. I cried because I'd thought I'd been loved, but it turned out I was just one more toy that Derek Chambers felt he owned. I cried because Chloe had found true love and happiness and, in doing so, she'd left me to fend for myself. I even cried because although Keo and I seemingly enjoyed each other's company, I couldn't be sure he wasn't more interested in my money than me.

When I was finished with my boo-hoo fest, it occurred to me that I'd only cried for myself. I hadn't cried for my *abuela* losing her only son when he was thirty-three, or for my boss, Steve Harrow, dying of a wretched disease. I hadn't shed a single tear for the solemn-faced little kids who quietly played outside the food bank while their felonious parents worked off their court-ordered hours boxing dented canned goods for people too poor to feed their own children. And, horrible as it was to admit, I hadn't wept a single tear for Starshine, who'd been found dead right in my own backyard.

I took a shower and then made a call.

"Lightner Lexus."

"May I speak with Ana Pueo, please?" I said.

"Ana isn't in today. May I direct your call to someone else?"

"No, thank you. Ana is my salesperson. She's the only one I'm willing to work with. When is she scheduled to be back at work?"

"I'm afraid she won't be back," she said. "Ana isn't with us anymore."

I felt a prickle of panic. What did she mean by *not with us anymore*? Had Ana died too?

When I didn't say anything, she went on in a soft voice. "She was let go about a week ago. I'm not supposed to say anything, but I think she's working at Costco now. If you'd like to leave your number, I'll tell her you called. She's a friend of mine."

I left my name and number. And then, as if to make up for being so self-centered earlier, I cried over Ana Pueo being fired from a job she'd worked so hard to keep.

🜲 🜲 🜲

At about seven o'clock that night, my doorbell rang and Pima dashed to the foyer and "assumed the position"—legs stiff, ears pricked, and mouth yapping. I grabbed her up before I opened the door.

"Miss Gomez?" said a good-looking 30-ish Asian guy. Next to him was the same dour-faced man who'd asked me if the shovel was mine, so I assumed the two of them were with the police department.

"Yes."

The Asian guy pointed to a gold badge clipped to his belt and said, "I'm Detective Glen Wong from the Maui Police Department, and this is my partner, Detective Art Baker. Detective Baker's here on assignment from Honolulu PD, and we'll be working together on this case."

I got the distinct impression Wong wasn't thrilled about Baker being called in to help, but apparently someone higher up had insisted.

"May we come in and ask you a few questions?"

"I've pretty much already told my attorney everything I know," I said. "Maybe I should call her to come over."

"No need," said Baker. "We're just here to confirm a few things."

I invited them in and we went into the living room. They sat on the sofa and I went for an upholstered chair. As we jockeyed for position, I could tell Wong was not pleased when Baker suddenly got up and changed places. This left Wong marooned in the middle of the sofa, with Baker scrunched knee-to-knee with me.

Wong pulled a notepad from his shirt pocket and said, "How long have you lived here, Miss Gomez?"

It seemed like a ridiculous question. What did it matter how long I'd lived there? At this rate, we wouldn't get around to Starshine's body in my yard for another hour.

"I don't want to seem uncooperative, detectives, but I fail to see the relevance of the question. Can't we skip the small talk and get to what you really want to know?"

"And what is it you think we want to know?" said Wong.

"If I'm the one who killed Starshine. That is, Lindsey Durrell. I knew her as Starshine."

"So, you were acquainted with the victim?" said Baker.

"I have a hunch you already knew that," I said.

Wong frowned and tapped his pen on the notepad. "Perhaps we'd all be better served by taking a ride to Wailuku," he said.

"What for?" I said.

"I'm just thinking that taking your statement down at the station might be a better idea."

"I think we're doing fine here," said Baker.

Wong looked stung. "I need a minute with my partner." He glared at Baker. "Outside."

Wong got up and headed for the door.

Baker sighed. After a few moments of hesitation, he followed Wong outside.

Oh great. As if things weren't bad enough already, it appeared I was caught in an ongoing snit between two guys who didn't work well together.

By the time Wong and Baker finally left at ten o'clock that night, I was exhausted. They'd said the ME determined Starshine had died from cranial blunt force trauma sometime between ten o'clock Tuesday night and three o'clock Wednesday morning. I'd been here in the house that entire time.

I closed the door and dragged myself into my bedroom to get ready for bed. Before nodding off to sleep I reviewed what facts I had. Apparently Starshine had died from a blow to the head. The shovel in my backyard had blood on it. And she'd been killed within a five hour window while I was at home.

From the cops' point of view, from eleven o'clock on I didn't have an alibi. Not only that, my fingerprints were probably all over that shovel since I'd moved it before I'd left with Derek. It was no secret that Starshine and I had clashed. I'd probably told at least a half-dozen people I was sure she was the one who'd keyed my new car.

The way things were going, it wouldn't be long before I'd be named a "person of interest" if not an outright suspect. I prayed something would turn up that would exonerate me—or at least make me look less culpable—but Starshine had been dead for twenty-four hours, and, as far as I knew, nothing else had surfaced.

Lisa Neville had told me cops call the first forty-eight hours the *golden time*. During that period, they generate the best evidence and nail down the most likely suspects. So, here we were halfway through *golden time* and, at this point, I was pretty much "it."

CHAPTER 33

Bev called the next morning. She said Derek had agreed to the price she'd suggested after doing the CMA, and he'd given her the go-ahead to list the house

"Do you want to go with me when I do the inventory?" she said. "It might help get your mind off things."

"What's an inventory?"

"Like a lot of high-end homes, Derek is selling his house fully furnished. I need to itemize all the personal property that will be included in the sale."

"I've never been in Derek's house before," I said.

"Really? I'm surprised. It's a beautiful home, half-again larger than your house because it's got a lower level as well as the main level. He had it professionally decorated. C'mon, I'm sure you're curious to see the stuff you're going to be missing out on now that the two of you have called it quits."

I wasn't at all curious, but I was bored. The media vans were gone and the police had removed the crime tape from across my driveway so I could now leave. The backyard was still taped and I'd been warned not to go back there, but from all outward appearances, Paradise Ridge was back to its pretentious version of normal.

I parked at Bev's house and the two of us walked over to Derek's. Bev was chattering on about how grateful she was

that Lindsay, aka Starshine, had been killed after the gala and not before, since the media had made a lot of noise about Starshine working at the food bank.

"The fund raiser was a complete success," Bev said. "We actually showed the biggest profit ever. When you only have to feed a couple dozen people instead of a hundred, it really makes a difference."

I wasn't in the mood to sing Derek's praises, nor to think about anything associated with the food bank. I wished I'd never even heard of it. Keo still hadn't called, and I felt like a fool for acting like such a pathetic slut on Tuesday night. And now that all fingers were pointing at me, I wondered if Bev would visit me in prison. I knew better than to ask if she'd watch Pima for me, but I hoped she'd at least help me find a suitable pet sitter before they hauled me off in handcuffs.

Bev unlocked the door to Derek's house and, as we stepped inside, we both gasped. Derek may have had his delusional moments, but he'd been realistic about one thing: his house was a pig-sty. Clothes, food, and dirty dishes were strewn everywhere. It looked as if bears had broken in for one final binge before going into hibernation; or an angry loan-shark had ordered his minions to toss the place in an effort to find the cash he was owed.

"Whew. This is going to take some staging," said Bev. I could tell she was disappointed in Derek's complete lack of housekeeping skills. I'm sure it didn't jive with her "king of all that" image she held of him, and it certainly didn't jive with his claim that he'd had house cleaners working there just a few days earlier.

"I'll tell you what," she said. "Why don't we start on the outside and work our way in? I'm going to call in some top-notch cleaning people I know. After they're finished, it will be much easier to do the inventory."

We went out to the front yard. Derek's landscaping was done in a somewhat Zen-style, with a little sand area that was raked into an interesting pattern, and a few knee-high bonsai trees planted among clumps of ornamental grasses.

"Huh," said Bev. "I could've sworn there was a little stone pagoda right over there."

She pointed to the near edge of the sand area, and we walked over to check it out.

"See? It sat right there."

There were four small dents in the sand, spaced to form a square. "It was the sweetest little thing. Derek told me it'd been a gift from a business associate in Hong Kong."

"Looks like someone ripped it off," I said.

"In Paradise Ridge?" Bev's voice was shrill. "Well, I guess that's what we get for allowing people who aren't licensed and bonded to work up here. One minute they're snaking out your toilet, and the next minute they're helping themselves to your yard art."

We cataloged the various "yard art" that hadn't been stolen, including a four-foot tall bronze crane statue, a beautiful red lacquer bench, and a covey of small concrete birds that reminded me of the quail in Southern Arizona.

Bev took photos of both the front and back yard, careful to get the best angle on the expansive ocean view.

"Should we tackle the garage?" I said.

Derek had a five-car garage that seemed to include nearly as much square-footage as the footprint of the house.

"No, let's let the cleaners muck it out first," said Bev. "You look tired. You want to stop over at the house for a bite of lunch?"

When I pulled into my driveway later that afternoon, I was surprised to see Wong and Baker sitting in their car outside my gate. I parked in the garage, and before I could close the overhead door, the two of them appeared in the doorway.

"Mind if we take a quick look around?" Baker said.

I'd seen enough cop shows to know I probably should've demanded they get a warrant, but I didn't want to appear uncooperative. Besides, what did I have to hide?

They poked around while I killed time watching the afternoon soaps. I chuckled at the various plots: Copper's new boyfriend had supposedly killed her mother and had gotten away with it so her family hated him; Tipani's baby probably wasn't Reed's after all, but Leighton refused to take a paternity test.

Ha! I thought. *If they need to come up with more crazy stuff for their story lines, they should give me a call.*

At four-thirty, Ana Pueo called. "It was good to hear from you yesterday," she said. "I'm sorry I couldn't call back sooner, but I work most nights until ten. I'm off tonight, though. You want to go get a drink somewhere?"

"Thanks, but I don't know if I should. I'm afraid I've got a lot going on right now," I said.

"I know. I saw you on the news. That's why I thought you might need a friend—and a drink."

We made plans to meet at eight that night. She suggested Momi's, but I asked if we could make it Roy's in Ka'anapali instead.

"Ooh, spendy," she said. "I'm afraid I don't get paid until tomorrow."

"No worries," I said. "My treat."

"*Mahalo*. Then I guess I'll see you at Roy's."

I clicked off the call and heard the man door that goes from the house to the garage slam shut. Pima pricked up her ears.

A few seconds later, Detective Wong entered the kitchen holding out a thick plastic bag about the size of a small pillowcase. He held the top in a tight grip in one hand while supporting the bottom with his other hand, as if the contents were heavy.

"What can you tell me about this?" he said.

I peered through the cloudy plastic of the bag. Inside was a square light-gray object about eight inches high and six inches on each side. Reddish-brown stains were visible through the plastic.

Seems Wong had come up with Derek's AWOL "yard art" without even realizing it was missing.

CHAPTER 34

I called Lisa Neville and she made it to my house in fifteen minutes. Pima put up her usual racket as Lisa came to the door.

"I see you're a pretty good watch-dog, after all," she said.

I could see her filing that away for future reference. *"But, your Honor, her dog would've gone ballistic if an intruder had been in the back yard."*

No wait, I thought. That would make my defense even weaker. If the dog didn't bark—isn't that what cracked a well-known Sherlock Holmes case? I guess I should've listened up in my sophomore year high school English class.

"What's this nonsense about additional evidence?" Lisa said to Wong.

"We found what we believe to be the murder weapon in your client's garage," he said.

"Do you have a warrant?"

"Don't need one," he said. "She allowed us inside."

Lisa shot me a "you're not making this easy for me" look and asked to see the evidence.

Wong took her outside to his police car and Baker stayed inside with me.

"You know, if you confess, I could ask the DA for leniency," he said in the same tone one would use to order a vanilla latte at Starbucks.

"If I'd done anything wrong, I might take you up on that," I said. "But I haven't."

"From all accounts, the victim was making life difficult for you. She allegedly damaged your car, and some folks believe she may have kidnapped your dog. One witness claims she overheard Miss Durrell bragging about dumping a rotten fish at your house."

"I didn't know she'd done that."

"Maybe so, but I'll bet you had your suspicions. Harassment is tough, because it's hard to prove. I guess some people might feel the only way to stop it is to stop whoever's doing it."

Lisa came back inside and Wong followed close behind.

"Either charge my client or leave right now," Lisa said.

Baker spoke up. "We'll be on our way. But tell your client she needs to stay put. If this does turn out to be the murder weapon, we'll be back to follow-up."

They left, and Lisa turned to me. "They were doing us a favor, you know. They didn't have to alert you that they found that ...whatever it was."

"It's a stone pagoda," I said. "Yard art. And I'm pretty sure I know whose yard it came from."

Lisa raised an eyebrow. "Are you going to make me ask?"

"Uh, no, sorry. It was from my former boyfriend's yard. His name is Derek Chambers. He's the guy I broke up with on Tuesday night."

"Huh," said Lisa. "And where might I find this Derek Chambers? I'd like to send my private investigator around for a little chat."

"He's on a business trip," I said. "In the Middle East. Most probably Dubai or Saudi Arabia or someplace like that. He's in the oil business."

"In-ter-es-ting," she said, dragging the word out in four distinct syllables.

"Yeah, it is interesting. I'm not exactly sure what he does, but he makes a boat-load of money doing it."

"No, what I meant was, it's interesting that he chose to go to a part of the world where the United States has no extradition treaties."

"You don't think..."

"Right now my entire focus is on your defense," she said. "I don't care whether this man is guilty or not. My sole concern is to create reasonable doubt. Short of proving your innocence, of course."

Lisa left and I began getting ready to go meet Ana at Roy's. I was looking for my keys when my cell pinged that I had a text message. I checked, and it was Derek.

I want the rubies. Lv at front door. Bev will pick up.

Technically, I didn't have to return the jewelry since it'd been a gift. But with the most recent development in the Starshine murder investigation, I thought it prudent to not provoke him.

Will do, I texted back.

I checked Pima's food and water before making made my way out to my car. It was seven-thirty, so I had half-an-hour to get to Ka'anapali. Just enough time to drop off the rubies and still make it to Roy's on time.

ᘓ ᘓ ᘓ

I parked in Derek's driveway and left the car running as I went to the door. I looked around to find a safe place to stash the jewelry case and settled on tucking it behind a potted bonsai tree.

As I started to straighten up, an arm shot around my neck, squeezing tight.

A low voice said, "One word and it'll be your last."

I felt something sharp poke into my side.

"Yeah, that's right. It's a knife. Hand over your purse."

My mind scrambled. Had a robber intercepted Derek's text to me? But the voice sounded a lot like Derek's. But Derek was in Dubai, wasn't he?

I wanted to scream, to plead, to ask what was going on, but the choke hold had cut off my windpipe and I was beginning to lose consciousness. I felt a shove and the arm released the hold on my neck. I sputtered and coughed as I heard a door slam. When I looked up, I was inside Derek's house.

"What are you doing?" I said, once I could breathe again. My eyes focused and Derek was brandishing the biggest knife I'd ever seen. It was curved, like a sickle, with Arabic letters carved into the two-inch thick blade.

"I'm doing what any guy with a decent set of balls would do," he said. "I'm taking back what's mine."

"What are you talking about? I returned the rubies. What else is there?"

"Look, I don't answer to you," he said. "In fact, from now on, you answer to me. That's how it is, so get used to it."

I stared at him. His face was flushed, and he was breathing hard. Deep in his eyes I saw the remorseless look of a coyote going for the kill.

"You think you can make a fool of me and get away with it?" he said. "You and that other damn bitch? I'm on to you both, you know. How the two of you were scheming behind my back. She told me everything. *Everything.*"

"Who are you talking about?"

"Who do you think? That meth head you stuck me with at the fund raiser dinner. A dinner I paid for, I might add. Well, he who laughs last, right? I made sure she won't be pulling shit like that on me anymore. Now it's your turn."

"Are you talking about Starshine? Did you kill her? Why?"

"Shut up," he said. "Like I said, I'll be the one asking the questions from now on. But first, you gotta make amends. Step nine, right?"

He put the tip of the curved blade to the back of my neck and marched me down a hallway. I wished I'd taken the time when I'd been there with Bev to walk through the house. Where were we going, his bedroom? A bitter taste rose in the back of my throat. I was pretty sure what he had in store for me and I could handle it. I'd comply, be submissive. Hopefully the wound on my elbow wouldn't open up and bleed all over the sheets.

About halfway down the hall, he grabbed my bad arm and pulled me to a halt. I cried out in pain.

"Shut up," he said.

He fumbled with his key ring and unlocked what appeared to be a closet door. He shoved me inside and snapped on a dim light. It wasn't a closet, after all. The door led to a short flight of narrow carpeted stairs which led down to another closed door.

"Get down there," he said.

I stumbled down the five or six stairs. Derek jangled his keys and reached around me to unlock the door.

When he pushed the second door open, I noticed it was at least four inches thick and it had a metal lining on the back side. Beyond it was a pitch black room. Anyway, I assumed it was a room. I couldn't see walls or a ceiling, only a carpeted wedge of floor visible in the faint light from the stairs. Derek pushed me inside. With a grunt, he pulled the heavy door closed between us.

I heard a bolt fall into place and the air around me became still and deadly silent. Blackness engulfed me like water rushing into the lungs of a drowning swimmer.

CHAPTER 35

I spent the first hours I was entombed exploring my unseen surroundings by touch. It was odd how the darkness seemed to burst into flashes of color when I encountered something new: the metal rivets on the back of the door or the inch-thick seams where the nubby fabric covering the padded walls had been pieced together. I was never able to make contact with the ceiling, even when I jumped as high as I could, but I figured it was also padded like the walls. I also assumed there might even be lights in the ceiling, but that was just a guess.

The pitch-black chamber must've been built as some sort of "safe room." A place where a rich guy like Derek could take shelter if he was ever under siege by armed robbers or if he needed to wait out extreme weather, like a hurricane. The mystery was why he'd never put a single stick of furniture in there. If he'd had to wait out a storm or hide until help arrived, it would've been just that much more tedious sitting on the floor.

For me, the room wasn't a sanctuary, it was a prison. Derek could hold me incommunicado for as long as he wished without worrying about anyone spoiling his fun. I prayed the novelty would wear off soon and he'd let me out because I'd never been a very patient person, and ever since I was a little kid I'd been afraid of the dark.

Even more pressing, I had to go to the bathroom. In my exploration I'd quickly come to the conclusion there were no "conveniences" of any kind. No toilet, no sink, not even a bucket. How had he planned to literally weather a storm with "nary a pot to piss in?"

If it had been anyone but Derek who'd abducted me, I would've been thinking this was some kind of kidnap for ransom. I could just imagine the kidnapper's frustration when he tried to find someone to hit up for my ransom money. After all, I had no family, no business associates, and the few friends I had would have no way of accessing my accounts. I suppose if the perp had done some research he might've come up with John Dease, my Arizona attorney. But John had been adamant about not becoming my trustee. *"Sorry, kid, but I've got my own neck to think about here,"* he'd said. *"I don't want it anywhere near Steve Harrow's chopping block."*

After what seemed like a few hours, I resorted to peeing in a corner. I had a hunch I'd probably pay dearly for sullying Derek's carpet—even though the carpet upstairs was filthy—but I felt immeasurably more cheerful once I'd emptied my bladder. Even cheerful enough to sleep.

I awoke and thought I heard something: a scrape of furniture across the floor above, maybe a footfall, I couldn't be sure. So, I began screaming. At first I screamed "help." Then, after my voice grew raw and became barely more than a whisper, I made a guttural sound that didn't tax my vocal cords so much.

I'd paced off the entire space and estimated it to be about twelve by fifteen feet: four strides across one side and five on the other. I'd yelled in different parts of the room, including each of the corners and then the middle, but I reasoned I had the greatest chance of being heard over by the door. I huddled with my mouth pressed against the crack where the door met the wall, making keening noises until I was too weak to stand. I hoped that if anyone was upstairs, they might hear me and become curious about the odd sounds coming from behind the locked door in the hallway.

Hadn't Bev said she wanted to get the house on the market right away? Wouldn't she be showing the house, even if it was only to other realtors, to drum up interest? And what about those house cleaners that both Bev and Derek had talked about? Maybe they were upstairs right that minute trying to get the house ship shape for potential buyers. Wouldn't they say something to Bev about a locked door they couldn't access? Or would they just assume it was "owner's storage" and move on?

After my voice gave out entirely, I crumpled to the floor and once again, I fell asleep.

۞ ۞ ۞

When I awoke, I panicked for a few seconds. Believe me, waking in absolute darkness with no sound and no air-flow is a startling experience. It took me a few beats to recollect where I was and who had put me there. The "how" and "why" were fuzzy, and anyway, it wasn't something I wanted to think about.

My stomach was growling and my mouth dry, but other than that I had no idea how much time had passed since Derek had closed and bolted the metal-clad door. I was wearing a watch, but the watch face wasn't luminescent. In the inky-black of the room, time-keeping—like water, food, and fresh air—were luxuries I no longer enjoyed.

After a while my abduction came flooding back to me, as if someone had switched on a full-color video in my head. I saw my cell phone screen with the text from Derek asking me to return the rubies. I visualized standing at his front door, the knife at my throat, and Derek admitting he'd killed Starshine. I couldn't quite recall his exact words, but I assumed she must have also done or said something to set him off.

I stayed awake puzzling over how Derek had known Starshine. After all, she hardly ran with the same well-heeled crowd he did. I should've been more inquisitive at the fund-raiser. But I seriously doubt either one would've told me the truth. But what could a tattooed, surly, food bank worker have said or done to enrage a wealthy oil speculator enough to make him kill her? Nothing was adding up, and just thinking about it taxed my already depleted resources.

I went back to sleep.

🙾 🙾 🙾

I tossed and turned and once again awoke with a start. The carpeting that had felt smooth and spongy when Derek had first shoved me in there now felt like burlap over concrete. I thought about Pima and hoped someone would find her before the water in her dish ran out. Had I put the toilet lid down before I left? For once, I hoped I hadn't and Pima would resort to drinking out of the toilet.

I tried to get up but couldn't muster the energy. Was I giving in to hopelessness or was it something more serious, like oxygen deprivation? How long had I been in there? A few hours? Or even a day, maybe two?

I'd expected Derek to make an appearance after a few hours, even if only to pile on more threats or slap me around, but he hadn't showed. Had he kept Starshine in this room before he killed her? I pushed that thought out of my mind and closed my eyes and fell asleep again.

I dreamed of old TV shows like "I Love Lucy" that I used to watch with my *abuela*. She loved Lucille Ball. She called her "*Pelo Rojo*" or "red hair." She used to come to my room and alert me when the reruns were on TV.

"Come quick, *mija*, Pelo Rojo is on."

As I lay there in the dark, it suddenly occurred to me that my *abuela* must've seen Lucille Ball somewhere other than just on reruns of "I Love Lucy." How else would she have known she had red hair? The "I Love Lucy" show in the nineteen-fifties was filmed in black and white.

I began playing video games in my head. I liked the old stand-bys: Plants vs. Zombies, Bejeweled, Zuma's Revenge. I mentally won and lost numerous games, marveling at the dazzling colors on my mental computer screen.

After a seemingly endless game of Bejeweled, I realized I didn't feel hungry anymore. I guessed by that time I'd been in there two days, maybe three, but I'd only peed once. I was ridiculously thirsty and would've happily written a six-figure check for a bottle of water. But the thought of food made me nauseous.

۞ ۞ ۞

I made peace with the darkness, but the silence still felt menacing. After that first illusion of noise I never heard another sound. No squeak from footfalls upstairs, no rustle of wind, no whoosh of passing traffic. It was as if time had stopped, and sleep was the only proof of my existence.

I dragged myself over to the corner of the room so I could sit up with my back against the wall. Funny, how things come to you in times like this. I thought about winning the money, and how all the money in the world couldn't save me now. There was no one to hire, no one to bribe, no fancy gadget or glorious bobble I could trade for my freedom.

I knew that if I ever got out of there I'd be able to see money for what it really was. When I hadn't had enough,

I'd imagined money equaled freedom. If you had enough money, you'd truly know what it meant to be free. Now I realized it merely offered opportunity. Opportunity to do more, learn more, and help out more. Too bad I'd been a slow learner.

I was inching toward accepting I was probably going to die in a sealed room in Derek Chamber's house. And, if so, I really wanted to grasp the last bit of self-control available to me. To die on my own terms. I tried holding my breath, but after a count of thirty-two I exhaled: gasping and sputtering like I had when Derek choked me.

Acknowledging I'd used up the last vestige of my personal power saddened me and I cried. No tears, though. I was too dehydrated for that. Instead, a series of dry wracking sobs convulsed my body until I was exhausted.

As my mind drifted into the infinite blackness, I prayed I wouldn't wake up. But I knew God may take a while to answer. It was only fair. I hadn't been in touch with Him ever since my *abuela* died, when my obligation to attend church slipped from mandatory to optional. I hoped the Almighty might cut me a little slack, though, especially under the circumstances.

Periods of wakefulness and sleep continued, seemingly without end. I stopped trying to determine how much time had passed. It was impossible to know. I remembered reading that a person can go up to three weeks without food, but most people die within a week without water. My shriveled tongue and scratchy, burning eyes signaled my seven days was probably about over. Sharp spasms shot through my back. Were my kidneys shutting down?

I crawled back over to the door and lay down, crossing my arms over my chest as if I were already in my coffin. I didn't want to give Derek the satisfaction of finding my body in a pose of desperation. If nothing else, I'd die with a shred of my dignity intact.

ↄ ↄ ↄ

I awoke to a loud mechanical whine and a blinding light fell across my face. Was this the "bright light" people spoke of who'd had near-death experiences? Then a shadow blocked the light and I heard the muffled sound of foot-steps on carpet. I felt something soft and wet against my cheek. I squinted, trying to recognize who had come in, but the light stung my eyes and I clamped them shut.

I was lifted by hands digging under my shoulders and the back of my legs. Had Derek come back to finish what he'd started? I fought to make out the face of the person carrying me, but my eyes wouldn't focus. When I tried to speak, my cracked lips and shriveled tongue refused to function. I sent up one final prayer for mercy and, once again, slipped into darkness.

CHAPTER 36

I had a sensation of floating above, looking down on the scene. My "angel self" observed my inert body being laid on a soft narrow bed and rolled along a bumpy path to the open doors of a brightly-lit compartment. As I passed along the path, I made out a few familiar faces: Bev, Max and his wife, Nancy. Even Keo Kekane was there. He was holding Pima and she tried to wiggle free as I went by. I felt a slight sting in my arm and my world went black again.

I awoke to blue-white light and unfamiliar smells.

"Am I dead?" I said to the mahogany-skinned woman standing over me.

"You came awful close," she said with a wry smile. "I'll ring for the doctor to let him know you're awake."

"Am I in a hospital?"

"Yeah, and not any too soon. Do you want me to stay with you until the doctor shows up?"

Her voice was low and caramel smooth, and I reveled in the joy of hearing it.

"Maybe just a little while."

I wanted to go back to sleep but fought the feeling.

She said, "You know, you had us all pretty worried. Can I get you anything? Water? Something to eat?"

The mention of food made my stomach clench and I gagged.

She carefully laid a hand on my shoulder. "Don't think about it. We've got IV's going so you're being rehydrated. You're gonna be okay."

"What happened?"

"We don't need to go into that just yet. The doctor's on his way."

I began to drift away. The white ceiling, sharp smells, and pinging noises felt overwhelming, and I ached to return to the comfort of nothingness. Then I recalled the black room and I snapped my eyes open.

"I need to talk to the police," I said.

"All in good time."

"No, I need to tell them who killed Starshine."

"You mean that other girl? Seems they already have a pretty good idea. Once they found you, they put out an all-points on the man who owns the house where you were found." She flicked at an IV bag hanging above me. "What you need now is rest. The doctor will be here real soon."

The clock on the wall read 10:47. I watched the second had sweep around the face and marveled at the beauty of it. As I took in the hospital room—the chair in the corner, the pitcher of water by the bed, the TV mounted to the ceiling— everything seemed incredible. I wondered how long I'd feel this way before going back to not noticing.

"What day is today?" I said.

"It's Thursday."

"Really? I think I went to Derek's house on a Thursday."

"That sounds about right," she said. "On the news, the police said they'd been looking for you for the better part of a week."

"I thought people died if they went a week without water."

"Most do. Seems you're a lucky girl."

The doctor came in, head down, flipping through pages on a clipboard.

He looked up. "Good to see you back with us. You came in severely dehydrated, but other than that, you're in a lot better shape than we might've expected."

"How did I get here?"

"Ambulance. The police had all but given up when your friend showed up with your dog."

"Is my dog okay?"

"Your dog's fine. That dog saved your life."

"Wait. I'm not following you. What happened?"

"I guess a friend of yours took the dog to search for you. When they went into the house where'd been locked up, the dog located you right away. It's all over the news."

"What friend?"

"A local man. On the news reports he said he's a friend of yours from the Maui Food Bank."

"Max?"

"Could be. I don't recall the name."

The nurse came back in the room and the doctor asked if she remembered the name of the man who'd found me.

She grinned. "Oh sure. It was Keo Kekane, that nice local boy who runs the food bank here in Wailuku. When my sista lost her job, that place really helped her out. We took her in, but she's got four kids. No way I could feed all of 'em on my salary."

She shot a bit of *stink eye* at the doctor. "You see, we don't make even half what these doctors here do."

"Keo found me?"

"Yes, and it was a good thing he did," said the doctor. "The paramedics reported you flat-lined at least twice on the ride over here. Let's check you out. You may still have some bruising from the defibrillator."

The doctor palpated my chest and abdomen and I winced when he hit a few tender spots. But I was so happy to be alive I kept quiet.

"You're in amazingly good shape," he said. "I'd like to keep you here for the rest of the week, just to be sure nothing pops up, but by Sunday, you'll be free to go home."

"Great," I said. But things weren't great. There was no denying the eight-hundred-pound gorilla in the antiseptically-clean room that no one wanted to talk about, including me.

The doctor headed for the door, but at the last minute, he looked back at the nurse. "I'll lift the ban on visitors. But no media and no police, understood?"

"No worries," she said. "At home my husband calls me a 'pit bull in a *mu'u mu'u.*' Any of those folks try to get through this door, they're gonna have to go over me or under me. And what comes out the other side won't be pretty."

The doctor threw her a *shaka*—that Hawaiian wave with the thumb and pinkie finger—and walked out.

I shut my eyes and when I woke up again, there was a commotion in the hall. I tried to sit up, but with IVs running in both arms and the sheets tucked tightly to the bed, I must've looked like an overturned beetle trying to right itself.

A few seconds later, the door opened and Bev peeked in. She was holding a large bouquet of protea flowers.

"Are you decent?" she said.

"As decent as anyone can be in a nightgown that's split open in the back." I continued to struggle to sit up. "It's good to see you."

"Let me help you," she said. She bounded over to my bedside and placed the flowers on my over-the-bed tray table. Then she grabbed a remote control that was hanging at the top of the bed. I heard a low hum and my upper body began to tilt upward.

"*Mahalo* for the gorgeous flowers," I said, fingering the soft plush of one of the saucer-sized blooms. "And thanks for getting me upright. I had no idea this bed could do that."

"Haven't you ever been in a hospital before?" she said.

"No, when I was little my *abuela* just patched me up as best she could. She even set a broken arm for me one time." I tenderly felt along my left forearm, trying to locate the bump where the bone had healed somewhat misaligned.

"That's terrible," said Bev.

"No, that's how poor people deal with things," I said. "What's terrible is Derek Chambers murdering Starshine, and then trying to do the same to me."

"Why is everyone saying that?" Her strident voice echoed off the pale green walls. "There is absolutely no way that's true, Monica. You've been through a horrible ordeal, but you must stop making these unfounded, and frankly, offensive and unwarranted accusations!"

The nurse pushed through the door, her brow furrowed. "What's going on in here? This patient is on total bed-rest. That means no yelling. If you can't keep your voice down, I'm gonna have to ask you to leave."

She bustled over to check the beeping machines on the side of the bed. "Look at that. This patient's BP is up thirty points. I've a good mind to call security to escort you outta here."

"No, I'm fine," I said. "I was just telling my friend about my ordeal. I guess thinking about it got me a little worked up."

Bev crossed her arms but said nothing until the nurse left the room.

"What on earth are you saying?" she said in a low hiss. "Derek had nothing to do with any of this. He's been in Dubai since before you disappeared. The only reason I've been waiting in this wretched hospital for an entire sleepless night is to ask why in the world you broke into his house."

"Bev, I didn't break in. Derek shoved me into that safe room at knife-point. He locked me in there."

"That's preposterous. When I called him to alert him that you'd gone missing, he was frantic. He offered to fly home right away, but I told him there was already a huge search underway. He even offered a reward for finding you. Why would he do that if he was the one who'd put you in there?"

"Because he's nuts, Bev. He admitted to me that he killed Starshine. He lured me to his house by demanding that I return his jewelry, and when I got there he pulled a knife on me. He left me there to die."

Bev bit her lip and sat down hard in the guest chair.

"I just can't believe this. I've been in that house at least a half dozen times since you disappeared. Everyone thought you'd left the island to avoid being arrested."

"What I'm telling you is true," I said. "And if Derek wasn't in Dubai when he called you, he probably is still here. I'm a little worried about what I'm going to do when I get out of here. I don't want to go back to my house."

"I'd offer to have you stay with me, but since I live next door..."

"It's fine. I'll check into a hotel under a fake name. Would you do me a favor?"

"Of course, anything."

"Find me a place that will let me have my dog."

CHAPTER 37

Soon after Bev left, Keo showed up with a huge exotic-looking plant sporting pink and white blossoms the size of my hand. It didn't look as if it had come from a florist, it was in a too-small green plastic bucket and it listed to one side. He grinned and ducked his head as he placed it on the bedside table.

"Sorry about the screwy-looking orchid," he said. "It looked a lot smaller when I dug it up."

"It's beautiful. And you dug it up? Did you steal it?"

He laughed. "No, I have orchids at my house. This is one of my favorites."

"Then you shouldn't have dug it up. I want you to take it back and re-plant it. Bring me a cheesy stuffed animal or balloons or something."

He shrugged. "No worries. I've got lots of 'em."

"I'm sorry about what happened to Starshine," I said. "And I'm so grateful to you for finding me. I...uh..."

How do you thank someone for saving your life? I hadn't had time to think it through, and I was scrambling for the right words.

"It was dumb luck," he said. "I went to check on Pima after I heard you'd gone missing. I went every day to feed her, and then one day it just hit me. If you were somewhere close by, she'd find you. Turned out, you were. And she did."

"I'm curious. What did people think had happened to me?"

"The police went to your house on Friday morning—"

"To arrest me for Starshine's murder?"

"They didn't say. Your car was in your driveway, so they checked with the airport to see if you'd left the island. After coming up empty there, they gained access and searched your house. I came over while they were there and when Pima came out from hiding, I told them something wasn't right. There was no way you'd leave your dog behind.

Anyway, by about the fifth day, it hit me that maybe it would help to take Pima out to nose around a little. The cops had already searched Chambers' house, but when I called Bev and asked her if I could bring Pima over there, she agreed to let me in. The dog went nuts when we got to that locked door in the hallway. Bev didn't have a key for it. We called in the cops, and once they saw the second locked door downstairs, things moved pretty fast."

"Bev said Derek put up a reward for finding me. Is that true?"

He nodded his head. "Can you believe it? I gotta hand it to him, the guy's got balls. More than likely, he figured it would throw suspicion off him."

"Which it did."

"Not for me, it didn't. I had my own theory about his involvement in Starshine's murder."

"What theory? Why would he do it?" My eyes were getting heavy, but I was more than a little curious about the connection between Derek and Starshine.

"That's enough for now," Keo said. "You look wiped out. The good news is Pima sniffed you out and you're alive."

A few beats of awkward silence passed.

"Keo," I said. "I'm tired, but I won't be able to rest until I understand why Derek would hurt Starshine. At the fund raiser he told me he knew her, but he made it sound pretty casual."

He blew out a breath. "Well, she's gone now, so I guess I can talk about it. Starshine had a big problem with drugs. She got clean about a year ago, but at one time she was the 'go-to' girl for cocaine and tar heroin here on Maui."

He held eye contact with me as if hoping I'd figure out what came next.

My hand flew to my mouth. "What about Derek? Was he a drug addict, too?"

"You saw how stressed the dude is. Seems he uses a good chunk of all that money he rakes in to party pretty hardy. One thing about addicts is they all think they're getting away with it, like it's all on the down-low. But on an island like this, everybody knows."

"You knew he was an addict?" I said. "Why didn't you warn me?"

"I tried to, remember?"

"So, you hired Starshine to work at the food bank when she got clean."

"Yeah."

"But she acted like you two were way more than just boss and employee."

"Well, that's 'cuz we were. I was her NA sponsor. You know, Narcotics Anonymous. Her first sponsor was a woman, but that didn't work out. You're supposed to have a sponsor the same sex as yourself, but Starshine didn't get along with women. Mommy issues, I guess. Anyway, after she'd run off all the women in her group, I agreed to do it."

He shook his head. "It was the toughest job I ever had."

"Huh. So, if you were her sponsor, does that mean...?"

"Yeah, I'm an addict too. I've been clean for nearly seven years now, but you know what they say, 'If you *were*, then you *are*.'"

The door opened and a different nurse came in. She shot Keo a flirty smile and said, "Sorry to intrude, but I'll need you to step out for a few minutes. I want to get our girl here cleaned up."

Keo nodded. "I should be getting back to the office."

I reached over and grabbed his hand. "Please don't leave."

He wrapped his warm fingers around mine.

"Okay. I'll be waiting right outside."

➥ ➥ ➥

Keo was still there when Bev showed up again at four o'clock. I felt guilty about asking them to babysit me, since I slept so much, but the thought of waking up alone was terrifying.

"I swear I've gone to every decent hotel on Maui," said Bev. "But none of them is keen on housing a long-term guest with a dog. I've tried bribing, pleading, you name it. I even opened my blouse a bit and hinted to one especially oily manager that I was single and always looking for a 'good time.' But he didn't budge on the dog issue. Come to think of it, I probably should've been insulted."

I had to choke back a laugh. The thought of tightly-wound Bev Strong seductively undoing the top few buttons on her silk Donna Karen blouse to give a smarmy hotel manager a peek at the goods was a visual that would crack anyone up.

"Well, I'm not willing to leave Pima. I guess I'll have to go back to my house and hope for the best."

"Not a chance," said Bev. "You and your puppy will move in with me."

She choked a little on the word, *puppy*. "I'll hire a security guard."

"You think that's a good idea?" said Keo. "I mean, Chambers is still on the loose and his place is right next door. It's dangerous, even with a security guard."

I shuddered at the thought of ever seeing Derek's house again, but kept quiet.

"You should stay with me," Keo went on. "I've got room, and no one will ever find you there."

"The sooner I can get out of here, the better," I said. "Every time someone comes in this room I panic, thinking it's going to be Derek."

"No need for panic. There's a police officer right outside your door," said Bev.

"There's a cop in the hall?"

"Yep," said Keo. "Twenty-four/seven,"

Bev added, "And I'm doing what I can to keep them there. I have Sam's Saimin bringing in lunch and dinner every day to keep 'em happy. No one should expect Maui's finest to eat nasty hospital food."

"Speaking of food," said Keo. "I really should get back to work. I left Makaila to deal with all of it: Starshine's memorial service, the media hanging around, Chambers' bad check—"

"What bad check?" I said.

"Yeah, pretty lame, eh? Seems he stopped payment on his fund raiser check before it could clear the bank."

"I didn't want to tell you," said Bev. "Because I was hoping it might've simply been a bank error. But as it turned out…"

I already hated Derek, but stiffing the food bank was the absolute last straw.

"Seriously?" I said. "The check bounced?"

Keo shrugged. "It happens. But now we're scrambling to keep the doors open."

He turned to go, but I called him back.

"I'll stay at your place," I said. "On one condition."

Keo laughed. "Don't worry, you can have the bedroom. It's got a lock on the door. I'm fine sleeping on the sofa."

"I'm not worried about that. My condition is you let me pay rent."

He and Bev shared an indulgent smile.

"*Mahalo*, but wait 'til you see the place," said Keo. "We're talking a nine-hundred square-foot *hale* with floors that haven't been mopped since the Bush administration—the first Bush, not the second. If you'll help me cook, that's enough."

"No, I insist. And I'd like to move in tomorrow."

"I thought the doctor said they're keeping you here through the weekend." said Bev.

"I'm done with being held against my will," I said. "I'm outta here tomorrow."

CHAPTER 38

On Friday afternoon after an especially uninspired hospital lunch, I got out of bed and slipped on the robe Bev had brought me from home. I told the cop at the door the doctor had ordered me to get some exercise so I was going for a short walk. He offered to go with me, but I assured him I'd be fine and I'd rather he kept an eye on my room.

When I got to the end of the hall, I took the stairs down to Bev's waiting car. She'd packed me a bag of street clothes and I wrestled into underwear, pants and a top in the car. Fully dressed, I could really tell I'd lost a lot of weight. My pants gaped around my waist and my shirt hung from my shoulders like a child playing dress-up. But it felt good to be out of bed and back out in fresh air and sunshine.

Bev turned onto the Hana Highway. "The police aren't going to be happy when they figure out you've escaped."

"Why? I'm no longer a suspect."

"True, but they told me you're considered a material witness. And Derek still hasn't been found. They want to keep an eye on you."

"Maybe after I got rescued he actually did go to Dubai."

"Hard to know. According to the news, they're still searching. Apparently there's no record of Derek's passport being used to get on an international flight."

"But he could've flown to LA or Seattle and then gone on to the Middle East," I said.

"Maybe, but supposedly the authorities checked the national database and his passport hasn't shown up as being used anywhere."

My hands felt clammy. "Do you think if he's still here he'll come after me?"

"I have no idea, but you probably should stay with Keo until they find him."

ꙮ ꙮ ꙮ

Upcountry Maui is so different from Kapalua it's like going from Phoenix to Flagstaff in Arizona. Same state, totally different surroundings. The rolling green hills and blooming purple jacaranda trees on the flanks of Mount Haleakala are as visually stunning as any sweeping ocean view, but it was hard to imagine we were still on the same island.

Keo's blue truck was parked at a spot where a gravel road met Baldwin Avenue. The narrow roadway was unmarked except for a weathered wooden sign nailed to a fencepost. The sign's fading paint showed a smiling Buddha sitting on a cloud. I inwardly chuckled, remembering how Keo's calm composure had reminded me of Buddha the day I'd agreed to join the food bank advisory board.

Bev pulled over and stopped. "I hope you don't mind me not taking you all the way to the house. But I just had my car detailed and, as you can see, that road's pretty rough."

I gave her a sideways hug and thanked her for helping me make my getaway.

"Don't thank me," she said. "I got you into this whole mess. I'll never forgive myself for what Derek did."

I assured her I didn't hold her responsible, and got out.

Keo gave me a perfunctory hug before helping me up into the passenger seat. We started down the rutted driveway and a minute later, four large rambunctious brown dogs bounded toward us. Keo kept the truck moving forward, the dogs dashing away seconds before being run over.

"See what I mean about you being safe up here?" he said. "That's my top notch security detail."

By the time the tiny brown house came into view, the dogs were frantically leaping and barking against the driver's side door. Keo got out and grabbed the biggest one by the scruff of the neck and tossed it aside. The dog landed hard but got up, barking and bounding back for more. I figured these must be some pretty tough dogs.

"What kind of dogs are they?" I said.

"They're *poi dogs*," he said. "You know, mutts. The animal shelter calls me every now and then if they've got a big one they're gonna have to put down if I don't take it. They've figured me for a sucker, I guess."

"Is Pima here?"

"Yeah, I picked her up from Nancy's this morning. She isn't too crazy about hanging out with these guys, but I'll bet she'll be glad to see you."

The house looked more like a gardener's shed than a house, but it seemed solid and safe and that's all I cared about. Pima was in a front window, peering out. When she recognized me, she began howling and the other dogs stopped in their tracks to listen. Then they started up again, barking and leaping with such renewed gusto it was as if Pima had egged them on.

"Let's get you in the house," said Keo. "These dudes won't let up until I'm out of sight."

We slipped off our sandals and went inside. In contrast to Keo's earlier remark about the floor not being mopped, the small space was spotless. There was even a branch of delicate white orchids in a pop bottle vase.

"This is really nice," I said.

"It's not even close to what you're used to, though."

"It's great. It feels really homey. My *abuela's* house wasn't much bigger than this."

The house had one room which served as living room, dining room and kitchen. There was a door off to the side that must've led to the single bedroom and bath. The living area was furnished with a vintage rattan sofa and side chairs with worn Hawaiian-print cushions. A faded rag rug covered most of the floor. A plain wooden table with two ladder-back chairs designated the dining area and the tiny L-shaped kitchen had a window over the sink which featured a framed stained glass piece.

I pointed to the kitchen window. "I like your stained glass."

"My brother made it."

"Oh? Your family lives nearby?"

"Honolulu." He practically spat out the word.

"I take it you're not big on city dwelling," I said.

"Nope, not big on the city, and not too big on my family, either."

Keo insisted I take the bedroom so I went in and unpacked. When I came out, Pima was curled up in Keo's lap.

"I really should get up and feed the dogs," he said. "But I didn't want to disturb her."

I smiled as I took in the scene. "It'll probably take a while for her to settle down, but once she does, she'll be fine."

"Yeah? I suppose the same could be said about you."

"True. I think I'm still in shock. You know, I really expected to die in there."

"Yeah. I'm sure."

And then, for the first time since I'd been rescued, the horror of it slammed into me. I started to shake and tears coursed down my face. Like windshield wipers that couldn't keep up, I couldn't swipe the wetness from my cheeks fast enough.

Keo came over and pulled me into a tight embrace. "It's okay. You're safe now. Anybody comes up this way will have to get through four former death-row dogs and me. No contest."

"I'm sorry. I feel so awful. Not just about being locked in that room, but everything. You have no idea how screwed up my life's been this past year."

He dropped his arms and gestured toward the arm chairs.

"Take a seat," he said. "

I sat and he stood behind me. He lifted my hair off my back and draped it to one side of my shoulder. Then he rested his fingertips on my neck. He slowly began kneading the knots in my neck and upper back, his strong hands taking on the rigid muscles like a potter to clay.

"How's that feel?"

"Great."

As he massaged, I felt small bursts of pain as the muscles surrendered and softened. I hadn't realized how stiff and sore I'd become from my ordeal and the rock-hard hospital bed, and I felt myself tipping forward, my body melting like candle wax under the heat of his capable fingers.

"Are you nodding off on me?" he said.

I jerked awake, unaware I'd drifted off.

"I guess I am. Sorry."

"No, it's fine. Why don't you go lie down for a few minutes while I make dinner?"

"I should help."

"Nope. My place, my rules. I'll come get you when dinner's ready."

ꕥ ꕥ ꕥ

He'd grilled chicken breasts and made a chopped salad. "Hope you don't mind the simple grinds, but I try to not eat better than the folks I work for."

"Work for? Aren't you the boss?"

"The way I see it, the people we feed are my boss. If it wasn't for hungry people, I'd be out of a job."

"I doubt that."

"Believe it. I came to managing the food bank the hard way."

We cleaned up the dishes and he made a pot of green tea. He ushered me outside to a sagging sofa on a covered lanai that stretched along the back of the house. The dogs gathered around as if this was a nightly ritual. Pima had calmed down and sat in my lap like a cat. The back of the house must've faced west because soon the sky was ablaze with the pinks, purples and eye-popping oranges of an up-country Maui sunset.

"It's gorgeous here," I said.

"It's peaceful. In fact the name of this place is, '*Hale Lewalani,*' or 'House of Heaven.' But I'll bet you miss your fancy digs up in Paradise Ridge."

The mention of Paradise Ridge made me shudder. "You know, I only lived there a few months. The place I really miss is Southern Arizona."

"You still consider that home?"

"I guess so. My *abuela*'s buried there. I think more than missing the place, I miss her."

"Do you have a close *'ohana*—you know, family?"

"Not exactly," I said. "They had a bad habit of leaving me."

I told him about my father's murder and my mom's death less than a year later.

"No brothers or sisters?" he said.

"No. Not even any real aunts or uncles."

"You saying you had some *unreal* ones?"

I laughed. "You'd be surprised who crawls out of the woodwork when you win a bunch of money."

A beat went by and I added, "So, tell me about your life. I was orphaned as a teenager and then left to die by a crazy boyfriend. You think you can top that?"

He took a deep breath. "I don't know. You see, what happened to you wasn't your fault. But my lousy history is all 'my bad.' Nobody to blame but me."

"Is that what they teach in your twelve-step program?"

"Yeah, more or less. But I knew it before. Every addict I've known got that way 'cuz of their own stupid choices and bad behavior. But addicts are liars, so you'll hear a lot of shaming and blaming—they had a tough childhood, or lousy parents—stuff like that."

"Was Starshine a liar?" I said.

I felt a prickle of uneasiness. I knew it was wrong to speak ill of the dead, and I braced myself for Keo to call me out on it.

"Yeah, and your pal, Derek, too. Starshine would toss around BS even when there was no good reason. That's why she could never stay clean."

"Do you miss her?"

"Yeah, I guess I do. She didn't deserve to die like that, for sure. I feel like I failed her."

I didn't agree, but it was useless to argue. One thing I'd learned from my *abuela* was you have the right to feel how you feel, even if it doesn't make sense.

By now the sky was a deep navy blue, with pinpricks of stars scattered across it. Keo reached over and stroked Pima's head and she trembled and snuggled in closer.

"So, how did you end up running the Maui Food Bank?" I said, changing the subject.

"I was the son of a rich man," he said. "My father owned a real estate development company on O'ahu and he made a lot of money. I was sent away to boarding school and became addicted to cocaine when I was fourteen. By seventeen I was dealing. When I got convicted of multiple felonies at nineteen my father disowned me. I did some prison time and when I got out I had two options: get clean or die.

"No one would hire me, so I volunteered at the food bank in order to eat. After a while, they gave me a paid position. I was able to go to community college and then I went on and got a degree in public policy from UH Maui. When I graduated, the food bank offered me the job of running the place. I've been there ever since."

"What about your mom?" I said.

"Ah, her. She ran off with an old boyfriend when I was four. After that, my dad had a bunch of girlfriends but he never remarried. My dad got rid of all the pictures of my mom, so I'm not even sure what she looked like."

"Wow. That's sad. But you say you have a brother?"

"Yeah. Two years older. He's a lot like my dad, but at least he still speaks to me."

"Does the twelve-step program just not allow drugs or are you not supposed to drink, either?"

"Some people in the program drink. But I figure if I'm gonna stay clean, I also gotta stay sober. I guess I'm just an all-around boring dude. Don't drink, don't smoke, don't dance."

He laughed. "Okay, I've been known to dance a little at weddings."

"And you live out here all by yourself."

"Yeah." He lightly stroked Pima's back. "But for the next month or so, it looks like I'll have a couple of housemates."

I wanted to lean over and kiss him, but didn't. Our previous make-out session aside, it felt as if the bond between us was tenuous and green. As if falling together willy-nilly would tamp down any opportunity for it to grow into something more.

Instead, we sat in silence for a bit longer and then we got up and went to our respective rooms to sleep.

CHAPTER 39

Early the next morning I borrowed Keo's cell phone and went outside to call John Dease.

"I haven't talked to you for a while, so I thought I'd get in touch," I said.

"Good thing you did," he said. "I was beginning to worry. I sent you a FedEx package and it came back 'undeliverable.' When I called you to see what was goin' on, I kept getting your voicemail. I thought maybe you were goading me into flyin' over to Hawaii again."

I laughed. "I'm not *that* cruel, John."

I told him I'd been dating a guy who lived in my neighborhood and he'd flipped out when I broke it off, so I'd been staying with a friend. I fibbed and told him the guy had snatched my phone in the break-up, but I was hoping to get it back when things settled down.

"Whattaya mean, *the guy flipped out*?" he said. "Okay, that's it. You're coming home. I'm afraid the news in the FedEx I sent isn't good. I want you to pack up and get back here ASAP."

"What's the news?"

"Steve Harrow passed away two weeks ago. The settlement you made with him became part of his estate and the heirs want all of it—in cash and right now."

"And that means..."

"That means I need your signature to liquidate a big chunk of your investments to get Harrow's family their money. With that, you'll be down to about twelve mil, give or take, counting your Hawaii property. But don't worry. If you sell the Hawaii house and come back you'll have enough to live pretty comfortably here in Arizona for the rest of your life."

"I doubt I can sell the Hawaii house," I said.

"Why?"

"Well, first a big sinkhole opened up in the back yard. That brought in the local cultural commission who claimed the house was built over a Hawaiian burial ground so they made me move out. They were making noise about demolishing the house and reclaiming the land. Then, about two weeks ago, a girl's body turned up in the sinkhole. So you see—"

"Damn, girl, why didn't you call me? I'm gonna be on the next thing smokin' to come over there and get you."

"I'm fine, John."

"You are *not* fine, young lady. You're losing money like a coyote pissin' on a rock, and now you've been run out of your own house. I want you back here where I can keep an eye on you."

It probably was a good thing I hadn't let on about Derek kidnapping me and leaving me to die.

"I need to settle a few things here, John."

"You just said you were homeless. What's to settle?"

"I just need a little more time."

There was a pause. "Look, Monica, I want you to call me every week, you hear? If seven days goes by and I haven't heard from you, I'm gonna haul ass over there. And I can assure you it won't be pretty."

"I know. So, assuming my four-and-a-half million dollar house is worthless, what have I got left?"

"C'mon, girl, you can do the math. You're looking at seven and a half, maybe eight if you're lucky."

"Thanks, John. I'll call every Saturday."

"You better."

🐢 🐢 🐢

Keo came outside to tell me breakfast was ready. His dark hair was still wet from the shower and a few dark curls clung to his forehead. He wore a plain blue t-shirt and khaki shorts. Now that I thought about it, I'd never seen him in anything else except the night of the fund raiser.

"Is that your food bank uniform or something?" I said.

He looked puzzled.

I pointed to his shirt and shorts. "Blue shirt, khaki shorts. Do you have to wear that outfit, or are those the only clothes you own?"

He smiled. "Well, yes and yes. I have to wear this, because that's all I've got: three t-shirts, two pair of shorts, and a couple changes of boxers. I like to keep things simple."

"But the night of the fund raiser you had on a nice aloha shirt and long pants."

"That was Bev's doing. She actually bought me three nice shirts, but I took the other two back and bought a coffee maker and a few more mugs for the break room. Don't tell her I did that."

We sat down to scrambled eggs and toast and I said, "Do you own this place?"

"I wish, but I'm just a squatter. It's leased to the food bank, but I get to live here as long as I keep it up. You know, mend the fences, keep the weeds down, that kinda thing."

"How big is the property? I mean, how much land?"

He narrowed his eyes. "You're starting to sound like Bev. Why're you asking?"

"Just curious."

"It's about eighteen acres, not counting the easements for the road and the cell tower. The guy who leases it to the food bank was hoping we could farm it, but so far we haven't been able to swing it."

"Why not?"

"Costs money to get something like that up and going. You gotta get equipment, outbuildings, irrigation, greenhouses, and the like. I looked into it but the start-up costs were more than our annual budget. As you know, we're barely keeping the Wailuku warehouse going as it is."

"These eggs are great," I said, changing the subject. "You got a secret recipe?"

"Fresh, that's the key. I got a few hens running around out back. They think I don't know where their nests are, but they're wrong."

I cleaned up the dishes while Keo went outside to feed the dogs. I was amazed at his well-organized kitchen, but then with such little space it was necessary. Most of the dishes and pans were nested in tidy stacks inside the open cupboards. I wiped out the large cast iron frying pan and carefully placed it on a shelf above the stove.

Keo came in the back door as I was finishing up. "Do you feel good enough to come in to work with me?" he said.

"It's Saturday, why are you going to work?"

He looked pained. "I called an emergency board meeting for this afternoon. I've got to tell them about Chambers' bad check and see if they have any ideas about what we should do."

"I'm kind of nervous about going back there," I said.

"Why?"

"I still feel like people blame me for what happened to Starshine. And now this bad check thing."

"Don't worry. As they say, there's good news and bad. The good news is that court-ordered people are used to having people they know die young, so they don't judge. And the people who are volunteering are too polite to say anything."

"And the bad news?" I said.

He held my gaze. "The bad news is I'm afraid more than a few of them are glad she's gone."

"How're you dealing with it?" I said. "I mean, you were her sponsor and all. You must've been close."

"I did what I could."

He swiped a hand across his mouth and looked away.

"You don't have to play the tough guy with me, you know."

He slowly shook his head and his face crumpled. "I've second-guessed myself a hundred times since that night. I had a hunch somethin' was going on with Chambers, but I just let it happen. I got so caught up in making sure we got his money... "

His voice trailed off. He flicked a finger at the sides of his eyes.

Now it was my turn to offer comfort. I put my arms around him and leaned into his chest. I heard his heart hammering, and smelled the detergent scent of his t-shirt. I reveled in the feel of him, all solid muscles and massive arms, but then I winced at my reaction. I was there to console, not lust.

"You must think I'm a big baby," he said. "You know, in prison they called me a 'Banana.'"

"Do I dare ask why?" I inched my hip away from his groin, lest I find out first-hand.

He pulled back and laughed. "Yeah, I guess that sounds kinda sketchy, especially for a prison name. But no, the Banana thing is a guy who's tough on the outside but soft on the inside. It isn't a compliment. In fact, it cost me a tooth when some guys jumped me in the exercise yard."

He tapped his front tooth and said, "The prison dentist made me a pretty good fake, though, don't you think?"

"Give me a few minutes to shower and I'll ride in to work with you."

ᖽ ᖽ ᖽ

He was hanging up from a phone call when I came out of the bedroom. I tore a check from my checkbook, folded it, and held it out. "Before we go in to work, we need to get a little business out of the way."

He looked down at the folded check.

"Remember?" I said. "You agreed you'd let me pay rent for staying here."

"Ah, so I did."

Keo unfolded the check and tossed it back at me.

"You don't have to do this, Monica."

But his eyes betrayed him.

"Yes, I do. And I've already moved in here, so it's too late to renegotiate the price of rent."

We stopped at a bank on the way to the warehouse, and we both got out and went inside. Keo signed the check and slid it across the counter to the teller.

She looked at it, eyebrows raised. "We'll have to put a hold on these funds for a week. After five business days the money will be available."

I said I wanted to speak to the bank manager. After a few phone calls, the guy agreed to reduce the hold to just three days.

"I'd rather you didn't tell anyone about this," I said as we walked back out to Keo's truck.

"But Makaila already knows the other check bounced. And I've told a couple of the board members, too."

"Fine. But technically the money came from you, since the check was made out to you."

He seemed to struggle with the logic, but as we pulled into the food bank parking lot, he squeezed my hand.

"*Mahalo,* Monica."

Keo informed Makaila that he was cancelling that afternoon's meeting.

"Oh, yeah?" she said. "Can I ask why?"

"The fund raiser money was covered by another donor."

"Praise the Lord." She patted her heart. Then she looked at me.

"What?" I said. "It wasn't me. I'm just glad it's over."

Keo told Makaila she could begin writing checks to pay the bills starting on Wednesday.

"Where'd you get the money?" she said.

"From a Good Samaritan."

"That's all you're gonna say about it?"

"Yeah. Now please get on the phone and let our creditors know they'll be paid in full next week. But don't call the landlord. Get his check in the mail today, but put next Wednesday's date on it. As soon as he gets the check, he'll stop talking eviction."

I'd had no idea the situation had been so dire, but I didn't say anything.

Keo went to his office to begin calling board members. I stayed with Makaila.

She eyed me suspiciously. "That's some big *kokua nui* whoever bailed us out, eh? I think you know more about it than you're lettin' on."

I shrugged.

"Well, I'm gonna be talkin' to Beverly Strong. She'll find out who did it. No way that nosy woman gonna tolerate not knowin'."

"I'm just glad it's over," I said again.

I thought, but didn't say, it was too bad the other horrors Derek had inflicted on us couldn't be fixed so easily.

"And our poor girl, Starshine," Makaila went on, as if reading my mind. "The police say they're still looking for that Chambers dude, you know. I saw him and Starshine at the fund raiser dinner, laughin' and carryin' on. And then he goes and kills her and then ties you up like that. You and him were *ipo*, eh? You know, sweethearts? That man's the devil hisself."

I had to agree with her about Derek's character, but I chose not to clarify the rumor that I'd been tied up. Apparently the newspaper had reported I'd been bound and gagged. I guess being locked in a soundproof room behind a four-inch steel door didn't make a good enough story to sell papers.

When Makaila went to the break room to get coffee for Keo, I used her computer to check my email. Derek had taken my phone and Keo had no Internet service at his house, so it'd been more than a week since I'd checked.

About halfway down the hundreds of messages in my inbox, I saw a message with yesterday's date and the subject line: YOU R DEAD. The "From" line was a bunch of letters and numbers at a gmail account.

I didn't open the message.

I exited my email account and waited for Keo to finish up. As I sat there, I decided John Dease was right: I wasn't safe here on Maui. But then, as long as Derek Chambers was on the loose, I'd never be safe anywhere.

CHAPTER 40

On Saturday night, Keo made another simple dinner: chicken and rice. And again, I insisted on washing the dishes. He was helping me dry when he cocked his head and said he ought to check on the dogs.

"They're like little kids," he said. "When they get too quiet, it usually means they're up to something."

A few minutes after he left, Pima began whining and I shushed her.

"Don't get your panties in a wad," I said. "He'll be back soon."

It amused me how quickly Pima had taken to Keo. *That makes two of us*, I thought.

I was stacking the last plate in the cupboard when I heard footsteps out front. Pima rushed the door, snarling and barking as if someone had insulted her mother.

"Calm down," I said. "It's only Keo. You just saw him leave a little while ago. Can't that little doggie brain of yours remember something for ten minutes?"

I opened the door and something solid slammed into my face. I gasped, and when I tried to breathe, blood rushed into my nose shutting off my nostrils. Later, as I looked back on it, it seemed odd I hadn't been more wary of blithely opening the door.

"Thought you'd make a fool of me, huh?" said a deep voice from far down my tunnel of pain. "You know what happened to the last girl who tried that, right?"

By now, even though my face was ablaze with agony, I recognized Derek's voice. I scrambled back into the house, tripping over Pima and falling to my knees on the rag rug.

A hand gripped my hair and shoved me flat to the floor.

Pima went after Derek, and then I heard her whine. There was a thud, and when I looked up, she'd hit the wall. Her head was twisted at a bad angle and she wasn't moving.

"You killed my dog!" I said. It came out sounding more like, "Oo, keyed ma dah," because by now blood had filled my sinuses.

"Good. I've heard dogs don't like it when their owners die and leave them all alone."

I struggled to get up. I was able to lurch into the kitchen area before he once again got a grip on my hair. As he pulled me back, I tried to lunge forward. The shelf with the cast iron skillets was a foot away.

I reached out to grab something—*anything*—from the shelf but my fingertips were inches away. Then I saw my *abuela* standing there. She smiled and reached over and turned the handle of the bottom frying pan—the biggest one—toward me. I closed my grip around the handle and whirled around, losing a fistful of hair in the process.

I slammed the heavy skillet into Derek's temple. When I looked up, my *abuela* was gone. I dashed over to Pima and felt her chest. Her little heart was beating, but just barely.

I ran outside to look for Keo and the dogs. It was getting dark and after circling the house and not finding them, I ran back inside and called 9-1-1 on Keo's phone.

"I see you're calling from a cell phone," said the dispatcher. "Can you give me your address?"

"I'm upcountry. I don't know the address. It's Keo Kekane's place—the guy who runs the food bank. I've been attacked and I can't find him."

Then I started crying.

"Turn on the porch light and all the lights in the house," she said. "That will help the police find you."

"The house is about a quarter-mile off Baldwin Road," I said.

Then I remembered the Buddha sign. "The place is called "Hale" something. It means "House of Heaven" in Hawaiian. I described the little wooden sign at the end of the driveway.

She repeated the information, and told me to stay on the line. I looked over at Derek's crumpled body and thought I saw him twitch. After that, I have no memory of anything until the police showed up.

🐢 🐢 🐢

Once again, I was in an ambulance headed for Maui Memorial Hospital. Since I hadn't been properly discharged from my last visit, the emergency room nurse let me know she wasn't about to "take beef," as she put it, from me.

"We got rules here, you know," she said. "For your own safety and security."

I asked about Keo but she wasn't willing to disclose anything. Maybe she didn't know. "How about my dog? I have a little miniature Schnauzer named Pima. She was badly hurt in the attack."

"This isn't no animal hospital," she said. "If the police found your dog, they pro'bly called a vet. But I don't know anything about that."

I was admitted to a room. This time, the doctor's order barring the police from talking to me fell on deaf ears. I was pretty high on sedatives when Detectives Wong and Baker showed up. My face was bandaged and my eyes nearly swollen shut.

"Seems you've got quite an arm there, Ms. Gomez," said Detective Baker. "Last I heard, the Seattle Mariners were looking for a new relief pitcher."

Detective Wong shot him some "stink eye" but Baker ignored him.

Baker went on, "You want to tell us what happened?"

"I'll tell you everything, but first I want to know how my friend, Keo Kekane is doing. And my dog, Pima."

The detectives glanced at each other as if deciding who was going to talk.

Wong said, "Mr. Kekane is in surgery. Seems Derek Chambers caught him in the back with a pretty nasty knife. He's got some internal damage, but they're working on it."

I could visualize the knife in question, but didn't say anything.

"How about my dog?"

Once again, the two of them silently conferred.

"We don't have any information on that," said Baker.

"Will you keep me informed of Keo's condition?"

"It works both ways," said Baker. "You tell us what we need to know, and we'll tell you how your boyfriend's doing."

"I'm kinda drugged up," I said.

"No worries," said Baker. "We got all the time in the world. Right, Wong?"

Wong glared at Baker. "How many times do I have to ask you to knock that off?"

"I think it's catchy," said Baker. "What do you think, Ms. Gomez?"

I smiled.

"See? She gets it," said Baker to Wong. "She's not *that* drugged up."

I gave them my statement. I covered the entire scenario, from when Derek texted me to lure him to his house to the moment when I bashed him in the head with the skillet. By the time I stopped talking, I was exhausted.

"I gotta hand it to you, Ms. Gomez," said Baker. "You took a heckuva beating and still managed to clean that perp's clock. Medical examiner says the guy's neck was broken. So, what is it? You got friends in high places? Or are you just lucky?"

"Both," I said.

EPILOGUE

Keo Kekane, aka "Banana," turned out to be tougher on the inside than his prison comrades imagined. He sustained a deep, curving wound that sliced through a kidney, ruptured his spleen and nicked his abdominal aorta, but the surgeons managed to patch him up. Thankfully, he remained infection-free until he was released from the hospital about a month and a half later.

His *poi dogs* underwent a similar recovery period. They'd been lured away from the house with rat poison-laced meat. But Derek had brought only enough to kill one dog. They'd each managed to snatch a bite or two, but the vet had acted quickly and the antidote worked.

Pima suffered a broken leg and a concussion. Ironically, the attack didn't make her more timid, but less. For weeks she wore a doggie "cone of shame" on her neck while her leg was in a cast, but when she was pronounced healthy, she raced around Keo's yard like she owned the place.

And, in a manner of speaking, she did. While Keo was in the hospital, I took what was left of my money and made an offer to buy "Hale Lewalani." The owner accepted.

Keo and I began shopping for farm equipment the day after he got home. We opted for an upscale vegetable farm where community service workers could learn to grow heirloom tomatoes and fancy artisan lettuce, and volunteers could enjoy some time in the cooler climate of upcountry

Maui. It made more sense to grow expensive produce and sell it for top dollar than try to meet the ever-growing demand for plainer, more affordable vegetables for the food bank.

The irony of me getting back in the produce business wasn't lost on me.

I had plans drawn up to build a good-sized house on one end of the acreage for myself, and to expand and remodel Keo's smaller house on the other side. But it turned out we only needed one house.

We were married almost exactly a year after we first met in the produce section of the Times Market in Honokowai. The food bank workers and board members came to our outdoor wedding ceremony at Hale Lewalani, and everyone brought their kids.

Max was Keo's best man. Bev cried when I asked her to be a bridesmaid, and even though I hadn't been able to serve as Chloe's maid of honor because I was still healing from Derek's attack, I asked her to be my matron of honor and she accepted.

Even John Dease flew over and this time he brought his wife.

"See what you've done," he grunted to me at the reception. "Look at her. She loves this damn place. Now she's talking about us flying over here every year."

I am a lucky girl. And to think, it all began with a display of passion fruit.

AUTHOR'S NOTE

As always, there are many people to thank for helping me get a story out of my head and onto paper (or into cyberspace). I will start with the most important people—my readers. Without you, this wouldn't be nearly as much fun. I love hearing from you on my Facebook page, JoAnn Bassett's Author Page, or on my website, JoAnn Bassett dot com.

But I'm also grateful and humbled by the many people who toil away on these books, some without remuneration, some asking only a fraction of what they are truly worth to me. My beta readers, Tom Haberer, Diana Paul, Francesca Moses Schelenski, are troopers. They read the initial draft and make much-appreciated comments and suggestions. Then, KC Spiker Curtis picks up at final draft stage to catch pesky inconsistencies and typos. (But if you spot any that we missed, I'm always grateful for a quick message on my Facebook page as I can fix them—and I will!). I must also thank Debora Lewis at Arena Publishing for her wonderful work in crafting a mere Word file into Adobe Acrobat so the fine folks at CreateSpace can work their magic in making it into a paper book.

And, although there are some authors who might take me to task for this, I'd like to thank Amazon for giving independently-published authors a shot. Yes, they are the 800-pound gorilla that we all must obey, but for the most part, they are a friendly primate. Without them, it would be impossible for a writer like me to put a book in your hands (or your device) without getting the blessing of the 1,000 pound gorilla known as the New York publishing industry. And believe me, that ape isn't nearly as generous.

Mahalo and *a hui hou*!

Look for other titles by JoAnn Bassett:

The Islands of Aloha Mystery Series
Maui Widow Waltz
Livin' Lahaina Loca
Lana'i of the Tiger
Kaua'i Me a River
O'ahu Lonesome Tonight?
I'm Kona Love You Forever
Moloka'i Lullaby
Hilo, Goodbye

The Escape to Maui Series
Mai Tai Butterfly
Lucky Beach

Visit JoAnn Bassett's website at: www.joannbassett.com

"Like" her Facebook page at: JoAnn Bassett's Author
Page

Made in the USA
San Bernardino, CA
18 May 2019